The Devil in
Buenos Aires

The Devil in Buenos Aires

A Novel

Lily Powell

THE LYONS PRESS
GUILFORD, CONNECTICUT
AN IMPRINT OF THE GLOBE PEQUOT PRESS

For Fred, in Grateful Memory

Printed in the United States of America

Book design by Casey Shain

1 3 5 7 9 10 8 6 4 2

Library of Congress Cataloging-in-Publication Data

Froissard, Lily Powell.
The devil in Buenos Aires / Lily Powell.
p. cm.
ISBN 1-59228-299-7
1. World War, 1939–1945—Secret service—Fiction. 2. World War, 1939–1945—
Argentina—Fiction. 3. Buenos Aires (Argentina)—Fiction. I. Title.
PR6066.O93D485 2004
823'.914—dc22
2004000714

A quiconque a perdu ce qui ne se retrouve

Jamais, jamais! à ceux qui s'abreuvent de pleurs

Et tètent la Douleur comme une bonne louve!

Aux maigres orphelins séchant comme des fleurs!

—CHARLES BAUDELAIRE
Le Cygne

The Devil in Buenos Aires

CHAPTER ONE

THEY WALKED UNDER THE HOT FEBRUARY SUN, past show windows and holes-in-the-wall where old shoes, umbrellas, and ponchos were auctioned off to customers on the sidewalks, till they saw in a decayed three-story building the Hotel Bolívar and stepped into the night of its vestibule.

The manager's pallid eyes appraised the young couple who asked for connecting rooms. They were well dressed, quiet, and self-possessed: the girl slim and pale, black hair, liquid, almond-shaped eyes; the boy tall, a bronze glow on his skin, hair, and eyes, a straight nose with mobile nostrils and a wide, powerful mouth. With all the difference in type, they bore a strong resemblance, the same wistful look in their eyes, the same self-assured grace in their carriage. They looked like children, yet not young—too perfected for the muddled transition of adolescence, too perfect still to have been marred by adult life. Through their unlike features broke the spiritual likeness of brother and sister, or great lovers.

The manager found their German name hard to pronounce; but they spoke flawless Spanish with the colloquialisms of *porteños*—children of the port of Buenos Aires—and used expressions out of fashion since long before they could have been born. They said they were brother and sister.

He disliked them spontaneously for being of a type foreign to his narrow experience, confined to businessmen, shady politicians from the provinces, and an occasional country family. Since nothing justified his uneasiness, irritation sharpened his antagonism.

Yet business being what it was, he led them to the cagelike elevator. They followed him along the badly lighted hallway—darkly papered, flanked by enormous double doors—looked dejectedly at the towering

ceilings of the rooms, and asked for the price, which he raised with spontaneous ill temper, to 380 pesos a month. They agreed as if they had no idea
of how much they were overcharged. Their registration disclosed that they
were indeed Germans just arrived from their country.

"Where did you learn your Spanish?" he asked.

"Our mother is Argentine," answered the girl politely, but with such
reserve that the full stop after her sentence was almost visible in the air.

The bare, windowless dining room was crowded. The hotel, a lone survivor
of the times when this downtown district had been a residential section,
now catered to the owners and employees of the textile firms that had taken
possession of the neighborhood. The entrance of the girl and boy in carefully tailored suits caused a stir among the all-male patrons, through which
they walked as if alone on a plain.

They chose their lunch with the swiftness of those accustomed to
dining out and became absorbed in a subdued, yet intense and lively conversation, their hands remaining in repose, but their strange, tranquil faces
growing vivacious and tense in turn.

Two men were watching them with unconcealed mirth. The older kept
whispering and the younger laughing. Neither took his eyes off the girl, till
the young couple changed seats, so the boy, rather than his sister, was facing
them. He frowned, "You mean, the fat, bald man and the young one with
the slick hair and the mustache?"

"Yes."

The boy continued to frown, his displeasure turning from the offenders
to their own condition. "That's what comes from going around alone. We're
too young. People take us for adventurers. Mother wanted to let the family
know . . ."

"It's all right," she said. "I don't want people to feel under obligation to
us. I want . . ."

"To be Antonie Herrnfeld," he concluded dryly. "Clever, self-sufficient
Tony who can go it alone."

"Not alone, Peter," she smiled. "With you."

He returned her smile. "You're the strength, dear, but I'm the reason.
And I'm afraid we'll need people. I can't offer my services at some estancia

2

like a day laborer; and for the moment you have no idea just what you could do . . ."

"We'll sleep on it. Meanwhile let's get a paper and look for an apartment or something. I wonder if we couldn't do better for the price."

They walked back through the gloomy vestibule into the glaring daylight. At the corner of Avenida de Mayo they bought a newspaper.

Returning late, they went straight to their rooms. From the dark walls the jumbo flowers pressed in on them. There was a fine, persistent draft even in the windowless bathroom with its chipped, badly functioning fixtures.

When they said good night, Tony suggested, "let's keep the connecting door open."

They lay down in the strange beds, pulled the coarse covers over themselves, and fell silent. Tony stared at the tall glass door leading into the bathroom. It was depressingly ugly but left her unemotional. She had not yet broken away from the last room she had slept in before taking the boat, a bright room with touches of the nursery it had once been.

The balcony door closed badly, trembling every thirty seconds at the screaming passage of a streetcar; and as time went by, each passed right through her brain. Peter did not seem to hear them in his young sleep. But she was not alone. He was there.

Single pictures arose. An autumnal wood, aflame in the setting sun. A tired horse grazing in a clearing, its rider looking down onto a lake, grey and calm in the evening haze. A large, old-fashioned automobile stopping before the sprawling manor house. A schoolgirl getting out, a book satchel under her arm, walking toward the entrance.

The modernistic outline of the Westend School. A girl, not a friend, someone whose name she could not recall; like the others of her grade, in oxfords, pleated skirt, and sweater. But her little sister, interrupting their recess chat to ask the older for a sandwich, was wearing the brown leather coat and the black tie with the swastika pin. Blushing, the older girl propelled her out of the classroom door.

Once more she stood in the courtyard, part of a swastika formation, silent while the others sang the *Horst Wessel Lied*. She did not have to sing. Her father was Jewish. But she must stand there, part of the design.

3

No, she now told herself, this is the past and dead. This is not what I want to remember. I want to think of the things I intend to go on living with, that are worth remembering, essential to be preserved.

But as she tried to think of her pretty mother who had given her the shape and color of her eyes, she could only picture her at the top of the stairs, welcoming guests—diplomats, intellectuals, noblemen, industrialists of all nations. Dolores Herrnfeld had enjoyed the company of statesmen but hated politics, and so the subject had been banned from her home.

Tony remembered an evening, she did not know the date. It must have been after 1936 and before the beginning of 1938, for her father still owned his steel plants, but the Kronprinz had ceased to be his guest. That night she had noticed a change in his attitude, had watched him in genial conversation with a South American consul. His profile was turned toward her; looking at the narrow nose and firm, gentle mouth over the blond goatee, she had thought that if ever she fell in love it would be with a man like him. It now occurred to her that Peter resembled him and she wondered what his wife would be like.

She remembered that specific night because it was when the change had taken place. Hugo Herrnfeld felt no great respect for Latin American consuls and had usually been polite but aloof. Now he had sought out this particular man, and Tony later learned that, by and by, a certain amount of money was being deposited abroad for her and Peter. One afternoon he told her of his perilous transactions and suggested that she and her twin finish their studies at a foreign university.

"Why don't we all leave?" she had asked.

"I have thought about it, you know that," he replied, "but do you think your mother could live as a nearly penniless refugee? And then, if we all fled the chaos, who would remain to fight it? I'm not just any Jew with a prosperous business. My career has acquainted me with the very same industrialists who are pulling these political strings to the best advantage of their businesses. My father has known their fathers, my grandfather their grandfathers. I believe I can still exert some influence on some of them. I think I ought to stay as long as possible. But you two can't waste your time here."

Tony had sometimes dreamed of an existence abroad, had placed the home of her childhood, the familiar woods, their close family life, in another country. But it had seemed unthinkable to go alone. Now she thought

4

how insane it had been, because, withal, they had not been blind; they had anticipated what might happen. Yet no threat, however great, had seemed capable of breaking through the protective power of their father's presence. They could imagine no catastrophe, no brutal force ruthless enough to split the sacred unity of their devoted, unworldly family.

And yet it had been split, not only once, but twice. Lying in this strange hotel room, she realized for the first time that nothing was left except childhood memories which, as the years went by, would represent a very small part of a lifetime. She also realized that it had all been gone long before she had left it behind, even before the *razzia*.

They had come at night, drunk Burgundy from water tumblers, ripped kitchen knives through old masters, thrown Dresden against the wall where she was standing, her blood so cold it made her body stiffen, the last hold giving way within her. She could feel it crumble, not leaving her weak, just empty and numb. They had taken Hugo Herrnfeld with them.

Dolores had gone to the Argentine Embassy, had requested and received visas for her children. She had stayed behind, waiting for her husband's release—but she heard nothing.

Her twin was stirring. "Tony," it was a whisper, "are you awake?"

"Yes, Peter, what is it? I thought you were asleep."

He came to sit on the edge of her bed. "I've been thinking about Potsdam and our childhood and what life was like and what it's going to be."

"So have I."

He touched her arm, his voice tense. "For God's sake, Tony, let's not ever talk about it to anyone!"

She sat up and locked her arms around her knees. "Why not? What do you mean, Peter?"

"Remember the stories about refugees? Remember the one about the dachshund in America who said that back in Germany he'd been a Saint Bernard?"

"I know. You mean, it would be in poor taste to reminisce about Potsdam."

"That's it."

"Let's keep it to ourselves."

"Good night, Tony." He rose. A few minutes later they were both asleep.

5

CHAPTER TWO

THE CITY'S SYSTEMATICALLY LAID OUT STREETS seemed an immense confusion to them. They did not know where to go. They had no idea what their money was worth, or where to spend it. Dolores had told them of Buenos Aires. They knew of Florida Street with its exquisite shops, of the Alvear Palace Hotel, of the racetracks and Palermo Park, of the Colón Opera and the residential suburbs, but nothing of the small apartments, one of which they now intended to rent, or about the modest restaurants where they meant to take their next meals. On board the ship someone had recommended the Hotel Bolívar, and they had gone straight there.

They had spent two days trying to take the initial steps toward settling down, but it seemed like attempting to move a mountain. On the third morning the telephone rang in Tony's room, and the voice of their mother's cousin, Antonio Guerida Paz, said, "You ought to be ashamed of yourselves, children. We had to hunt you down. Why haven't you called? You mother wrote you'd be at the Alvear, where she has always stayed."

Having accepted a dinner invitation, Tony said to Peter, "How very much like mother. 'At the Alvear where she has always stayed.'"

The taxi took them out of the narrow downtown streets, through the residential section of the north that Tony eyed longingly, and then sped along white Avenida Alvear. From well-kept gardens shone ornate palaces. Into the open windows of the taxi swept the intoxicating summer scent of the jacarandá blossoms the trees had spread over the wide sidewalks.

On their right the dense tree groups of Palermo Park fled back, green lawns flashing under arc lights or mysteriously aloof in the glow of old lanterns. The taxi left them before an overpowering wrought-iron gate. The gleaming front of a palatial mansion towered over them under the dome of a star-studded sky. For a long moment they stood in silence, until a look passed between them, a mixture of awe and amusement.

"Let's brave it," Tony said at last. Her voice sounded small in the magnificence of the night.

A white coat flashed in the darkness. A butler swung back the heavy gate. "Buenas noches, niños."

He led the way into the house, through a hall of Italian marble and into an elevator where Peter whispered in German, "Imagine going up and down your own sweet home in an elevator."

"Hush," she said, "you're just envious." They were left alone in a reception hall the size of a hotel lobby, among high-backed Renaissance chairs and walls hung with priceless tapestries over parquetry covered by three immense rugs.

"I like it," said Tony.

"Oh, you do?"

"You don't understand. It isn't just grand. It's fine and sober. I guess they're nice people."

Through a carved door entered a gentleman in his late fifties, tall, spare, and very erect. "Well, children, here you are." He took one hand of each twin and looked at them with a frank curiosity that, too kind to be embarrassing, made them feel welcome and at ease.

Tony reflected that his was the most ill-shaped nose she had ever seen, very long and hooked and quite red, but the sparkle of his small, intensely green eyes left even this enormous nose in their shadow. Before the thought had truly crystallized, the words slipped out. "I'm glad you called."

Still holding their hands, don Antonio said, "You're at home."

While they were settling down to a drink, doña María Teresa Dorrego de Guerida Paz came into the room, voluble and sweet, her stout body pressed into an excellent Paquin gown, her white hair crowning a round face once known for its beauty. She came sailing toward the twins with a kind of heavy grace and kissed them in a manner that made them feel like a couple of the countless cousins who stopped in every so often.

"Carlota will be down in a minute," she said. "Antonie, you are beautiful! Even more so than your mother, and she was lovely! My brother—you'll meet him—used to have quite a crush on her.

"Give me a Scotch and soda, *hijo*," she told her husband, settling herself in a chair, crossing thick legs with fine ankles, her small feet not quite touching the floor. "And now you tell us all about Dolores. You look a lot like your father, don't you, Handsome?" she asked Peter.

It was a matter for speculation whether she would have given him time to answer had Carlota not come in at this moment. She had all her mother's prettiness, combined with her father's impressive carriage. A dark blonde with large eyes the color and brilliance of don Antonio's and sparkling teeth, she was tall and athletic, the antithesis of Tony, who somehow felt that this dynamic Artemis must be bewildering to her mother and an extremely satisfying surprise to her father.

"I'm so glad you're here," she said, pouring herself a sherry. "You must have had a terrible time."

"I don't imagine they're out of it yet," remarked Antonio. And from then on the siblings answered a crossfire of questions about themselves, Dolores, and their father's fate. It was quite depressing, and they were glad when dinner was announced.

The dining room had all the splendor of a ballroom; the towering Sèvres vases on sideboards and consoles and the Venetian mirrors were too ornate to be attractive. Tony had a sinking sensation of disappointment, though she felt a spontaneous contact with the Brussels cloth, the smooth cool curve of her Limoges soup bowl, those household appurtenances that arrogantly divided classes and reached across frontiers to serve and unite the privileged.

The lengthy dinner was taken up by don Antonio's inquiries concerning the political situation in Germany.

"When will there be war?" Carlota asked, shockingly matter-of-fact.

"That's hard to say," replied Peter. "Last September it seemed inevitable, yet peace was saved once more."

"With Czechoslovakia thrown into the bargain," remarked don Antonio. "This year your friend Hitler will bare his teeth again, and Mr. Chamberlain will throw him another bone."

"England and France aren't sufficiently armed, *hijo*," said his wife. "Everybody knows that. Wouldn't you like some more beef, Antonie?" she asked, as her cousin let the platter pass. "How do you like Argentine beef, children? I imagine your mother has missed it all her life."

8

"England and France are weaker than Germany now," continued her husband, without heeding the change of subject. "Two years from now they'll have doubled their power, no doubt. But so will Germany, at the very least."

"Do many Argentines feel like you?" Tony asked, surprised.

"No." He shrugged. "They read and hear what's happening in Germany. But they say the accounts of the refugees aren't reliable; they've suffered from the régime and can't be objective, they exaggerate . . . But they do believe the propaganda leaflets from the German Embassy. And there are the Fascist officers who are invited to Germany and return with glowing descriptions of stadiums, highways, singing, organized youth—all forerunners of the coming war."

"You're a fanatic," said doña María Teresa. "I think these twins have had enough of Nazis and war threats and want to have a good time."

"They will, don't you worry, Mamá," laughed Carlota, "once they've sat it out with the family and got to know some interesting people."

She turned to Tony. "Not even Papá judges the Argentine attitude in its real pathetic light. He dramatizes. It's true that they don't believe anything they hear. The reports about concentration camps are exaggerated. The Germans, after all, are so *gemütlich*. Their wines are good. The Wagner Society is as popular as ever. They don't bother about the political aspect at all. As far as they're concerned, the Germans are excellent people, and Hitler must really be a genius to fascinate the masses as he's doing. Nobody troubles to study the situation, except a few Nationalist officers who dream of the *Gauleiterschaft* of Chile or Uruguay."

"What rubbish," said María Teresa. "After all, you twins, you're in a free country, a democracy, now. By the way, why didn't your mother come with you?"

"She's waiting for father," said Tony, as quietly as if there were no cause for wonder.

"Can't the Argentine Embassy do anything for him?" asked Antonio.

Peter shook his head. "As far as the Germans are concerned, Mother has lost her citizenship through marriage, and Father is a native-born German. We'd considered buying a Central American citizenship. If you could spend enough, it was easy, but dangerous."

"Is that all the Latin American diplomats are doing over there?" asked Antonio.

Peter smiled. "They also exchange pounds against marks, at five times the official rate. Tony, stop kicking me. Why shouldn't one say it?"

The Gueridas laughed.

When they left the table, Tony was hoping that coffee would be served in the enchanted-looking garden. But they went into the Louis XVI salon to sit on gilt chairs covered with Aubusson.

"How did you manage to get money out of Germany?" Carlota asked with surprising insight.

"Oh, we smuggled some out," Tony said noncommittally.

"Also the consuls?" chuckled Antonio.

"In part. But there were 'businessmen,' too." She laughed. "One was particularly adroit. He came to Berlin to live cheaply on traded marks. When he suddenly vanished—the police were looking for him—his ex-friends, the consuls, put their fingers to their lips and with their long hands made the gesture of stealing and said they'd never really known him very well."

It had always struck her as funny, but now it sounded acid. "Still they've all been square with us," she added earnestly. "We've nothing to complain of."

"No, you have nothing to complain of," don Antonio repeated with mock gravity.

The twins bought chocolates on their way home, as was their wont when they felt despondent. Now they sat in pajamas in Tony's room, munching absentmindedly. It was two o'clock in the morning.

"They're good people," said Peter, "and yet they depressed me no end."

"There's nothing wrong with them," she replied, leaning back on the bed. "It's us. We've got to get used to being refugees. They'll always ask us all those questions. Everybody will. And we'll just have to keep harping on our problems and sounding pathetic."

"But we didn't really," he objected. "We didn't complain at all. We gave the facts, as we should have."

Tony bit into a piece of nougat. "Amounts to the same. That stuff hurts my teeth. We'll have to look for a good dentist. You're right, brother, we need the family's advice. But what I mean is that all our talk about the consuls and such just made us out as the poor abused lambs."

She laid what was left of her chocolate on the night table and Peter picked it up. "That's probably so. I guess we're refugees all right, with all the trimmings," he said. "But, and that's the trouble, we don't belong with them, and we don't belong with the others either."

"Goodness, that house of theirs!"

"Oh, that's come down to them from Papá," answered Peter somewhat contemptuously. "The old man bought that stuff in Paris with the money Grandpa's cows made." He yawned. "I guess I'll turn in. Tomorrow I'm going to Antonio's office. We want to talk about my work. I have an inkling he's got room for me on one of his *estancias*."

Antonie laughed "At about 15,000 acres each, there ought to be room for just a little fellow like you." But once the lights were out, she anxiously faced the prospect of living without Peter.

He told her that Antonio was sending him immediately to the larger of his two estates in the province of Buenos Aires. Tony managed to appear pleased, told herself that it was really wonderful, but could not help feeling a slight ache, realizing that he so little dreaded leaving her.

As though reading her thoughts, he said, "Antonio says they want you to live with them."

"Preposterous!" she exclaimed, more harshly than she would have, had she not just been hurt. "I'd rather die than act the part of the poor relative!"

Nothing changed her mind. The Gueridas made sincere attempts to make her accept their offer. But to tell the truth, they weren't too sorry when they failed. After all, this beautiful second cousin was a stranger they were sure to get along with splendidly as long as it was a question of visits. But that was a far cry from adopting her.

CHAPTER THREE

AFTER PETER HAD LEFT TOWN, Tony stayed on at the hotel. Every morning Santiago, the houseboy, brought breakfast to her room, wearing a soiled white jacket, chewing the stump of a toothpick between his rotten teeth.

In the afternoon she would pass by the manager's appraising eyes into the sitting room to write long letters to her mother. Dolores's letters made pathetic reading and were hard to answer because, no matter what one wrote, there always recurred sentences like, "You must write the truth; I feel that you are concealing something to spare me, and yet I worry much more when I have to rely exclusively on my imagination."

Tony knew that many mothers in Germany wrote such letters.

She often was aware of the men who had bothered her in the dining room on her day of arrival. They watched her from the doorway, loudly voicing their impressions of the foreign *chica*.

Then two noisy men moved into the room that had been Peter's. She never saw them, but they called out to her through the thin connecting door, inviting her out to dance, and often continued their one-sided talk for hours until Tony bit her hand to keep from screaming. One night after she had turned off her bedside lamp, she noticed a thin ray of light coming through the connecting door and found a small, round hole.

On the following day she rented the very first flat she was shown, two impersonal rooms and a small vestibule filled with department store Empire. The neighborhood was lovely, however, and she could close a door and shut out strangers.

This accomplished, she set out to find work, a quest she faced without the slightest preparation. Right up to their precipitous departure it had occurred to no one that they might not continue their studies at a foreign university. The sudden interference of events had not only advanced their departure but interrupted, perhaps cut off, the slow clandestine flow of capital abroad. Whatever they owned, cash and jewelry, must remain as intact as possible for their parents who, if ever they were to join them, would not be likely to bring with them anything but the officially permitted ten Reichsmark. On the boat the twins had quietly and resignedly agreed to strike the ivy halls from their future plans, and the only other word they ever lost over it was Peter's wisecrack, when in Buenos Aires they first heard of the political role of Latin American schools. "Lucky guys, for them there's nothing academic about higher education."

Tony spoke four languages fluently, knew how to use a typewriter, and had taken a shorthand course in preparation for the now-eclipsed lecture halls. Thus endowed, she went to hunt for a job, surprised when her first try succeeded; not a full-time job, but after-hours office work for the manager of an export-import firm. After he had dictated the first letters and offered her a sherry, she knew that she would have to look for another job. But her luck did not turn; they were always jobs "after closing time," and her employers acted as surprised at her rebuffs as she at their advances.

She decided to put a clearly worded advertisement into *La Prensa*, offering her services as a secretary or translator, and received two letters and a telephone call in return. The first letter came from a gentleman who needed an efficient secretary during the day and a sympathetic companion in the evening; the second suggested an obviously shady business deal. The telephone call was from Antonio, who asked her to lunch.

As soon as she arrived, he chuckled, "Antonie, you are an *enfant terrible*. Who on earth told you to put that ad into the paper?"

"Nobody. How did you happen to see it, and what's wrong with it?"

"I didn't, but María Teresa's brother did. He's an idle old chap with nothing to do but read the paper from cover to cover. The rest of his time is employed somewhat differently, which probably accounts for his watching ads such as yours. And that answers your second question—what's wrong with it. Don't you know what it conveys, Antonie?"

"No," she said blandly.

"Antonie, my dear, in this country, if a woman advertises as a secretary, it means but one thing. The word *secretary* is almost synonymous with . . . " The rest of the sentence was replaced by another chuckle.

"Lord!" Tony said, and paused to digest this.

"Look here, you're quite an admirable child to have the desire to work. But it would be too bad for a girl of your class to spend her youth in an office taking orders from some gringo merchant. I wouldn't want you to do what I wouldn't let my own daughter do."

This seemed kind, if very ineffectual to her. "But I must do something," she insisted, irked by the sensation that her words fell into a benevolent void. "I have a little money and some jewelry, but I can't sit around and use it up. Besides, I want to work. At home it is just as shameful for a woman not to do anything as it would be for a man."

On entering, María Teresa and Carlota had overheard the remark. "It isn't shameful for either," María Teresa said, piqued. "There are many excellent boys in our own family who'd rather live modestly on their mediocre incomes in order to cultivate their artistic abilities."

"Or their inartistic but prosperous wives," concluded Carlota. "You have some money to last you for a while—until you can 'cultivate' one of the splendid marriage candidates I've already got lined up for you," She said, laughing.

When Tony left the mansion on Avenida Alvear, where she was always so warmly received, she felt more lonely than she had on her arrival in Buenos Aires. Crossing the stately avenue, she walked in Palermo Park, which was flooded by the red and turquoise sunset, with clusters of old trees standing out like black silhouettes. She sat down on one of the benches being gradually vacated by moody-looking nurses and quiet children in stiffly starched clothes. As she watched the white-piqué children trip toward their white nurseries, and the sun go down, and the fog veil the radiant landscape, she realized for the first time that there was as much of an abyss between her and her Argentine family as, in a different way, between herself and her preposterous business acquaintances.

On the following afternoon she was crossing Plaza San Martín for cocktails with Carlota at The Copper Kettle on Florida. Although Carlota was trying to tease her out of her plans, she might know of some type of work a girl could do. During the night, Tony had conscientiously re-tailored her depressions into dogged purposefulness to fit the need of the hour.

The sun was bright and warm, but it was no longer a summer sun. She walked with long strides, marveling at how she was going along, free and fearless. The newness of this adventure had not yet worn off and always made her remember. Her mother was still hoping for some help from the embassy. Tony herself had seen someone at the Foreign Ministry, but the answer had been: "Those are internal matters of the Germans. We can't interfere."

Carlota arrived, as usual somewhat late, in the unexpected company of two young men. One was lame, slightly dragging one leg with a lateral motion of the hip and supporting himself on a cane. He had a fine head with dark hair, regular features, and intelligent, though rather cheerless eyes. They had already made arrangements for dining out, and Tony knew that it would give her no chance to talk to Carlota.

In the powder room, she asked, "Who is this Romero Basualdo?"

"He's from a very good family. Arch Catholics, too. Not much money, though." Carlota put some soap on a run in her stocking. "Poor chap, he's had polio. I didn't mean him for a candidate."

"He's nice, though. I like to hear him talk about French plays. He sounds as if he were writing."

Carlota covered the run with her narrow black skirt and made some contortions to see if her seams were straight. "He translates, anyway. Can't do much else. Must be pretty grim to live like that."

When Tony got home, she hung up her suit, leaving it out for daylight inspection, for it would be the last for a long time to come. She cleaned her shoes and washed her stockings, and then, not sleepy, went to the kitchen for a midnight snack.

She was thinking about Carlota, whom she liked for being smart and stylish, witty without being sharp, terse without being cold, and, above all, natural. She was a far cry from her mother's description of Argentine girls, warning her that she would not be able to do this, or say that.

Still there were reservations. She tried to figure out what they were. You're jealous, she told herself. That's the only reservation. But of what?

Don't you have enough self-assurance not to be jealous of anyone? Yes, but I live on my self-assurance, support myself on it, while Carlota doesn't have to use hers at all. There's never any need for it. All she has and has been, is and will always be. There's nothing to be explained, not more than one impression to be gained from her. Her lovely appearance is mounted before a perfect background of spacious rooms, Irish linen, and a very visible and effective family. Her parents need no help, and it would be in very poor taste indeed to question her about her financial setup. In all likelihood she doesn't even know what it is. No matter how much I may have some day, I'll never regain that status.

Tony rinsed off her plate and knife because the charwoman had already complained about the amount of work. This is my background, she thought wryly. Then she told herself: You're developing the mentality of an embittered little typist, or else you're scared to death.

CHAPTER FOUR

AT FIRST SHE HAD MET FEW OF HER RELATIVES because the wealthy spent the summers on the beaches. Their absence had made her realize that the Guerida Pazes had returned early to the hot city just to receive her and Peter. Though the sacrifice of a few weeks out of a three-month vacation may not have seemed a great gesture, Tony knew how upsetting such a sudden change in plans could be when the masters descended unexpectedly on a big house with half the servants on leave and the other half enjoying the comforts of the drawing rooms.

As March drew to a close, they began to take her around. Tony would stand, bewildered, among throngs of shrill-voiced women who talked with great emphasis, believed that they had a claim to all, that they did everything right and were of immense importance. The rest of the family, although polite, did not take her up as one of them. As the daughter of an Argentine society woman, their doors were open to her; as a foreigner, they did not actually beckon to her to come in.

Peter's letters spoke of the flat, wide *pampa* whose bare expanse had first depressed him and now gave him a grand sensation of unlimited freedom, told of the riches of the plains, the tough little *criollo* horses, the countless livestock.

Peter's settling down to a life of work and purpose made her even more resentful of her own idleness. But by now she had realized that she could not hope for outside assistance, and when she saw a public translator's sign on a house front, she walked in and asked for work. Though there was no vacancy, she made an arrangement to take urgent jobs that came up on weekends or at short notice.

Having achieved unassisted what everybody had told her was impossible, the achievement dispelled the dulling sensation of failure. Self-assurance regained, she began to look about, ready to be pleased. The urbane, rather unenthusiastic life of Buenos Aires and the stylish, tepid entertainments appealed to her. From among the chattering crowds she singled out Argentine women who were placid and unaffected, spoke beautifully and commanded an uncommon respect by their uncommon dignity. But her best hours were spent with Antonio, and with Romero Basualdo, who had called her the day after their first meeting.

They often drove out to the country, just kept driving, and had long talks or said nothing for hours. Sometimes they sang or recited poetry. Born interpreter that he was, Romero's expression and mood changed with the language he employed. Tony had a pretty soprano, inherited from her mother, who had taught her the songs of the age when, as don Antonio's generation said, the tango had not yet lost its soul.

She was not falling in love with Romero. A whole world separated them, a world of things that did not matter in friendship but that, she knew, would matter in love. Part of it was his upbringing in a devout, narrow-minded family that, though he gave no indication of bigotry or intolerance, must needs have shaped him through childhood and adolescence. The other part was intangible; a veil between them, not unpleasant, no hindrance to a great friendship, but one that people made to love each other would have lifted.

His attitude toward life was cheerful enough. His existence seemed stimulated, though quiet, and his mind had the gentle working of a very well adjusted person's. Still Tony felt stricken every time she happened to glance at his profile. Whether he was talking, laughing, singing, or listening, there were always his eyes, joyless, too hopeless for desperation or even bitterness. Those eyes, occupied in watching the road ahead, living by themselves, without relation to the serious, placid, or gay face, made her feel unhappy and impotent. She often thought that it would take great wisdom, strength, and daring for a woman to love him.

Later in the fall Carlota asked her to spend a weekend on their *estanzuela*—literally the "little one of their estates"—of some 3,500 acres in the province

18

of Buenos Aires. Antonio met her at the rural station, mounted on a grey horse beside a mail coach driven four-in-hand by a coachman.

A young man and two women were walking toward him, and he swung off his horse, took off his battered felt hat, and made the introductions. The young man's name was Fernando Belmán. One of the women seemed to be his sister.

When they were driving off, facing each other on the benches running down the length of the coach with don Antonio out of earshot, their talk conveyed that they were habitués of the estate. One of the women giggled. "I imagine you're quite shocked by this show of charming quaintness."

The man was slight, with evil eyes in a boyish face that constantly watched everything with an expression of blasé amusement.

"You must know," he told Tony in a mixture of mockery and admiration, "that his carriages have the merit of being more than mere replicas. They have been in his family for generations—that is, in yours, Milady," he added with an ironic little bow.

Tony smiled, but she did not like the scintillating eyes, the livid face, the miniature perfection of the body clad in Bond Street riding clothes. He did not look quite real, rather like a character in a drawing room comedy.

"Actually, we had no idea," he continued, "that don Antonio had the distinction of counting any Germanias among his delightful cousins."

Why did he not ever speak without irony? "The revelation fell like a bombshell into our eventless social life."

"Why?" she asked bluntly.

"Of course, we were charmed, my dear."

By this time she hated him.

"Are you going back?" inquired his sister.

"Oh no!"

"You aren't?" He was so astonished he was serious for the first time. And quickly, "Why did you leave?"

"My father is Jewish."

One of the women said, "Oh," and Belmán asked, sharp-eyed, "So you don't like the Germans?"

"I don't like the Nazis."

19

"That's all the same," concluded the sister with finality. Though Tony tended to agree with her, she did not like the supercilious tone of this young woman who did not know what she was talking about.

"So you're anti-Nazi?"

"Yes, I am." Tony was weary of this cross-examination. They were now trotting through a limestone gateway onto a dirt road bordered by eucalyptus trees. Right and left stretched flat country dotted with cattle and grazing horses. The long road ended at a paved courtyard surrounded by stables and coach houses, where don Antonio introduced his *mayordomo*, a husky, red-faced Scotsman, and then led them toward the bungalow that lay, white and sprawling, behind a magnificent lawn. The front of the middle wing was taken up by a porch where María Teresa and Carlota were entertaining guests.

Most were in expensive riding clothes, while María Teresa was wearing a shabby wine-red silk dress and a cardigan and Carlota well-worn jodhpurs. Her boots were shiny; Antonio's so old the leather was rubbed red and cracked where it touched the horse. He wore large time-stained gaucho spurs, and while his cotton breeches were ragged and discolored, there was no doubt who was the master of the land.

Only one other person seemed really to belong: Federico Dorrego Macín, María Teresa's brother. Tony had met him in town, where he had looked to her like a gentle schoolmaster, timid and rather sweet. The illicit amusements Antonio had ascribed to him had seemed oddly incongruous with his quiet, dejected appearance. Yet later, observing him beside his strident, bustling wife (who was reported to have all the money), she could picture the all too easy refuge this kind of man would have sought. The country air, and possibly the distance from his wife and her rivals, gave his grey skin a healthier glow and his carriage a new freedom and dignity.

She spent a pleasant half hour with him, but when the conversation became general, she felt somewhat forlorn. The talk was as fast as it is wont to be where people have known each other for a long time, with wisecracks darting back and forth, and allusions made in rapid succession to people she had never heard of, met with great mirth. One laughed at unfinished sentences full of first names, and Tony, a newcomer, could not get their point.

During lunch Carlota made an effort to draw her in. Oh yes, it was right, there was this exciting foreign girl! What interesting experiences she must have had! She ought to write a novel about it. And how did she like Argentina? Wasn't it wonderful to be here? Now everything else was forgotten, wasn't it? And her parents, were they here, too? No? Oh. But surely at the trial her father would be able to prove his innocence. He hadn't really done anything against the government, had he?

"You know, there's a girl from Austria," said Belmán. "She's some number. She says her mother was a baroness, but she's quite ill-mannered, really. Of course, baronesses often are—but not in exile!" he snickered. Someone insisted once more that Tony tell about her life over there. And had the Nazis taken their money away from them, as people said they did?

She answered in monosyllables, silently comparing the dachshund that had been a Saint Bernard with the ill-mannered Austrian whose mother had most likely really been a baroness. Changing into riding clothes after lunch, she heard in front of the open window Belmán's nasal voice. "I bet this slant-eyed sphinx is Nazi. Why else this mystery about her past? Real Jews always talk about what they've lost."

They mounted their horses. Rocking on a smooth-gaited criollo mare across miles of cattle-studded plain, Tony thought that their place in Potsdam had been a backyard compared to Antonio's "little estate." The wind was blowing the hair back from her face. Feeling once more the power and response of a young horse flow through her, the depression that had beset her at overhearing the comment on the porch gave way. She was happy, more herself than she had been in months.

She sat her horse well, but her pride vanished with all strict theory at seeing Antonio and Carlota who, as on photographs of the turn of the century, sat most unacademically close to the cantle, legs slightly advanced in the British style, erect but so loose-limbed they looked lazy, their reins almost slack, yet never losing contact. From Antonio's wrist hung a *rebenque*, a beautiful ornament of bleached rawhide and wrought silver. He looked shabby, picturesque, and dignified.

They cantered onto a narrow path in file, eyes lowered, bending over their horses' necks to avoid the thorns of the *acacias negras*, till at last, lifting their faces, they found themselves before the wide greyness of the river Paraná. A wet breeze swept over their hot bodies.

"How wonderful!" said Tony to Carlota who drew her mount up beside hers.

"It strikes a chord because part of you comes from this place and belongs here."

Tony knew then that they were friends.

CHAPTER FIVE

SHE HAD ENJOYED THE COUNTRY SO MUCH that Antonio began to take her along on many of his inspection tours. They spent three or four hours in the saddle, sometimes in conversation, more often in silence, a great understanding growing between them that bridged the gap in years and the difference in memories, experiences, and expectations. They were living the same moment in the same place almost with the same sensations.

She would not allow Antonio to stable a horse for her in Palermo Park, but she rode there regularly on rented horses, pleased with the well-kept bridle paths and carefully set hurdles, although it gave her an unreasonable feeling of guilt toward Romero. She had thought of asking him to the estate some Sunday, believing he should be physically able to ride. On one hand, she did not like for him to think that she doubted, but on the other she was not sure. Afraid to blunder, she said nothing, just kept the glow out of her voice when she talked about the estanzuela. At one time she had wondered why he never asked to see her on weekends, but now she was glad of it because it would have meant giving up her country escape.

One evening they drove up Avenida Costanera toward the port. For a while they stepped from the car and, turning their backs to the twinkling light strings of the amusement park, rested their elbows on the white parapet. She looked out onto the dark phantom river and felt sadness like a premonition, oddly incongruous with the merry-go-round tune that came pattering across the thoroughfare to dance and skip over the heavy breathing of the river.

"I wonder," she remarked, "why God has made sadness so predominant over joy. His children would surely not sin so much and be less hard if happiness were not so rare that they must hunt for it and then hold on to it, fight to get and fight to keep it."

"I don't think, Tony, that you can just say, 'sadness,' and make it every-body's sadness; not everyone feels unhappy about it. Of course, it is every-where, at every moment, even in bliss or ecstasy, in success and triumph. It is the background to life. One must be born, or learn, to live with it."

"But why? Why do most people smile *malgré tout* when it could and should be natural? Unhappiness is barren. Coping with it consumes ener-gies that could be put to some constructive use instead."

For a second the flame of a match pierced the night; then only the two red points of their cigarettes glowed in the dark.

"You mustn't fight sadness," he said quietly, "not even let it start to make you unhappy. You must accept it as a quiet black backdrop, like the velvet you see behind your lids, ever present, unchanged each time you close your eyes. And so you can set out from it and go back to it, using it as a gauge for your pleasures and joys that come and disappear so swiftly, fluctuate so that without your background of sadness you would have no basis by which to evaluate them correctly. I don't know if you understand. But I can always estimate my golden moments by stopping to see how much of the black they're able to cover."

"But do they often cover a lot?" she asked skeptically.

"Never." He laughed softly, the glow of his cigarette going out before it reached the water. "Yet, a little gold looks gorgeous on a lot of black."

"It takes a mellow mind to reconcile oneself to it," she said dryly.

"It's just a convenience. If you use it my way. I told you, sadness is ever present and always the same. In contrast to happiness, it doesn't disappoint us because we're not led to expect any blessings from it; it never cheats us be-cause we do not wish to be deceived by it; and it cannot ever hurt us brutally because we know it for what it is. We ought to be afraid of happiness, which we know only casually and which may turn on us at any moment, rather than of this long familiar sadness."

This conversation had given her an insight that, to some extent, leveled the abyss between his eyes and the rest of his face.

With the coming of winter, Antonio began to look upon the European sit-uation with anxiety and worried more about Dolores and her husband, al-though Carlota maintained that in case of war the Germans would be too busy to bother much about the Jews. At the Jockey Club he broached the subject with the Foreign Minister, who instructed the embassy in Berlin to make a request to the German government to release Herrnfeld and allow the couple to leave the country. It seemed an arduous enterprise and little progress was made. But Tony knew that at last something was being done, and everybody assured her that the Germans would not refuse such a small favor to a country that could be of great use to them.

She felt confident and rather happy, although she missed Peter. They wrote to each other several times a week, but she lacked the presence of someone who had shared her past, who needed no explanations or descriptions and understood half finished sentences. When she said to Antonio or Carlota or Romero, our orchard, my dog, my way to school, she knew that, were they to draw what she described, she would not recognize it.

But then, she told herself, she had made within a very few months three great friends, more than she had hoped for. Carlota had come to rank very close to Antonio. They met almost every day, and her cousin kept introducing "candidates" to her, fortunately without pressing the point.

In Palermo she had seen Fernando Belmán again who kept a white Arab, small and spectacular like himself, and sported an astonishing collection of antique riding crops and stock pins. He courted her in an insolent manner, often slippery, yet so diluted that most of its offensive sting was lost. She saw through every one of his fibs, every stretch of comedy, and every crooked move of his mind. As before the eyes of one who is farsighted, the shocking picture she had perceived at first became blurred at close range, giving way to amusement.

"I'll tell you, Tony," said Carlota one afternoon at tea, "I don't mean for you to take up Fernandito. He's no good. But there are others. For God's sake don't get too deeply involved with Romero. He's a nice boy, but you'd have to be a saint to live with an invalid for the rest of your life."

"It's never occurred to me to marry him," protested Tony. "Neither has it to him."

"I know how you feel," insisted Carlota. "You pity him. Everybody does. He's such a splendid person. Even good-looking. And all that bungled by an infirmity. You tell yourself that it doesn't really matter, not to you, but to most others. So you feel called upon to give him his one chance. But pity isn't any foundation for marriage because it isn't the stuff that love is made of. You know, it would be like living on a volcano, always taking precautions until finally it blows up under you all the same. It would end in revulsion, or even hatred."

Personally Tony had no objection to this carefully prepared piece of advice. Carlota was right and she had no intention of marrying Romero. Nonetheless, it hurt that his eyes spoke true: that he was considered well nigh a freak, that nobody just said, "what a nice boy," that they all added, "what a pity . . . "

"I don't feel sorry for him," she said defensively.

"That's what you think," murmured Carlota.

Ignoring it, Tony added, "Romero is perfectly happy and that is precisely what makes him good company. I wouldn't enjoy him if he made me sad. I'm not going to marry him, though."

"That's the girl," nodded Carlota, discarding the top of her sandwich. "You know, by the way, that he has a girlfriend?"

Tony noted with relief that the news did not rankle. "No, he hasn't told me. Who is it?"

"It's a funny thing. Some time or other, oh, perhaps two years ago, he met a girl who had some infirmity herself. She had no money and he paid for all her treatments until she got well. Quite a morbid, and if you want, romantic story."

"I think that's great." She was wondering what need she was filling, since this other attachment, rather than just erotic, seemed to be a true friendship.

July brought plenty of work, as well as a succession of dinner dances, evenings at the theater and opera, and the meeting of new, often interesting people. But her heart was only partly in it. The Argentine Embassy in Berlin had so far obtained nothing but promises "to look into the matter." Dolores had again been without news from her husband for a long time. She wrote that she had sold their home. *Sold.* What did the word mean in a letter that had to pass censorship? Everything across the sea had become one gigantic, menacing question mark.

26

One night, half an hour after he had taken her home, Romero called her on the telephone, his voice depressed and urgent. "Tony, I must talk to you. People are so perfidious! So lowly! So . . . "

When he picked her up, he did not turn his face toward her, and his hands pressed down on the steering wheel as if holding something down by force. "You must think I'm mad. If I could explain!"

"What happened, Romero?" she asked quietly, but her heart contracted and waited for a blow, she did not know what kind.

"I never knew people could be so perfidious!" he repeated, as deeply shocked as he must have been at the first moment. But then he tried to sound matter of fact, though he was shaking with excitement. "You see . . . I know a girl . . . I don't love her. Not any more, anyway. Even at the beginning it was only pity. She was so weak, spiritually resourceless, had nothing to fight back with in adversity. She's unintelligent and even quite common. Maybe I once imagined myself in love, had some attachment. But even that has been over for a long time; and I should have known! But no one with a bit of decency in him could imagine such baseness. A clean mind just can't!"

He raised his hands and threw them back onto the wheel. "Anyway, tonight, just now, I went to see her to tell her that everything was finished between us. Because I like you so much better, Tony. And . . ." He stopped because bitterness, rage, and despair were strangling him. "I found her with a man!"

He swerved violently to avoid an oncoming car. "How vile! How unspeakably dirty!"

Tony said nothing. There were many things she could have said, trivialities she would have told any other at this moment: If she is that kind of girl she isn't worth crying over, or, You wanted to break with her, would you have preferred to hurt her instead?

But she knew that his hurt had not really been caused by the girl, who had only torn open a long-existing inner wound. She saw it so distinctly; a girl, just some kind of a girl, with a big, healthy man; and in the doorway Romero, slight and dark, leaning on his cane, all his power in his fine, manly face, unable to defend himself, once more confronted by the fact that what he lacked was important.

He went on, but the intoxication of rage that had made his anguish somehow bearable had spent itself; and now without the effervescence of rebellion, only the stale excitement and the raw, ugly hurt remained.

"It didn't really matter at all because, I told you, I don't love her. I don't want to be with anyone but you any more. That's why I went to see her tonight. But the way it happened! If she had come and told me, 'I want to be free, I love someone else.' But this way!"

"I know, Romero, I know," was all she found to say.

They were driving alongside Palermo's bridle paths. The white hurdles shone ghostly through the night and poplars whispered surreptitiously under the sharp breeze blowing from the river into the open window. He was as exhausted as a child after a tantrum, the calmed surface still rippling with hysteria, when at last he headed back to town, silent until they reached more urban streets. Then he began to apologize for having disturbed her at so late an hour.

"Don't apologize, I'm grateful."

He stopped before a white apartment house. "Will you come up with me, Tony, just for a little while? Please, I need you so."

In the haste with which he seized on her instant of hesitation, he failed to notice its swift passing. "I would never have told you, had I not gone there tonight to make a break, nothing else."

He put his arm around her shoulder just as she was about to say, "Come to my place for a drink and a midnight snack," and now pressed her head against his face, seeking her mouth. She disengaged herself gently and said, without irony, "Romero, not all out of Germany is ersatz."

CHAPTER SIX

A WAIL FLOODED THE NIGHT. Tony sat up in bed. It came from far away, reaching across the sleeping metropolis like a giant arm to clutch at her heart in frightened appeal. It penetrated into each single room of the city, wildly beating about everywhere at the same time, screaming people out of their slumber. To the straining ear it seemed to die down, but it went on and on and on until at last it faded into an exhausted sigh.

She sat, motionless, wondering if it could have been a nightmare, for there was only silence and blackness. Then the telephone at her bedside rang in familiar shrillness and there was Carlota's voice. "Tony, have you been frightened? That was the siren of *La Prensa*. It's war."

"God," she said. A thousand thoughts crashed into her mind like steel bars and lay there in a jumbled lot.

"Let's talk for a while," suggested Carlota. She could picture Tony in the dark of her lonely apartment, knew the implications of the single "God" at the other end of the line.

There was a pause while they groped for something to say, except what was foremost in their minds. Finally Tony asked lamely, "What's Argentina going to do?"

"We'll keep out," said Carlota with the brutal calm that was hers whenever she felt indignation. "Our generals are too convinced of a German victory to bet on a loser, and the government wants to play it safe. If the Germans win they'll take vengeance; but the Allies will gratefully embrace any latecomer to organize a swift, seamless peace. They've got it all figured out."

"Oh," said Tony listlessly. There was another pause.

"Do you want me to come over?"

"Oh no, don't! After all, it had to come sometime. Maybe this will be the end of the nightmare."

"I'm sure it will be, Tony. Aren't you?" Carlota asked softly.

"Yes, I am. Good night, Carlota. Thanks for calling."

"Good night, Tony."

Carlota's description of the official attitude had been accurate. However, except for a group of vociferous youngsters who called themselves nationalists and resented "British investments and Yankee imperialism," the general public gave roaring applause to the Allies' newsreels, never doubting the final victory of the democracies.

Hearing many rumors about espionage, they worried about every foreigner. Tony sensed suspicion in their questions, heard it in their jests, without understanding. She had no idea that a neutral country, separated by an ocean from the cause and effects of the war, could be a place for spies. Even in a country at war, espionage was to her something to be read about in paperback thrillers.

She told Romero that Belmán called her "X-24, the German spy," and was surprised, almost shocked, at his reaction.

"How beastly," he said, his brows contracting into one dark line. "You've suffered too much at the hands of the Nazis to deserve such insults."

"But it was a joke," she laughed, her laugh stiffening at the sudden memory of how sharply Belmán had watched her response.

Romero, who knew that she would always fight the Nazis, approved of her attitude, but could not understand her desire to see Germany at bay.

"After all, it's your country; you can't want it mangled," he said. "No matter what should happen in Argentina, it would always be my country and I would love it."

She had not tried to argue. There had again been the veil that had not lifted. Explanation should have been unnecessary. Since the stormy winter night so full of despair and failure for him, they had continued to see each other. Never mentioned, nothing having changed on account of it, it had been the touchstone of their friendship, while this evening's remark made a change. He could not fill her need for understanding and approval at a moment when she realized that there were very ugly suspicions under people's puzzling attitudes toward her. But, characteristically, she did not try to force the veil apart, and thus no dissonance followed.

But when Belmán once more called her "X-24," she flared up. He raised his eyebrows and, making his gold-mounted crop slide through his fingers, asked, "Why this violence? You used to understand jokes."

Tony moved with a jerk, her horse bounding under the accidental touch of the spur. "You might as well jokingly call me a murderess!"

"You're very touchy, my dear."

When she told Antonio, he laughed. "Don't you know Belmán is a little snake who won't hurt you as long as you keep your foot on him?" he asked. "He simply loves to see people get into trouble, mainly to give him occasion for a wisecrack, but also—as he has a very curious mind—to see what will come of it. He has an extremely unpleasant habit of circulating rumors that he's made up just to watch the stone rolling or to get one of his snickers out of it."

"The meanest thing is that he makes these remarks usually when others are around. When we're alone he's too busy talking about himself. And I can't help being embarrassed like I used to be in customs, though I hadn't smuggled anything."

The next move, however, came when they were alone. They were letting their horses graze without dismounting, and she was reaching into her pocket for a cigarette when Belmán said solemnly, "let's ride over for a drink at the *boliche* by the lake. This is a day to celebrate."

"Celebrate what?" she asked, astonished, her hand with the unlit cigarette suspended in mid-air, wondering what prankish idea or romantic farce was behind this.

"Don't you know? Today it's been eight months since you arrived in Buenos Aires. You don't realize what it means to me. I happen to be in love with you."

She was sure that she had never mentioned her exact date of arrival and was already so uneasy that his knowledge made her wonder. Yet she had also learned caution. "Don't be a clown, Fernandito. But I don't mind a drink." She took up the reins. The cigarette, uncharacteristically in one corner of her mouth, she headed at a sharp trot toward the lake heedless of the asphalt, an unusual act of negligence. He was a good observer.

31

When she told Carlota, her cousin asked, "You know where he got that? He has some kind of soft job as a court inspector, which gives him access to police records."

"But why go to all that trouble?"

"Just to impress you," laughed Carlota. "You'd be surprised to find how much effort and hard work this loafer will go to for the sake of a prank."

Tony began to isolate herself. Except for Romero and her family there was nobody she wished to see. While the changed attitude of some embarrassed her, that of others, like Federico Dorrego Macín, was even less welcome.

One afternoon on the estanzuela, don Federico said, "I admire the Germans. They're hard but they're strong, and that's what counts in this world. From economic shambles and political discord they've built up a magnificent country that can challenge the whole world. And they're going to win this war."

The hero worship of the defeated shone in his tired eyes. Seeing the stiff line of Tony's mouth, he added, "Of course, what they're doing to the Jews is terrible. But they'll get over that."

"Maybe," Tony remarked icily, "but their victims won't."

There was no pleasure in social gatherings where war was a constant topic, and hers seemed an odd twilight position. She concentrated on her work, which she had found to be the best drug for depression, until even this modest delight was marred. The Belgian Legation, giving her employer a harmless commission, inquired who was going to do the job. Paradoxically, they demanded not only impossible proof that she was a genuine refugee but a certificate of good conduct from Nazi Germany. The assignment was given to someone else, and she never again worked without this memory at the back of her mind.

A week had passed without a letter from her mother. Although it was to be expected that after the outbreak of war mail would be held up or snowed under with censorship, times were too uncomfortable for easy guesses. Peter was also without news and advised her to go to the German Consulate. Talking to a German government official was a distasteful prospect, but she knew no other way to make inquiries.

As she walked down the one flight of stairs from her apartment, she heard the janitor's voice in the hall: ". . . it seems that she's a German spy."

She stopped dead and held her breath. ". . . spoke like an Englishman . . . all kinds of questions. . . ." The interjection was but a murmur. ". . . always had a hunch . . . mail from Germany . . . so-called translations . . . elegant lady, doesn't really need to work." She walked on and turned into the vestibule, where the interlocutor was facing the wall.

For a moment she stood on the street, lost, like a stranger with nowhere to go. Then she took a cab to Avenida Alvear. If people did not understand the tremendous accusation they were making, their abhorrence was less than hers.

She spread her indignant anger before Antonio who tried to reassure her. "You mustn't get so upset over what strangers say or think. Of course, the Allied embassies investigate everybody in your position. You wouldn't want it otherwise. And, naturally, people will have all kinds of strange ideas. What matters is that we believe in you, Antonie."

Her sore, hypersensitive mind took exception to the words, "What matters is that we believe in you." Why had he deemed it necessary to make their position clear? So they, too, must have doubted but kept their faith. It had sounded to her like a plea not to disappoint him.

Another week without word from Dolores. Silence out of Germany was neither accidental nor negligent. She sent a cable and received a prompt reply: "Perfectly all right. Love. Mother." Dolores used to sign herself "Mamá," but maybe greater formality was logical in a cable. Another week went by without a letter. I must, after all, go to the consulate, she told herself one evening, shortly before the telephone rang.

"Tony, it's been a long time . . ."

Half an hour later Manuel Giles was at her apartment. He had been on the staff of the Argentine Embassy in Berlin, the only foreigner who, on the morning after the *razzia*, had called to ask how they had fared. Tony knew from her mother's letters that he had never wavered in his friendship. But now he, too, had joined the exodus of minor diplomats and had arrived this very morning on a Spanish ship.

Before he had time to sit down, Tony asked, "What's wrong with mother, Manuel? Except for a cable, I haven't heard from her since before you left. Won't they let her letters through, or is she in hiding, or what?"

He looked at her, trapped. Her heart missed a beat.

"Tell me frankly," she said. "I'm prepared."

He spoke swiftly, expressionless, as though it were the only way to bring himself to say it: "Your father died suddenly and, I suppose, mysteriously, in the concentration camp. Someone came to tell your mother and to inform her that now, as a 'German Aryan,' she would receive an exit permit to join her children in Argentina if, here as well as there, she showed herself willing to act as such.

"She told me that she cut them short, 'I am one hundred percent Latin, the widow of a Jew and the mother of half-Jewish children,' whereupon they objected somewhat lamely that her children were Christians like her. I advised her to agree to everything because, goodness, once here, who could have harmed her or you? But she seemed to feel that she must identify herself with your father beyond death. She informed them that she would adopt the Jewish faith. They came to arrest her, but she . . . she shot herself."

"Shot . . ." Tony repeated stiffly. She had sat all this time staring at his torn face, petrified in her nightmare. And with that same nightmarish sensation of unreality she went on as if arguing him out of something illogical: "Mother hated to even hear a shot. She distrusted Father's gun when it lay unloaded in his desk. She only wanted to have a good time. Don't you see? She had such a horror of any kind of weapon that she wouldn't even hunt, although we all . . ."

She stopped short and, as if coming out of the dark into blinding light, gave him a wild stare and closed her eyes, shaken by sudden, tearless shock waves.

"I know, Tony. Love and suffering have made a heroine of your mother," he said lamely.

She reopened her dry eyes. "What for?" There was a peculiar harshness in her despair, more painful to watch than tearful abandon. "Now we're completely alone. Now there's nothing left of our lives. Now we must seek new values to make our existence worth living. But what?" She stared at him.

"New love . . . people disappear from our lives, Tony, but children are born."

She kept looking at him without moving. "Children who may one day have to go through things like this? Children of whom they would know nothing?" Then her gaze turned inward, shut him out. "I'll have to tell Peter."

CHAPTER SEVEN

WHEN PETER CAME THEY BURIED THEMSELVES in the apartment. Once she had broken down, Tony could not pull herself together. Peter's hurt seemed to tie him in knots, made him hard and tense.

She found him changed. He had put on weight and muscle. His bronze skin had darkened, and that made the eyes look amber rather than brown. His speech was slower and more coordinated, more mature and less spontaneous. He carried himself more erectly and with a flexibility that did not make him look young, only more powerful. It was as if he had prematurely reached middle age.

Although wishing to remain close, they drew an invisible chalk line across the room. Tony, who lay awake crying, knew that Peter on the living room couch was awake, too. He did not stir, while normally he would have turned around several times, cleared his throat, then sighed in his sleep. Apparently this taut silence was his way of crying.

For one week they uttered only abrupt sentences. But when on the eve of Peter's departure they sat over a cup of tea, he said harshly, as if laying down a program, "We must forget. Thousands must forget, not we alone."

She shook her head. "I can't. I felt no real hatred when they smashed our future. But I can't forgive them for trampling on our past."

Peter passed a hand over his sun-bleached hair. "It's not a matter of forgetting and forgiving. I shall always hate . . . hate actively. Passive resentment is barren."

"What do you mean?" she asked, discouraged and in no mood for a diatribe on political philosophy.

"Oh, you could never learn, Tony. Because you feel differently. I've seen it in your letters. Ever since we arrived we've taken different routes. I chose mine on that first night at the Hotel Bolívar when you thought I was asleep until I spoke to you. Remember how I said I'd been thinking about home?"

"Yes. So had I."

"I know." He rose to stand by the fireplace, the way his father used to do when an important decision was to be reached in the family. "And I also know in which way. I'm sure our conclusions were very different.

"That night I, too, revisited Potsdam, smelled the leaves in the woods, heard them rustle under hoof in the fall, and the women sing in the fields. I dropped in on drink-sodden old Jacob who used to drive four-in-hand for grandfather, and found him in his quarters in back of the gardeners' house listening to Radio Moscow, despite the death penalty and the fact that he didn't care for communists.

"It was good to go back, but at the same time I realized that such personal things were what had held Father. That everything else was make-believe."

As Tony stirred, about to protest, he took a step forward. "His pride needed a heroic excuse. That was all. He simply couldn't disengage himself from the spell of the woods and lakes, the language of his poets. He didn't have the spirit to blot out what had built him and what he had built in a lifetime. To admit that his entire marvelously full fifty years had been a delusion, less than worthless, like a capital wiped out by bankruptcy, would have crushed him. He preferred to live a great tragedy to compromising with drabness—and that way came damn close to sacrificing us all."

Tony was silent. What Peter said was irrefutable. But it left their lives bare of all spiritual values. She was not so willing to chastise herself for the sake of reason.

"And I don't think," he continued, "that you quite realize what he has done to Mother, who had no convictions one way or another! His personality was so potent that she acted it out with him in her grand, spectacular manner, finished it for him, beyond his end. But martyrdom without a cause is nonsense. They were very foolish heroes, if they were heroes at all."

"What do you gain, Peter, by stripping yourself of past values?"

"My freedom," he said brusquely.

"Does it steady you?" she continued softly, "It can only make you drift like an empty shell."

"I do remember, Tony, and I want to. There are very many things that I will never forget. That first night I lined them up in my mind: the brown jackets in school and the thousand and one humiliations. But even more than the personal persecution, the bestial organization for oppression and conquest that aimed for this war. All that and only that. On our first night in Buenos Aires you didn't stop to put that on the other side of your scale, or it would have tipped over. Like mine."

"I know you're right, Peter. But I can't make myself feel it intensely, even now. I can't hate trees and songs and individuals. I guess I have no character. I'm just terribly sad, that's all."

Peter put on her shoulder a hand that was still fine and slender, but heavier from an amount of manual work. "It isn't easy, I know. I, too, have felt all you feel. But I had to get away from that part of myself if I wanted to be of one piece. I had to have something solid to build my life on."

"How strange. You survive by shedding. I, by preserving."

He sat down and lit a cigarette. "Don't think that I'll be one of those refugees who after a few years don't remember they were born elsewhere, who say "we" when they refer to Argentina and talk about the Germans as if they were saying "the Japanese." The trouble with us, dear, is that we belong nowhere. Or, maybe, it's to our advantage. We're the really free because our conscience won't ever be confused by the fact that we're both judge and party."

This first exchange of ideas since their tragedy had taken Tony out of her inarticulate despair and made her conscious again of her own person other than a link meaningless without the chain. She lived once more, though not very gladly.

One day she called Carlota to offer her an invitation she had received to the *vernissage* of the spring salon.

"We got ours," said Carlota. "But how come you did? They're going by the Social Register. Terribly stuffy affair." And with typical irrelevance, "Let's go. What? What rubbish! You're not going to spend the remainder of your life without reading a book or looking at a picture!"

On the same afternoon a letter from Romero asked her to call him any time she was ready to see him. She asked him to her apartment, although even this friendship was thrown off balance by a remark Peter had made while in Buenos Aires: "Your friend may be all right, but his father is pro-German." Nothing seemed to count any more except political opinion. Where was Peter's freedom of those who belonged nowhere?

Two days later she attended the opening of the art show with Carlota, who after a casual tour went off to her hairdresser. For Tony, at a picture gallery as in a library, it was hard to stop browsing, and while gradually the padded shoulders and flowery hats that had barred access to most pictures dispersed, she walked through the now almost hushed rooms.

A hall, frames, pictures, a door, arrows, signs, she thought, nothing of it exists for them. They're mute, blind, unconscious . . . not even that, they are not. No more than if they had never been. A vision of Dolores's hands brought tears to her eyes. It seemed senseless, unless there lay beyond death something besides the great void of which she had always been convinced and that she now preferred to doubt.

She stopped before a bucolic Fader, drinking horses, all in browns. It made her think of Peter, the peace on his estancia and the bitter comment in his last letter: "What a joyful present for year's end, the sinking of the *Graf Spee*. But, believe me, the 'interned crew,' which even now, I am told, is hanging out at the Richmond Bar, will soon be back in Kiel. Leave it to the German estancieros with whom the coast up here is lousy. They are busy refueling and supplying U-boats and smuggling in and out whom they please."

"Aren't you Miss Antonie Herrnfeld?" The voice was pleasant, but the long-unfamiliar German sounds made her start. The stranger who had stopped beside her was exceedingly tall and thin. His silky blond hair receded from a pale, vulnerable looking face.

"Yes," she replied slowly and as if in doubt.

"My name is von der Heiden. I've heard a great deal about you." He smiled a fine, forceless smile.

Tony was embarrassed. A German. What kind of German?

"I've been told that you worry about your parents. I may be able to help you."

She looked up into his gentle, attractive face and thought of the submarines. "Are you German?"

"Yes," he smiled ruefully. "Even a member of the embassy. It isn't what you would call easy, but, as we say in Germany, *mitgefangen, mitgehangen*."

His eyes were of a gentle grey and trust-inspiring, and she was glad that Peter had mentioned the submarines approaching in the hour of sleep.

"Where are your parents?" he inquired sympathetically.

"Don't you know?" she retorted, neither moving her lips, nor looking at him. She was so puzzled it was painful.

She felt his eyes on her profile while the sympathy in his voice turned into compassion. "I thought maybe you didn't. I happened to see a report on them, and when just now a friend told me, 'you see, over there, that's Carlota Guerida's beautiful German cousin I told you about,' I naturally remembered that report. I would like to help you."

Tony knew he lied to her with icy predetermination. And yet, through some intricate circumstance, her information might be inaccurate. She had no word from Germany since Manuel Giles's visit; either no one answered her letters or the answers were not getting through. The remarkably half-hearted investigation into which the foreign minister had been pressured by Antonio had so far brought nothing to light. Manuel had not been an eyewitness and had in the meantime been reassigned and left town. There must be some Germans left who were human, so perhaps . . .

"Where could we have a quiet talk?" he asked almost shyly. "I don't suppose you'd care to be seen in my company."

They went to her apartment. When he sat in her chair as if he were in his own home, and she could not shake off a sensation of trust. He had beautiful, narrow hands and a pleasant accent.

"I know that you've been without word from your mother for quite a while. The cable you received was a fake," he added contemptuously. "You didn't know, did you, that both your parents are now in Buchenwald?"

"No." They are dead, she thought, why does he lie? What does he want? Yet again, Manuel was no eyewitness; even he wouldn't know for sure. The wildest rumors circulate where free expression is impossible. She looked at the stranger's aristocratic forehead, his weak mouth. Maybe he is speaking the truth, wants to help . . . maybe all is not lost.

"You mustn't tell anyone, though, that I talked to you. It could cost my head."

"And why are you risking it?" she asked coldly.

"I come from a diplomat's family," he explained. "We've been in the service for generations. Besides, I'm German; my country has been stepped on, and now rises. I don't particularly appreciate the way in which it happens. I detest violence, and I despise anti-Semitism. Many of my friends are Jews. But, as I said, I am a German. Right or wrong, my country, if I may borrow the language of our temporary enemies.

"In spite of all this, I feel that I must help the innocent victims of this chaos of rebirth. I feel it to be my duty to counteract, within my limited powers, the cruel excesses any such upheaval carries with it. That's why I remain on the job, you see."

He had spoken slowly and somehow convincingly.

"Can you free my parents?" she asked in clipped syllables.

"Not that. I don't believe so."

"So what can you do?"

Von der Heiden, taken aback by her directness, was silent for a moment. Then he said, "If I were to put in a word for them, they might be given special privileges."

"And what reason would you give for your charitable intervention?"

"I would, of course, have to say that you'd be willing . . ."

"To pay for it," Tony concluded, wryly remembering Manuel's story of the recruiting of her mother.

Von der Heiden blushed. "That is perhaps correct. We live in a dirty world."

"In the fight against a dirty world. What do you expect from me?"

"You might be able to obtain certain information for the embassy."

"What kind of information?" She sat stiffly, every nerve in her tense, and reconnoitered the ground to find her line of defense.

Von der Heiden shifted in his chair, embarrassed. "Oh, nothing specific. Just whatever you hear. Don't you know quite a few British?"

"None at all."

"The British Embassy has okayed you." His voice had a slight edge. "You must have connections."

"I've been investigated like all Germans," she replied calmly.

"We'll find some way to put you in touch with the right people."

She looked into his pale grey eyes, held them for a moment, and then let them go like one would drop something one does not intend to use. "What makes you think I would do such a thing?"

"You love your parents. Besides, you're German yourself, and your country's not going to forget that you helped her on the way to victory."

"Are you so sure you're going to win?"

"Perfectly sure." It sounded sincere. "You work for the British Red Cross, don't you?" he asked abruptly and without transition.

"Sure. Unfortunately that's all I can do."

"You see, you do know Britishers." He smiled as at a child caught in a fib.

"Of course I know Anglo-Argentines."

"Why don't you go to the Red Cross more regularly? You see, they don't just knit and gossip, but entertain the sailors from the merchant ships, give them tea and cakes and little English girls to dance the Big Apple with so they won't go to the harbor joints, get drunk, and talk. You know, on the whole they're good dutiful boys, like ours. Too bad we must fight them.

"It will be only too easy for you to date them. Preferably have them come here. Of course, the embassy must first fall in with my plan. If they do, they'll furnish whatever you need. Scotch," he chuckled.

Tony clenched her teeth. "What guarantees do you offer me?"

"Your parents will be taken care of. But, Miss Herrnfeld, no one outside the embassy must know about this. It might cost my life—and most certainly those of your parents."

Stephan von der Heiden left the house, his mouth stale and bitter. He thought of the slender, erect girl with the bloodless face, the soft mouth, and the depressed eyes. Why did she betray her race, her ideology, all that she so splendidly seemed to embody? From despair, from fear—from love. For two people she loved she tore down her world, made herself vile. He had learned to mistrust love, and it had been a long time since he had let it draw close enough to be forced to step around it.

He did not care for the Jews; they were loud and insecure. The views, gestures, and voices of the few he had ever met had displeased him, but the Nazi methods against them more than displeased him, they revolted him. There was no valid reason to proceed in such a way against a minority that neither could, nor would become a danger to Germany and had given it considerable intellectual and artistic prestige. A government official who ought to know had assured him that the concentration camp stories were exaggerated; still, their very existence was a blot on German honor and culture.

So why did he consent to being a representative of such things, while he clearly understood that no half-agreement was possible, that one could only be for or against?

Though he truly came from a family of diplomats, his own father was a retired cavalry officer with a fervent hatred of the Nazis, "those artisans and bookkeepers in their grotesque policemen's uniforms who dared order Germany around." When they had come to power, he had withdrawn to his estates in Mecklenburg to bury his bitterness among the oaken walls of his library.

His life had ended there; but Stephan had been very young at the time. Unable to muster much interest in the breeding of Mecklenburg draft horses and his father's rusty weapons collection, he had lived in a Proustian dream cocoon and, when it came to choosing a career, had seized upon the diplomatic service. It offered the brilliance he sought but sidestepped, he believed, the coarser aspects of the new code.

He had had no idea of the inhumane nature of its real functions. Now he was in it, up to his slender neck, yet spied upon and surrounded by distrust because his father was no Nazi. Most of the time it had seemed worthwhile in a strangely negative way. For all his robber-baron ancestors' penchant for the good things in life, he failed to combine their boldness and laughing unconcern, their ignorant cruelty.

Antonie Herrnfeld, he reflected, was not strong enough either. She, too, was attached to individuals and single things and therefore could neither give in to nor combat Nazism. But she was proud and so, too, upright to bend, would probably break under the strain. He had never known a Jewish girl and she surprised him. She was not great, but she was fine. And clever. Did she believe him? Had she not wondered at an invitation to such an exclusive social event, which he had secured through an ambitious young Nationalist belonging to the outer, reactionary fringe of society? Would he be able to manage her? Probably, for she was desperate and depressed and she had not seemed totally hostile.

CHAPTER EIGHT

A PICKET FENCE OF DISTRUST BARRED THE EYES of the British Embassy official. "Doesn't he know you're here?"

"No," said Tony in surprise.

He kept staring into her eyes: "How'd you dare come then? Are you sure you're not being shadowed?"

"Shadowed? Oh! You think someone might have followed me?" Suddenly she felt endangered.

The man passed three fingers through his crew cut and laughed. "You seem to know darn little about this business."

"Of course." She had decided to take her information to the British Embassy, not knowing that it would get her into even deeper waters. She felt cold as if in a draft while the man looked pointedly at her trembling hands.

"You can still tell him to go to hell, you know. But it might not be safe—and I don't mean for your parents, even if they were alive. It wouldn't be safe for you, they'd fear an indiscretion—such as you're committing right now. On the other hand, if you actually work with us, we can, at least to a limited extent, protect you."

"What could I do for you?" she asked timidly, seeing only two open roads: into the fire or into the water. She shivered with the cold, but her head was burning and her hands were clammy.

"I couldn't tell you offhand. Whatever comes up. At any rate, you'd pass on information to the Germans. Carefully selected information!" he laughed as at a practical joke.

She hated him for his laugh. "Won't they find out?" she objected lamely.

"Leave that to us. It'll be hard to establish. And tell us all you hear—even when it seems unimportant."

"May I come back here?" she asked, worried.

"No. Tomorrow you'll meet someone at the Red Cross. A man who goes by the name of Hull. Now, about your remuneration."

She sat up. "No money, please. I need no money. All I needed was a solution. You've offered it."

"As you wish." He rose, smiling at her for the first time, a wintry smile, his eyes still barricaded.

The building dropped back like a protective refuge as she walked through the narrow streets of the banking district, which buzzed at this hour with traffic and pedestrians. A polyglot hum surrounded her. People crowded the sidewalks on their way to eat or to the department stores for hurried lunch-hour purchases.

She thought, I'm a spy, adding derisively, Mata Hari. She was afraid. Why must she, so normal and unadventurous, err into this kind of situation? Who had pushed her into it? Fate? She hated big words full of pathos, hated the pathos of her own predicament. From time to time she looked over her shoulder to see if she was followed and, doing so, felt ridiculous.

She liked to work at the Red Cross despite her feeling of isolation, there as everywhere, when she heard women talk of "their" country and "their" boys. It was always "we," and she belonged nowhere, her only attachment an idea she prayed for, not a country and a people she was proud of, eager to preserve. What she had loved and wanted to safeguard had ceased to exist.

This afternoon she had had her first experience of direct involvement. A road was now mapped out for her toward a concrete aim, and she told herself that it was good, that she had at last found a place in the world. But there was more apprehension than elation, and she cuddled into the warmth of this commonplace gathering, fearing the ticking of the clock, the street, being alone again.

She told one of the women that she would gladly help out in the canteen. "Oh, sure," was the reluctant reply, "but you won't enjoy it much. Those boys aren't very interesting. Still, it may give you an idea of how the British people live and think. You've probably never seen our type of boy."

When she poured tea for a blond sailor with a smooth, pinkish neck and square hands, nails bitten down to the quick, she wondered what the

English lady had meant by "our type of boy." He was just a boy with no label attached, the universal child of twenty-two, telling her about a schoolteacher, his father, his little sister.

"It's fun talking to you about home. You've never lived there and so it's all new to you. I can tell you silly stories without boring you. Or do I?" he laughed, embarrassed.

"No, you don't. All those small things compounded determine the kind of life we have," she replied absentmindedly, wondering when the man who went by the name of Hull would appear. "Do you enjoy being at sea?"

"Oh yes," he said. "Not at first though, I didn't. You see, I'd just started college. After the war I'll be too old to go back. And then what? All I'll know will be how to sink U-boats."

He smiled at her. "Still, it's grand to help. It's good to have something worth fighting for."

"I'll have to run now, but I'd like you to come to dinner tonight." She smiled at him.

"Sorry." He grinned sheepishly. "Me and two other fellows are going to the home of some old lady. They're awfully nice wanting to entertain us. But we have to accept every time and so we've got hardly any freedom. Makes us talk less, says the Old Man."

She left the Red Cross without having encountered the man who went by the name of Hull and was rather relieved to be leaving the building so eventlessly when a man in the doorway whispered, "Go to the subway."

Sensing him behind her, she walked on, went through the turnstile, and took the first train. The man grazed her in the car door: "Retiro."

When she got off to change trains he stayed behind but slipped out when the doors were already hissing shut, passed her when they got to Retiro, and from then on she followed him, up the stairs (he seemed to be avoiding the escalator) to the railway station.

She noticed that he was a very tall man with broad shoulders that just missed hunching. His walk was heavy but with a spring that gave his back a self-confident look. The impression of ease was accentuated by the unhurried coordination of his movements, which gave him a worldly appearance despite his sloppy clothes and badly worn hat.

She followed him into a train marked Tigre, and sat down by the aisle. He took the window seat beside her and opened a book. On the open page lay a piece of paper: "Stand outside. In Belgrano jump off at the last moment."

She walked toward the door wondering how she would bring herself to jump off a train in motion. He did not stir. She was learning, step by first hesitant step, how it was done; and she felt as if these crisscross train rides had carried her many miles farther away from her white room in Potsdam, a cool hand on her forehead during a childhood illness, the smell of apples picked off the tree. She touched her hair and throat with something like reminiscent tenderness.

Then she looked back at the stranger. Until now she had only seen his shoulders or sensed him at her side or back. He was very blond, with a blunt, strong nose. His lips were clearly outlined like those of reliable people, the forehead furrowed and the eyes, cast on the book, surrounded by many fine wrinkles, though he certainly was not past his mid-thirties. For a split second he raised toward her eyes of a clear Scandinavian blue, strangely old without being weary.

At Belgrano she stared ahead as if absentminded, finding some grim humor in the fact that espionage made acrobatic demands on her. He had left the car from the rear, and as the train pulled out she jumped, landing unsteadily on the platform, her heart beating fast.

The stranger passed her, and half hidden under sandy lashes was a vaguely comforting smile. He walked through the turnstile and climbed the green slope, cutting through the dusky park and zigzagging for a while past lovers on benches holding hands or in unconcerned embrace. Then he went down again; and once more she followed him upward, through tree-lined streets hushed in the evening fog. Mansion after mansion remained behind in the quiet aloofness of their dense and flowery gardens. And down again until he stopped before a barroom by the station and looked through one of its large windows.

This probably means that I should walk in, she thought. She took a table in the Salón de Familias, behind the wooden partition topped by dusty house plants that separated it from the exclusively male section, and a few seconds later he was sitting opposite her and introduced himself: "Hull."

"Antonie Herrnfeld."

"I know," he smiled, making her blush at the foolishness of her introduction. A waiter flipped with a sweep of his napkin a cloud of peanut skins and flies off the table.

"*Cafecito negro?*" asked the man who went by the name of Hull. She nodded without hearing him. Then he spoke swiftly in a low voice. "Did H. get in touch with you again?"

"Yes. But I couldn't make any date at the Red Cross. I imagine he'll be suspicious."

"Oh no, on the contrary. He couldn't expect anything else at first try. You know me now. This is Tuesday. Friday at three p.m. I'll be in the underground passage of Plaza de la República. You come only if you have something to tell me."

Tony nodded. Now he would go, without looking back, because it was the wise thing to do. She would again be alone with her strangling fear. You have to do it, she told herself gruffly, so at least make the best of it, try to be glad that you're good for something.

The stranger must have read her pinched face. "You'd better go as soon as you finish your coffee. But I want you to know that in this kind of work you're never as alone as you think." He smiled. "We don't let little girls walk alone into the lion's den."

Tony went back to the Red Cross, where she ran again into the same sailor. In the evening, von der Heiden came to see her.

"Have you made an engagement?" he asked, avoiding her eyes.

"Yes. A little sailor with gay childhood memories. He'll be here tomorrow evening. I'm ashamed, aren't you?"

Von der Heiden still did not meet the eyes that were looking straight at him. "Don't ever give way to pity. It would be the end."

The last sentence was more than a generality, and Tony spoke loudly in an attempt to give firmness to her voice: "You've got nothing to fear. I have my bad conscience well under control. In fact, I've done some soul-searching. Maybe you're right; my home stands on German ground and I suppose one remains, after all, too involved with the childhood one has spent on it to want to see it ravaged." Romero's strange words had now helped her over this barrier.

"That's fine," said von der Heiden, utterly unconvinced.

Now it was she who, embarrassed, did not look at him as she asked as dryly and matter-of-fact as possible, "What do you want me to find out?"

There was just the suggestion of reluctance before a decision. "This sailor. What's his name?"

"Ed."

He laughed. "Ed, that isn't much. Ed's ship has been here too long to stay much longer. You find out when it sails, its cargo and speed and whether it carries anti-aircraft or all-purpose guns. It may be hard to get it all, but he'll probably tell you some."

"And what happens then?"

He smiled. "You won't have anything to do with the rest."

Tony smiled back. Her glance fell on the Scotch he had left on the drop-leaf table by the wall. "Would you like a drink on the house?"

"Thanks," he smiled dryly. "It isn't me you want to make drunk. Or is it?"

She blushed. How clever they were, or how unskilled she. "I frankly doubt that anyone could succeed there."

Her blush had not escaped him. He looked at her pensively, but he refused to be suspicious.

The bottle of Scotch was half-empty. Used plates lay on the table and the still-warm smoke hung heavily over the room. Ed looked around with liquor-dimmed eyes, stood up, and stretched stiffly. "I guess I'd better go now. May I come back for a while tomorrow at seven, or would you care to go out someplace? I'd like to buy you a drink for a change."

For that time she had an appointment with von der Heiden. "I'm sorry, I have an engagement," she said. "Let's make it nine, all right?"

"I can't," he said, "We . . . " he lowered his head and made an ashtray spin like a top, "I'll be on duty." He had not foreseen the true drive of his nervous gesture. The ashtray careened off the table top and splintered against a chair leg. "Oh, I'm so sorry!"

In his blanching face there was all the dismay and consternation of his childhood blunders. This is how he must have looked, she thought, in his story about crushing a chocolate pastry on someone's silk settee.

✿ ✿ ✿

At three o'clock sharp on the following day, she was in the underground passage. The man stood before a show window, looking at the government exhibits in it. Since they were alone, she did not think it could be wrong to go and stand beside him. He neither took his eyes off the display, nor moved his lips. "Well?"

"They want to know the date, the cargo, the speed, and what kind of guns they carry."

"And the boy? Did he talk?" They could hear steps echoing in the vault. Hull passed on to the next showcase. When the steps had died down at the other end of the passage, she followed.

"I didn't ask, but he almost did. Enough for me to know that they'll sail tonight."

The man smiled into the window. "Smart, aren't you?"

"He spent all evening with me," she replied, "but as early as the first day he had mentioned sinking submarines. So they must carry all-purpose guns, don't you think?" She was a little proud of her deduction and hoped it was correct.

"That's right," he said shortly, as if her insight bothered him. "You say, anti-aircraft guns and tomorrow night. But you've already told H.?"

"No! I'll see him late this afternoon."

"Won't that be a little late if they're sailing tonight?"

His voice was completely flat, bare of any intonation, and she was at a loss how to interpret his remark. "Anyhow, I couldn't have told him the truth."

"Why not?"

"Without your instructions? Besides, if one said the truth . . ."

Again the hollow sound of steps from the distance. She looked at him. He didn't stir, and she moved on, though it seemed pointless. When he caught up with her, he said, "Tell them the boy's coming to see you again tonight."

"But they'll find out," she said, piqued at the suspicion in his remarks, resentful of taking such risks in exchange for so little trust and appreciation.

"I know. But they'll think he fooled you if you just stay home tonight and prepare as if for a dinner guest. I really don't think you have anything to worry about."

Odd how much friendlier he was when she did not quite understand; the impatience crept into his short tone when she caught on quickly. She wondered if he was like ordinary men who liked to teach and be superior, but she could not imagine anything as personal in him.

"There's quite a bit more to discuss," she heard him say. "But that requires time and this isn't the place. Tomorrow night at ten you'll meet a grey-haired man at the corner of Rivadavia and Larrea. We'll call him Bob."

"Didn't he tell you their speed?" asked von der Heiden.

"No, he didn't."

He frowned. "That makes a difference."

"Why?"

"Never mind. Tell me, your brother lives on an estancia, doesn't he?"

The question added another, unexpected worry. She had not told Peter, with whom she shared everything else, because she was sure he would want to participate, and this she was determined to prevent.

"I wouldn't try to use him. He's very immature."

"Is that so? Please be at Prietzmann's tomorrow evening. You know the place, don't you?"

"I can't."

"Why not?"

She must not tell an obvious lie. She would probably be followed. "I have a date."

"Then we'll make it ten in the morning, all right?"

She could not go to sleep, afraid of the next morning, which, it seemed to her, would bring the first real contact with the monster. Von der Heiden embodied in manner and looks so little the *Parteigenosse*, or even anything conspicuously and exclusively German. Like a voice over the telephone, he failed to impose a sense of direct confrontation. She badly wanted to sleep, to be free of her fear, though in sleep the new unbearable day would come more quickly. From now on all her days would lie before her like nightmares, every night such a short reprieve.

CHAPTER NINE

TONY AND ROMERO HAD OFTEN DINED under the green bowers of Prietzmann's garden restaurant, where colored lanterns cast a glow on goblets of Rhine wine and a string orchestra played Viennese music. At ten o'clock on a rainy spring morning it looked very different.

The interior, a large, unlovely hall with wicker chairs and grotesque wooden chandeliers, was deserted. Von der Heiden, usually punctual, kept her waiting. When he finally came it was not from the street but through a door behind the bar.

His tone was unusually cool. "Please wait a moment." He had not offered his hand and now walked back to the door through which he had come. As he opened it she heard voices as of many people gathered behind.

Von der Heiden returned with a short, stocky man who was bald except for a band of black hair. Rimless glasses shielded small, nasty eyes in a white and flabby face.

Von der Heiden made the introductions. "Mr. Lagen, Miss Herrnfeld."

The other slumped into the chair opposite her without as much as a phrase of greeting. "Fräulein," he addressed her as one would a servant girl, "do you know what you're doing?" The soft Austrian accent made the harshness of his speech uncanny.

Tony raised her eyebrows. "I'm in possession of my mental faculties."

"Sufficiently to make you realize just how powerful we are?"

"Oh yes, alas, for the time being."

He ignored her reservation as one would a child's attempt at unruliness. "Do you know that your information was incorrect?"

"Yes."

Von der Heiden, who sat between them, pale and anxious as if he, not Tony, were on trial, gave a start. Even the other was taken aback. Then he said cuttingly, "What do you mean, yes?"

"I mean that the boy didn't show up last night. So I assumed that they had sailed."

"That they have done." He tried to sound jeering. "Perhaps you didn't know that, Fräulein?"

"I didn't." She sat very upright, her face expressionless, but under the table the nails of her right hand left marks on the back of the left. "The boy himself may not have known when he made the date."

"You do a lot of reasoning," Lagen remarked caustically. "All the same, your debut is far from striking. I advise you to secure more accurate information."

He rose and left, and von der Heiden followed him without turning around. Through the swiftly opening and closing door came smoke. Tony's hands unlocked, shaking. As she got up and walked through the stained-glass door, she felt not only alone, but physically threatened.

The charwoman had left a note saying that Romero had called up. She so craved normal human contact now that she lifted the receiver without even taking off her gloves. Later, on their way to a rustic tearoom in San Isidro, the night closed in with all the moisture of late spring, and from the cottage wall where they sat down the heavy-scented jazmín del país was shining in luxuriant whiteness through the evening blue.

"You're nervous, Tony," he said. "I wish I could be of some comfort to you. But I know I can't."

His sincere compassion made her feel like a hypocrite. Her mourning, overshadowed as it was by glaring personal calamity, seemed a farce. Their eyes met. She felt something deeper than mere friendship drawing her to him now that they were both, in their own way, excluded from life in its normal sense.

"Tony," he said suddenly, "you're the only flawless person I've ever met. I love you. And I want to marry you."

A joy like seeing harbor lights while lost at sea rushed through her before once more her heart went under. Her life was not only today and this year and the next. It would be madness to jeopardize the entire span for fear of the next few years. She wanted love. If ever she should stop caring about herself to the point of renouncing that happiness, she would lay her life aside gently, without regret. But she was not yet exhausted, only frightened.

She did not know what to say. While casting about for an answer, she kept looking into his sad, steady eyes as if it could come from them. Finally she disengaged her glance. "Give me time, Romero."

His eyes reached for hers, forced them back. "I do want you to think it over. I'd be afraid that if I rushed you into consent you might some day tell me so."

Though in her first surprise she had only thought of herself, his words unwittingly confirmed her reasoning. Acceptance would victimize him no less than her. She did not love him enough to make him happy, but loved him too well to be willing to make him miserable.

"I want you to meet my parents," he said. "I don't mean to force anything by that, but I think it would help you make up your mind, one way or another."

She was not going to let him plan and dream, add another disappointment to his mangled life.

"It never occurred to me that you might feel that way about me," she said. "Everything between us has been different from other people. And it was good. But I'm not sure it's love."

His lashes fluttered for a second under the shock of the word "different," but his eyes neither shifted nor hardened. "I understand, Tony. Still, we can enjoy our 'golden moments.'"

You don't understand a thing, she thought. That you're lame has nothing to do with it. I wish I loved you so I could prove how little it matters.

But one didn't say such things; one would rather hurt people than be tactless.

By ten o'clock another shower had chilled the atmosphere. She stood shivering in the sharp breeze at the corner of Rivadavia and Larrea. Automobiles passed her by with everyday people going somewhere: home, to some amusement, to some kind of tedious duty, but each to a commonplace occupation. All knew where they were headed.

A cab stopped, the door opened, a grey head appeared, whispering, "Bob." She got in. He did not speak. As they drove through dark, unfamiliar streets, she remembered how Dolores had never permitted her to be taken home from an evening party other than in their own chauffeur-driven car. "You never know," she would say with a wise expression on her face, and truly no one had ever known which, if any, of Tony's young men she took for Bluebeard in disguise.

The taxi stopped. In a split second the man had vanished, leaving Hull in his place, and they drove off. She felt as pleasantly surprised, almost safe, as if she had met a friend. He leaned forward and whispered to the driver. Then he put his arm around her, his face close to hers. Was she dreaming . . . an espionage yarn, an amorous adventure, or both . . . had Bluebeard materialized?

His breath grazed her cheek as he whispered, "Don't worry." Then he let her go. She shook her head, smiling, relieved, into the dark.

They made a U-turn and then drove onto the sidewalk straight up to one of two steel sliding doors. It opened as if someone behind it were listening for the signal of the stopping of a car, and they entered a somber carriage door brightened by only a red shimmer underneath the step that led into the house. Hull paid the driver and helped her out. Private cars were parked in the shadows of the inner court, their license plates covered by black cloths. The taxi disappeared through the adjoining sliding door.

A waiter in a greasy tuxedo escorted them through the vestibule into an elevator hung with rugs. The second floor encircled the downstairs hall like a gallery, the wall pierced by door after door. Behind the door he opened was a square, windowless room with whitewashed walls, dingy and sad like a hospital emergency room at night. A wide bed was covered with a green cotton damask spread. Bathroom fixtures gleamed through a flimsy, ineffectual curtain of the same faded stuff. On the chiffonier lay a drink list and on one wall was a card with the prices per hour.

The man who went by the name of Hull locked the door and hung his hat over the keyhole, laughing nervously. "This is safe; here no one will get the wrong idea about us."

He had obviously made the same joke on previous occasions and she was not amused. She was looking around for a seat and, having followed her glance, he shrugged. "No chair."

She sat reluctantly down at the foot of the bed, Hull at the head, crossing his legs. "I hate to put you into this situation."

She smiled. "That's all right." She was genuinely bent on dispelling his gêne now. "It's an ugly room like any other."

"I'm glad you feel that way. What's new?" He held out a pack of cigarettes and seemed glad that she accepted one.

"They knew that the sailor hadn't come," she said. "They knew everything. They ordered me to Prietzmann's this morning. That seems to be a Nazi hangout."

"Yeah," he said dryly. "That's known."

"There was a man by the name of Lagen who cross-examined me."

"Lagen? That's not his real name, anyhow. What did he say?"

Tony told him.

"Who could that be? What did he look like?"

She gave him a description.

"You say he called himself Lagen? Jesus, Lagen . . . Nagel . . . how obvious can you get? He's a big fish."

Tony's face was a question mark.

"Will you see him again?"

"I hope not." She shuddered.

He leaned forward, his blue eyes bright with eagerness. "I wish you could make friends with those people. Nagel—an ex-Austrian and one of the very early Nazis—is accessible, but in your case probably too suspicious. And von der Heiden is considered too unreliable by his own crowd to have much top information."

Tony was silent. Hull was gnawing his lower lip, then he looked at her again. "I guess you'll have to try Nagel. You see, I want you to get some insight. Those gatherings at Prietzmann's, for example, are very interesting. When you see him again, be friendly. Free him of the bewildering notion that you're a lady. He's forever hanging around the dumps on Leandro Além. Allegedly because the girls tell him what the British sailors let slip, but mainly because he likes it."

Tony looked at him fixedly. He takes me for a machine. He talks like an automaton himself, yet he too must have or have had some sort of private life, a mother, perhaps a wife and children. How is he when he's not a machine? She could not imagine.

Her sad, pinched face made him suddenly sorry. "Have I said something ugly?"

"No, no. Only, you see, I can't give them a friendly look. I . . ."

"I understand. But you must try. Think of something beautiful when you're facing them, and look right through them at the beauty and smile at it."

He had turned on the sentiment for her benefit, got it out of his bag of tricks as he had previously done with his old gag.

He saw her hostile glance, and there again was his uncanny mind reading. He smiled, amused. "I read that in a spy manual."

Tony turned away and he came to stand before her. "Miss Herrnfeld—it would be easier to say 'Tony'—it isn't as bad as it looks. If you get panic-stricken, you're lost."

Had he guessed 'Tony' or had he learned that, too, from one of those ruthlessly thorough reports? She looked up, her eyes stinging with unshed tears. "I'm in no panic. I'm tired and . . ." She stopped herself. This stranger, unknown and foreign even as to type, exercised a peculiar influence on her, made her say things she did not want him to know. Such were probably the crack agents.

"We're a whole world fighting together," he said softly.

"That's so general," she replied impatiently. "I need something more concrete. If ever it became necessary, the world could not give me its hand, and I can't give it mine, can't sit beside it or say good night to it." She laughed. "You think I'm mad, don't you?"

"No, I don't. Everybody feels that way. I'm fed up with this lousy country myself. But I guess I'll sit here until we, too, are in it."

Tony was puzzled. "What are you at the embassy?"

"Nothing at all. I'm a private citizen. An American, in fact."

It occurred to her that he should not have told her even that much about his identity. But to conceal this glorious privilege was probably more than an American, even a secret agent, could bring himself to do.

"I still don't understand," she said. "From your accent I imagined you to be a Canadian. I don't see how . . ."

"You don't need to." It sounded secretive, a child playing Indians and giving himself importance. It was a first crack in his image and, she was afraid, in her saving trust in him as a technician.

"I hate this dirty business," he said. "We're in a so-called democracy and must hide, while the Germans are at liberty to make their propaganda and indulge in all the sabotage they please."

As he offered her another cigarette, she asked, "What was your peacetime occupation?"

"Once a newspaper man, always a newspaper man, in peace or in war," he said with mock pathos. "And if we should enter the war, because of my profession the government would probably keep me right here or put me somewhere else behind a desk."

"I want to ask a stupid question," she said. "I can't understand any of it because I'd never heard of it before." She saw him listening with interest, yet without the lurking attentiveness she had invariably encountered with von der Heiden or Lagen or the man at the British Embassy. "What are you doing? What is espionage in Argentina?"

"Espionage is what the Germans are doing. It confines itself almost exclusively to the kind of information one expects from you. This is followed by sabotage—bombs on British ships, or submarines intercepting them. After all, England must fight this war on Argentine meat and wheat. Luckily this government's pro-Nazi sentiment stops short of the pocketbook."

"There was something von der Heiden said," she said pensively. "I think I now know what it meant. When I told him I didn't know the ship's speed, he said 'that makes a difference,' or something to this effect. Can he have meant that it made it impossible for them to time a submarine?"

"Most likely. It meant they would have to lay a bomb. If they had found the ship, that is," he grinned. "But to come back to your question. Our work is counterespionage. We try to sabotage the sabotage."

"Why don't you denounce those people to the police if you know what they're up to? Why don't you lure them into a trap and have them caught redhanded?"

"By the Argentine police?" he chuckled. "But we're talking too much," he added with a glance at his watch. "Let me give you your instructions." She turned toward him, trying to look willing and intent. "You choose your own way into the organization. After all, it's you who talks to the people and you alone know your day-to-day standing with them. So your instinct is surer than all our calculations. Nagel is dangerous. He's shrewd, mean, and courageous. He shows up and vanishes. So far it has been impossible to establish just where he goes underground."

"And if you knew, what could you do about it?"

"Some young ladies ask too many questions," he smiled, the fine wrinkles around his eyes multiplying.

"I feel like a blind tool," she protested and saw him wince at the cliché. "Von der Heiden and you—pardon the comparison—everybody sends me on assignments and no one is kind enough to tell me what it is about, what I'm really doing. If one trusts me sufficiently to use me, one might trust me enough to tell me how things hang together."

"And if the Germans trusted you sufficiently to tell you, what would you do with the information?"

"Bring it to you."

"You see?"

Tony was indignant. "You mean you think I might . . . Don't you trust me, really?"

"To tell you the truth, nobody trusts anybody enough to initiate him totally. All of us know only fragments. And you're very new. Your ignorance protects you, not only the organization."

Again I belong nowhere, she thought, disappointed. Even now I am held at arm's length.

There was a knock at the door. Hull turned the key, and she heard the waiter: "One hour's up."

He returned with an uncomfortable grin. "We'd better go."

She rose, somewhat bemused. Then she said slowly, "if no other door opens, I might at least ask von der Heiden to dinner."

"I leave that up to you." He pulled the bedspread down and began to rumple the sheets. "We're not interested in Nagel so much when he's here," he continued, throwing the pillows on the floor. "We want to know where he goes when he disappears."

When they reentered the elevator and Hull handed the waiter a bill and some change, she tried to persuade herself that the situation was not embarrassing, yet it seemed that, after all, morality was what others believed.

CHAPTER TEN

DURING THE FOLLOWING MONTHS Tony developed contacts among the Germans. She tried in vain to join the women's organizations, which, like all German associations and welfare institutions, had ceased to be anything but the means to request, demand, or extort money for the Nazi war machine.

Her connections remained strictly business and male, but there it was surprisingly easy to get acquainted. Though they had scant respect for a renegade "almost Jewess," she furnished limited amounts of information and amusement. On the rare occasions when she attended a meeting in Prietzmann's backroom, they got themselves drunk on alternate swallows of Schnaps and beer and would put an arm around her and mix folk and Führer songs the way they mixed their drinks. Though she did not join in their chants, they had no qualms. They had been carefully briefed on her hybrid position, made the more plausible by the fact that she had indeed always avoided refugee circles.

Nagel attended every one of the meetings, von der Heiden none. In fact, he told her more than once that she was under no obligation to go through this plebeian ordeal, and had it not been for her orders to miss no chance to watch Nagel, she would have desisted with a sigh of relief and a good reason: Her perseverance was hard to explain to von der Heiden.

Ironically, Nagel was the only one to discourage her less than half-hearted attempts at sociability, though he alone was able to accurately gauge her value. He realized that she was more than the scared young girl who laughed slavishly at inane jokes and allowed herself to be impressed by Nazi power and its iron servants. He knew that she abhorred them all and fulfilled this duty for the sake of her parents. However, he trusted her very intelligence, of which only he was aware, to know that there was no way out, that she must stick by them.

She met Hull mostly in the hotels of assignation that filled the upper part of Cangallo, changing continually from the most discreet, where the car stopped in a patio before the door of the room; to the dingy bed-chair-bidet type that catered only to the most elementary of needs; to the most outlandish in Arabian Nights splendor. Soon they knew them all, sat on the edge of a grimy bed or sank into the cushions of a silken divan, and exchanged information.

One night when Hull handed a bill to the waiter, the man had no change. They waited in a shadowy corner of the vestibule while he scurried off for the money.

"Too silly," he whispered apologetically. "I always keep the right change handy. But we were longer than I thought we'd be."

Tony did not reply. Her eyes were fastened on a couple that had emerged from a room. The man supported himself on a cane. For a moment their eyes met, then he turned away.

"Don't worry," Hull said lightly. "I don't imagine you'll meet any acquaintances here. And if you did, they'd be in the same boat, which is a miraculous silencer."

The waiter returned with the change, and she walked out beside Hull, stiff with horror. The pain was so ugly that she was unable to get a grip on herself. Hull watched her from the side. "I know it's hell," he said sympathetically. Then he gave a sharp whistle. A cab stopped, and Tony got in.

"Our Father who art in Heaven . . ." she prayed, wringing her hands in the darkness of the automobile, saying the entire prayer once, twice, automatically underneath her thoughts, as one might count so as not to focus on a physical ordeal, yet fervently as one would clutch at something in such pain. She had not prayed since childhood and did not maintain the familiar relations more fortunate humans have with God. But lately she had taken refuge in this litany whenever she was at the absolute end of her resources and could only hope for some greater power, if such there was, to solve her problem for her. She did it without faith, as she did everything else.

61

Pity and shame mingled with self-pity and disconsolate feeling of loss. The ugliness of the situation was so pungent that her sensation of sickness was almost physical, and the knowledge that it was but a cruel yet irreversible distortion made the hurt only more unbearable. So she had done exactly what she had not wanted, had heaped another disappointment on the one Romero had hardly overcome. She remembered how, that winter night, he had repeated over and over, "how perfidious, how unspeakably dirty . . . if she had come and told me, I love somebody else . . . but in this way . . ." And later, "you're the only flawless person I've ever met. I love you. And I want to marry you." The memory was like a nauseous flesh cut. He had introduced her to his parents. Now he must feel that he had led a trollop into his home.

If she could have explained, it could never have set matters right, but he might have been less hurt and she would not remain in his eyes a girl who went to a dingy hotel with a bulky, sloppy-looking man.

She felt bitterly resentful toward those who expected her to sacrifice everything. She was willing to do her share and take a soldier's risk, who also was but a civilian not born to kill and to be killed; but it was expecting too much of her to make herself despicable in the eyes of her friends. I would give my life, she argued, but am not willing to ruin it. And then, with a rather contrived detachment: the eternal dilettante.

All through the night she kept chain-smoking and arguing with her life, a superior adversary who therefore could dispense with argument and at last made her understand that, however she rebelled, there was no way out, that she was caught in a tight net of ugliness. She realized helplessly that the loss of Romero might well be only the beginning, that the more she held on to those she loved, the greater was the danger of losing them.

The family's departure for Mar del Plata added to her feeling of isolation. Their invitation to spend the summer at their beach home was a godsend that for a few months would have freed her from her predicament. It had not occurred to her that the Germans might object, and they did.

One Friday afternoon she managed to drive out for a weekend with Antonio, who often spent the workdays in the city. Giddy elation made her talk and laugh and point like a child at grazing cattle and people by the roadside, and Antonio watched her rather silently, with a sad smile, humoring her like a false convalescent.

Their place, at some distance from the resort town with its urban turmoil and paved magnificence, lay by a not yet built-up beach. It had a colonial-style bungalow, flat and sprawling, with grilled windows, white and plain. At night in her room she could hear and smell the breath of the sea. She stood by the open window to see if the salty air could wash her clean of her confusion. For one day only she was at peace with the world, not even two, because the second would already be burdened again with the fear of the next.

Early on Saturday they went to Playa Grande because María Teresa wished to introduce her to their friends at the Yacht Club, where they spent the ritual beach morning between a dip and a drink. In the afternoon Carlota planned to take her to a thé dansant at the Golf Club.

"No," said Antonio. "You go ahead. I'm taking Antonieta fishing."

As the slim yacht carried them toward the open sea, Tony felt very keenly what people meant when they spoke of the intoxication of freedom; it was so very physical when alone on a ship with the shore shrinking away and the whole ocean before one. Crossed-legged, her back against the mast, she dreamed of escaping to liberty, to strange places where no one knew of her.

They anchored at a good fishing ground, threw out their lines, and for a couple of hours were caught up in the magic formula of sky and nature and physical exercise they had known at the estancia. When the evening sun made the distant beach look rosy and the air began to chill with fog, Antonio poured two tall drinks. They sat on deck, their eyes on the still waters.

"What's the matter, dear?" he asked finally. "I want you to tell me."

It seemed easy to talk out here, far from the entanglements of the shore. The ancient belief that the freedom of the sea releases one from the straight consequences of one's earthbound acts seemed to become valid for her. Nothing stood against shedding her burden of secrecy here where no eyes or ears could reach.

But as she turned from the sea, her lips parting to speak, the very glasses, the matchbook with the words of the city printed on it, even the mast and the wood under their feet recalled that but for these few hours was she free.

"What do you mean, Antonio?"

"You act like a sleepwalker. And as with a somnambulist, one is afraid to talk to you because you're just as startled. You either need a psychiatrist, or if you are in trouble you should tell me. Don't you think so?"

"There's nothing the matter with me, Antonio. I'm just not very merry."

He pushed his drink back and said bluntly, "You're not in this state on account of your parents. You were deeply shocked and unhappy when it occurred and for a long time thereafter. But this is different. You're at the edge of a nervous breakdown, and the cause is another. I want you to tell me."

Again the enticement to give herself up to the opportunity. She told herself that she would never blame herself for succumbing, that she would always, regardless of the consequences, understand this moment's weakness.

"Antonio," she said. "I'm not going crazy." She took a long swallow of whisky to drown out the last dry whisper of warning. It still found time to question, why this long drink? And she paused . . .

Antonio felt the struggle, wanted to help. "Is it Romero?"

This natural assumption, which in its very normality separated his world from hers, reawakened her to her own segregated reality. The mood of the moment had been a prisoner's dream. Nothing had changed, life remained outside.

Fear of herself made her voice tight and sharp. "I wish people would mind their own business."

She looked at him, aghast at her own rudeness, wishing ardently she had been serene enough to think of a friendly, noncommittal reply.

But he seemed not to have heard the offense. "Maybe you're right dear. I'm sorry," he said gently.

He took the glasses down into the cabin and started the engine. On their way back, he pointed out sites on the approaching shore as pleasantly as if no discourtesy had taken place.

They spent their next and last day on their own deserted beach, wading through dunes and swimming in the rough sea. When the sun had spent its strength, Carlota and Tony lay in the sand, one with a long stretch of pleasant summer before her, the other with the strangling apprehension of return to her life in Buenos Aires.

"Well, Tony, it seems you and Romero have called it a day."

"Yes, it seems so," repeated Tony, looking at the sky.

"That's what I was afraid of from the start. Not that I wanted you to go on. You know I didn't. But I wish you had called it off as soon as you saw that he was serious about it. It wasn't necessary to hurt him."

"I didn't hurt him," said Tony weakly.

"He proposed to you, didn't he?"

"Yes, he did."

"Poor chap. Why on earth did you give him so many illusions?"

"I didn't, Carlota. I told him I couldn't marry him," Tony said unhappily.

"Then why did you agree to meet his parents? It immediately became the talk of the town, and you can imagine that being booted that way doesn't bolster the self-assurance of a boy like Romero. He's completely broken up."

"How could it become the talk of the town?"

Carlota giggled. "Fernandito took care of that. Mrs. Basualdo, quite concerned about the whole affair, confided her anxiety to her bosom friend, Fernandito's mother. And that, naturally, opened the windows of hell, that is, Fernandito's mouth."

"I wish I could have kept him from getting hurt."

"Oh well, one of two always gets hurt, and I'm glad it wasn't you. Of course, people who would never go out of their way to do him a good turn feel that you've played him a dirty trick. But you needn't worry about that. I think you've done right—though it would have been more charitable to do it sooner."

The blood rose into Tony's pale face. "Goodness, Carlota, haven't I, too, a right to some pleasantness? Can't I expect anything for myself . . ." She stopped.

Carlota sat up and looked at her in surprise. "Tony, you talk as if your fate were sealed by tragedy. What's the matter?"

I must control myself, she thought. Once one is in the wrong light, it's no use trying to explain it away. I'm cut off from everyone, except for a thin thread of small talk.

Her life consisted of perfunctory translation work, tense hours with von der Heiden, and those unreal nightly meetings with the man who went by the name of Hull and who, at rare and very fleeting moments, came nearest to offering a human relationship.

❦ ❦ ❦

Often the exchange of information with the American took so little time that it would have been conspicuous to leave right away. So they formed a habit of discussing their preferences, literary and otherwise, their memories of a brighter past, and their hopes for a calmer future. She was surprised that she could follow him, convinced that with her own past irretrievably lost and her future a mirage, her present was a wasteland where normal pursuits could not exist and thought could only hurt.

She now knew that his first name was Pat and his last was certainly not Hull. At night she sometimes wondered what it might be: Donovan, McPherson, Fitzgerald, Lowell, Grant. She knew that he had grown up in the Hudson River Valley, which in his descriptions oddly resembled the hills and woods of her own childhood. While it appeared that most of American family life took place in the kitchen and that cakes and savory dishes were of undue importance, she could understand him when he spoke of his early years.

Though quite different in type, they had been brought up polyglot in a liberal, intellectual environment; had spent a peaceful, generous childhood in woods near the water; ridden and swum; and on long, white winter evenings copied poetry or tried to write some of their own. She was glad that no ocean separated them; it would have been frustrating if the only person she was allowed and able to trust had been totally alien to her.

More than four months had gone by and it was a winter evening when she put her soft, grey felt hat on the table and buried her hands in the pockets of her tweed suit. "Lagen is gone."

Pat looked at her in surprise. "Since when?"

"Since last night. Von der Heiden received some last-minute instructions from him—that's why he stood me up."

"How did you find out?" Appreciation in his voice.

She looked past him. "I acted angry and wouldn't be mollified till he gave a satisfactory explanation."

Pat laughed. "You must have great influence over him!"

"Very great," she confirmed without triumph.

"It's really none of my business. What do you intend to do? Or do you also know where he is?"

"I don't know anything."

He went to the window, gazed at the pale neon lights blinking on and off under it, then turned around. "Maybe we should give you a letter. You could say you received it through the mails, and you could insist that you can't give it to anyone except Nagel himself."

"Say 'Lagen,'" she insisted. "I'm always afraid I'll slip some day. What kind of letter?"

She came to sit beside him and saw reflected in the cheval mirror placed obliquely to the bed his large, tired face, sallow under the tan. "We'd have to think about that very carefully, but, just for example, it could tell Nagel, I mean, Lagen, that a German seaman is in hiding on an estancia and requires an urgent operation. Such cases are nothing new, neither for the German Hospital nor for most German doctors. It would ask him to make the necessary arrangements with a reliable surgeon. Something like that . . . we'll see. At any rate, it must be presented as pressing enough not to leave him time to check."

"But why should I get such a letter? I mean, it would seem illogical," she said.

"I was thinking about your brother. I would imagine, living up there . . ."

She shook her head. "No. Although we're twins, he's much younger than I, impulsive. Leave him out of this."

"We'll see," he said with finality, as if forbidding a child to argue. Tony gave him a discouraged look. As often before, she was appalled at his coldness. He was a stranger again with his own designs that took her into consideration only as long as she kept in line with them.

"And after they find out?" she asked lamely.

"Then we'll make it appear that Peter let himself be bamboozled by a big bad British agent. But it won't come to that, for Lagen won't have time to speak."

"What do you mean?"

After a moment's silence he said, "We just must act very quickly as soon as we know where he is."

"What are you going to do to him?"

"He isn't going to talk."

"Who will do it?"

"I don't know." He smiled at her reassuringly. For a split second their eyes met, hers dark and troubled, his clear and wistful. Then she looked away. Though he was nothing to her heart, he had by now become a person to her, almost a friend, and she felt pain at seeing him gambled. She knew his voice, the outlines of his face, his hands, the way he moved. It was not possible to keep thinking of him as the man who went by the name of Hull.

"Is that necessary?"

"Do you feel sorry for your *Landsmann*?" There was surprise in his voice.

"No. I'm afraid."

"Afraid of what?"

"For you," she said with sincerity, though without particular warmth.

"For me? Tony, I'm doing my duty as you're doing yours. I'm sometimes afraid for you, too."

"Isn't there any other solution, though?"

"No. The Argentine police won't help us. It's the only thing we can do."

CHAPTER ELEVEN

"YOU MUST GIVE ME THE LETTER. As far as you're concerned, I'm Lagen's personal representative. I can't tell you where he is." Von der Heiden straightened up as if to intimidate her by his height.

"Then he won't get it," Tony replied calmly.

"Your airs are preposterous. Do you by any chance think we trust you?"

"No. Nobody trusts anybody." She had to support her hands on her hips to keep them from trembling. At this moment no letter existed; what it would say and where it would call Nagel depended on his whereabouts. What if he asked to see the envelope? She had absolutely nothing. She should have thought of it, so should Pat. By now she had been arguing for a full hour and had given up hope of wresting Nagel's hiding place from this terse and stubborn man.

How long had her present silence lasted? Conspicuously long? How many thoughts did one think in one second or two? Or was it longer? As if from far away, she saw him sit down, wearily.

"All right."

She put a hand on his arm. "I'm glad you trust me, after all."

"How cold it is," she said when the waiter had shut the door after them. "Winter in June and Christmas in summer. I'll never get used to it."

"Did you use to have a Christmas tree?" Pat asked.

"Yes. Tall, very tall, with wax candles and silver balls and tinsel." She turned around. "And carols. My father played an asthmatic spinet."

"Being practical Americans," Pat smiled, "and living in a clapboard house, we had records and electric lights. *Silent Night, Holy Night . . .*"

"Stille Nacht, Heilige Nacht . . ." Their eyes met, laughing.

"That kind of Christmas will return, Tony. But we must do something about it. What's new?"

"I know where Lagen is."

"Fine. You're a smart girl."

She smiled gratefully. "German Old Folks Home, Burzaco."

"What was that?"

"Deutsches Altersheim, Burzaco," she repeated, settling down without any of the former uneasiness at the head of the gaudy bed. "When the Nazis came to power, they saw the opportunity. The poor old people, in order to gain access to the home, turned over all their earthly possessions. Now they have no other place to go and must work for the Nazis or, at least, keep their mouths shut. When people like Nagel have to go underground that's where they hide."

"How ingenious."

"I'd better go now, scandalously soon. But von der Heiden is waiting for me."

"Is it very bad?"

She met his eyes. "No, not very."

"If only the end of this were somewhere in sight. But it has only just begun."

She put on her brown derby. Its rigidity gave her face a soft and child-like expression. He was holding her coat. His glance, falling over her shoulder, met hers in the mirror.

"Sometime I'd like to kiss you, Tony."

His face in the glass lay wide open to her. She held his eyes and, even though there was nothing sultry in their mood, a curiously electric current ran through her, like happiness.

"Not here," she said.

"No, not here."

When she faced Nagel in Burzaco the fear that had never left her since her involvement with this was monstrously magnified. For the first time she was gambling herself.

He listened to her, read the letter and the enclosure she handed him, and then gazed at her a long time and with an intentional lack of concealment. She stood his glance without flinching, though she thought that at any moment she would grow dizzy from staring into the glittering disks of his rimless glasses.

On her way back to the garden gate, she saw old people walking awkwardly in the stingy winter sun. So that's what some of our active enemies look like, she thought, these old men and women who can't have any lust of conquest or arrogance left in them. A waiter crossed her path, carrying a tray toward the house. His face was familiar, she could not remember from where, and only in the train it dawned on her that she had seen his picture in a collection of the Nazi hierarchy Pat had shown her.

The message she had handed Nagel had been accompanied by what looked to her like a few perfectly forged lines of Peter's handwriting.

My dear,
My neighbor asks you to give this letter to his uncle in Burzaco, who owes him a wad of money. Don't mail it, so the old man won't pretend he didn't get it. He tells me he met you at a party but you didn't seem eager to give him your address, which I can well understand. He's a nice guy, though, absolutely no Nazi but, as his envelope, being sealed, proves, a bit of a boor.
As always,
Peter.

The enclosed message for Nagel had obviously been typed on a German keyboard. On an international typewriter with a trema key the *Umlaut* would have looked different. It was also written in the code used with Nagel's contacts on the coast, which the British had only recently cracked.

For her own and everyone else's protection, should pressure come to bear on her, she was indeed kept ignorant of what it conveyed, only knew that if Nagel followed its call he would that night go to where the Río de La Plata met the Paraná. The plan would only work if, left no time to double-check, he actually went, and went alone, and once there, he did not get away or kill his assailant. Only if nothing went wrong, would the German

Embassy fail to be alerted. If Nagel escaped with his life, Peter's life and her own were at risk.

The scheme did not seem quite logical. Shouldn't the man have someone else in the region? How did he know of her involvement? And why would he trust her?

Pat, perhaps for good reasons, did not provide a very clear answer, and she was unconvinced. Though unable to put her finger on it, she sensed that something was intrinsically wrong. She had also pointed out that Peter would not address her as "my dear," and for a moment he had frowned and then said, "Oh well, it doesn't matter."

She looked through the window of the commuter train while it rolled along an overpass spanning Palermo Park where a few late horsemen rode stableward through the evening haze. How far away, how far away. She asked herself why she was not more afraid. It must be because Pat did not seem particularly worried. She could not imagine that her life weighed so lightly on his scales. He must be pretty sure of their venture. Her trust in his judgment was so absolute that in danger, rightly or wrongly, her confidence was but the echo and mirror of his.

"At any rate he has disappeared," insisted von der Heiden. "And your letter must have something to do with it."

Tony, pouring the German Embassy Scotch, shrugged. "I tell you I don't know. Of course, it's possible. Maybe Nagel thought it wise to disappear for a while, maybe that's what the letter advised him to do."

She noticed him watching her intently. Something strange and confusing was in his gaze. She felt her blood stand still and a helpless void invade her head. She had said 'Nagel.'"

"Nagel," said von der Heiden pointedly, "hasn't taken a single piece of luggage."

"Nagel," Tony retorted just as pointedly, "undertakes nothing that isn't full of tricks and traps. When I read his real name on the inner envelope I knew immediately that Nagel was Lagen or Lagen Nagel, as you wish . . . anyway, I was always sure that even his name was a lie. Nobody's name is Lagen. Only the inversion is amazingly simple-minded, not worthy of him."

"You needn't give lengthy explanations," he interrupted with a gesture of his hand, as one would break up the hectic and senseless buzzing of a fly. "You needn't excuse yourself." He looked straight into her eyes. "Antonie, do you know what I would have to do if I should find out that you're double-crossing us?"

She had never told him that she was called Tony. Antonie sounded hard and distant as she had wanted it from him. At this moment she would have preferred to hear something more intimate and friendly. She held the cigarette case out to him. "You would do to me what you people do to all those who are in your way."

Von der Heiden lighted a cigarette. "You're an odd person. You work for us to save your parents and for that reason alone. So why do you fake a sort of enthusiasm before the others? Why do you show your feelings only to me, the only one whom it causes suffering?"

"Because the others are dumb and have one-track minds. They would distrust me for it. They don't understand that if an ideal enables people to bear plenty, necessity does a lot more."

She was wondering why she had indeed given up her feeble pretense of *Vaterlandsliebe* before von der Heiden. Why did she trust him not to give her away? Was it trust or weariness?

"We all bow to necessity," he said.

"What necessity? The need to satisfy your hatred, your greed? There are necessities imposed by love, and I think you know it. You're the only one who still seems able to glimpse that part of life, if only from a prudent distance. That's why I'm frank with you, though."

For a moment his face lit up, then he rose and went to lean, his hands in his pockets, against the yellow canvas window curtain.

"Nagel has disappeared. Where is he?"

Tony sighed. "I don't know. But I may be able to find out." She was playing for time.

Von der Heiden passed long, pale fingers through his hair. "Seven months ago I began to give you a few minor assignments, and now you're already trying to run me."

"The master race complex aroused," she remarked, staring into the smoke that curled up from his unfinished and apparently forgotten cigarette in the ashtray. Just string one word to another, on and on, not let a pause set in, gain time in which to think of a plausible answer. "I meant to . . ." she began, not knowing how to finish.

"How could you find out?" he interrupted. "I'm afraid for both of us, Antonie, don't you understand that?"

"No," she replied coldly. "I'm not afraid."

He looked at her, perplexed. "What makes you so sure?"

"Nagel's confidence." Was it a brilliant idea or a very bad one?

"What do you mean?" His voice was shrill. "What kind of madness is all this?"

"You are afraid, that's right. You're so afraid you're almost irresponsible. And that's why Nagel doesn't trust you, not because, perchance, you're not a good Nazi."

"Has he talked to you about me?" He came across the room.

"Sit down," she said not without gentleness, and he obeyed. "Nagel is gone. I don't know where. But I may receive more letters. I don't know who they will come from. I'm not supposed to know either. Now, those letters will give you instructions, not me. But Nagel trusts neither you, nor me, nor anyone. He just wants us to spy on each other. He has made some rather snide remarks about you. Just as he does, I'm sure, to you about me. That's why I wanted to talk as little as possible about the matter. But you insisted. At any rate, the ground got a little too hot for his comfort, but that's all I know."

"You don't mean to tell me that he trusts you more than me?" He still tried to sound ironical, but every syllable dragged a weight.

"By no means. I don't know any more than you do." She did not even know if the situation she had invented at the spur of the moment was possible in the workings of an intelligence service. She went on laboriously, as if twisting her own rope. "I don't know where he is, what he's doing . . ." (What next? she thought.) "Very clever, your superior, Nagel . . ." (And what now?)

"Superior! I'm a foreign service officer and he's . . ."

"Nothing but a little scoundrel who does the dirty work for the gentlemen of the diplomatic service."

"Antonie, please! But what did Nagel say about me?"

"Won't you spare me that?"

She saw with satisfaction that he was very pale. But no matter how hard she tried, she could find in her whirling mind nothing that would ring natural, without possibly upsetting the balance of the situation. So she put her hand on his and leaned toward him. He kissed her solemnly, wistfully, and a little probingly, as one would sample an unfamiliar, foreign wine. It was always like this.

When he was walking home, hat in hand, he thought of many things at once. Of Edmund Nagel's flabby face and suspicious eyes, of Antonie's clear-cut features, her smooth clean voice, of Adolf Hitler's execrable manners, of the Argentines who really believed in nothing and ate far too much, and again of Antonie's fine shoulders against his.

Why did he sit, evening after evening, beside her like a boy, waiting for her, one day, to make the first gesture? Was he not drawn to her? He found her beautiful, intelligent, fine. She had the innate, uncomplicated pride he lacked, no feelings of inferiority, no doubts. He even admired her. So why this hesitation? Was it because he knew that one day it would come to pass and therefore did not suffer but was unconsciously glad of the delay, afraid of the entanglement with the Jewish girl, Antonie Herrnfeld?

His father, who had shared his misgivings about the bewildering people, had nevertheless liked to tell of the handsome, ardent Hebrew women who in the past war had been part of the booty in Poland. His father knew so well how to reconcile things. But not this new régime and his personal code of honor. With a twinge he brushed the thought away.

And then he would have liked to be with her again, to make her surrender and break her reserve. But Stephan was never free of the notion that even a man, when he took, also gave himself. And he felt as sure of her contempt as of his father's, and that of all who had surrounded him in his childhood, and of the handful of college friends he had really valued, those who had turned their backs on him because he had struck a bargain with the devil. Stephan felt lonely and unhappy and wanted love from someone else, not always only his own love for himself.

✦ ✦ ✦

The tip of her nose against the window pane, Tony looked out into the rain that had burst from the thick clouds with sudden violence. The night wind howled and tore the tops of the plantains below, chasing sheets of water before it. A water curtain descended on the glass. She felt on her cheeks a warm flow, salty on her lips, the first tears of sadness rather than anxiety since Peter had returned to the country.

Pat would probably praise her for tonight, but she wished she had never known about these things. Not about Pat either? Of course not, I'm not in love. I cling to him because he's the only hold for my hands that shake with fear. I would probably feel this tenderness for any other happening to be on my side.

For example, von der Heiden. I don't even hate him, though he's my enemy, the negation of everything I believe. I'm tepid; they've murdered my parents but because he hasn't done it with his own hands I don't feel revulsion at his sight. He has good manners, fine features, and I feel an odd pity for him. I'm not afraid of him. Most of the time I just feel slightly uneasy, let him kiss me because it makes me feel a little safer. I could hate him only if I were afraid of him. What does he really think of me? He likes me. It shouldn't be too hard to make him defect; he doesn't really have the sacred fire. Oh rot! Tonight's improvisation has made me initiative-happy. I'm a goose.

And Pat? "Sometime I would like to kiss you," he'd said, as one would say, "Sometime I would like to dance with you." A friendly gesture like a pressure of hands. We work together, expose ourselves to the same dangers, share secrets, are young and almost friends. It doesn't mean anything.

There are also his uneasy glances, his probing questions, and the almost harsh remarks when I seem to understand too thoroughly for just an obedient tool.

You're dreaming. What do you care? Now of all times, are you becoming sex-conscious? What he really feels, if anything, is what a man who is constantly alone with a woman comes to feel almost automatically. Anyway, it seems to be catching.

You'd better think of what occurred tonight with von der Heiden. How did it actually happen? He gave me the idea that I would make him even more insecure if he were to believe that Nagel has a measure of trust in me. But when he wanted to know how I could find Nagel, I didn't know what to answer and wished I'd kept my mouth shut. I just said the very first thing that came to mind. But once it was said (that I might receive more letters), it occurred to me that this should let us continue to give him fake instructions. Which may have been wrong. I must never act on my own. Must follow Pat's line, period. Pat wasn't there, though. I was all alone, and I had to do something.

I wish I were like Carlota, like all other women. "I don't want anymore," she said in a loud whisper to the storm and the rain and the writhing trees. If only I could talk about it to someone. That's the worst part, not being allowed to talk to anyone.

Only to Pat, of course. But it isn't enough. All we do, actually, is talk, talk compulsively. I wish we could stop for once. But we don't dare.

The window pane was cool against her forehead and her clammy hands left imprints on the glass. Perhaps I'm feverish, she thought. Then I can stay in bed, needn't undertake anything for a while. Maybe I shall be ill for weeks. Maybe I won't get well. That would be too easy. Things aren't that easy for me. If he were beside me now. "Not here . . . no, not here . . ." I don't want to wait any more. I'm afraid. Perhaps there is no time to come.

You only think about that stranger, Pat Who? I want to name him, touch him, have him touch me. She shivered. Stop. Going crazy is no way out.

CHAPTER TWELVE

PAT WAS WAITING. He had asked Tony for ten o'clock, and now it was ten-thirty. Perhaps she had not come because someone had followed her. He wished it were not that, because there would be no way of finding out before morning and he would worry himself sick all night. If only they could communicate like common mortals. What a strange thought, he noted. We're not supposed to be a pair of lovers but—secret agents.

He thought of the knife he had held in his hand a couple of weeks ago. Would the war be over before he got used to it, before it would no longer make him sick to his stomach and then follow him around, haunt him forever? And yet this time it had been different. He had had a personal stake in it. Only his knife had interposed itself between Tony and calamity. It had had to find its target, come what may. He thought of the hills on the Hudson and of Tony's Potsdam. Those very Potsdam dogs were to blame for everything. Though without them they would hardly have met.

He reminded himself that it was, nevertheless, scarcely worth a world war. He rose, hands in coat pockets, and looked into the tarnished mirror over the chiffonier, which reflected the room under a dusty, shadeless ceiling light.

From the adjoining room came suppressed voices, the loud laugh of a woman, shrill with embarrassment, and silence again. He was glad Tony was not there, had not heard the laugh.

Was there no other meeting place? Nothing as safe. She had taken it naturally, never lost a word over it. Her breeding held her suspended over any environment so it never really touched her. He thought of fields and meadows, trees and sky. The most desirable thing in life seemed a walk with Tony.

He was frowning into the mirror. He liked to have things straight, hated to stir up someone else's emotions just because he felt himself momentarily off balance. Why had he made the foolish remark, "Sometime I would like to kiss you"? It had troubled him ever since. Flirtation had no place in their relationship. Their situation was such that in its frame everything they did, every word they said assumed weight.

And yet I'm serious, he told the calm blue eyes in the glass. I'm thinking of a home, and her, and children. I'm not daydreaming. I've lived many years without wanting to remarry.

And if, someday, I could take her back with me? How would she fit into our way of life? Or rather, how would it suit her? He could see her raise her eyebrows in good-natured amusement as she did whenever he was carried away by the enthusiastic American delusion that at home everything was just a little better than anywhere else. And he could hear the drawling voices of American housewives: "She's a foreigner . . ."

How familiar that voice was. It was Jean's. Jean, blonde and strong, cool and extremely efficient. Whatever she was doing she did well—driving a car, cooking a meal, playing golf, getting along with her in-laws. Only, this apparent perfection had the limitation that she had never attempted the things that did not come to her easily and automatically. Perhaps, he thought, it was the secret of such smooth, unruffled people never to venture out of their boundaries, to stay smugly in their spiritual village where they knew their way around expertly.

His own profession and main interest—foreign affairs—had never drawn a comment from her except, "They have a lot to learn from us." She never referred to Latin Americans, English, French, or Germans as such but as dagos, limeys, frogs, and jerries; and he had not forgotten the frustrations of his first foreign assignment where his social contacts with the host country had more often than not come to a politely cool end when Jean in the crudeness of her kitchen Portuguese (the strictly minimum vocabulary she needed for her maid) had tried to give them, the poor ignorant savages, a notion of the American Way of Life. One was not offended but smiled and did not care to impose this uncouth company upon one's friends.

Then Jean's brother had come down for a visit. This word "down" had in their language the actual ring of descending, and so he had descended to the level of those dagos. Wanting to show him how attractive people could be even beyond the borders of "the good old U.S.," Pat had made the hopeful mistake of introducing him to a Brazilian couple, then taking him to a party at their Copacabana Beach home.

South Americans drank astonishing amounts without becoming objectionable and rarely overstepped the point where they would grow melancholy, mellifluous, unduly euphoric, or amorous at most. Unlike his compatriots, they seemed to draw within inebriety an apparently self-determined line. He remembered them sitting in a circle, on sofas, chairs, or on the rug, carrying on a liquor-enlightened philosophical discussion. Then his brother-in-law's fourth drink too many had blown a spark. He stood up and, weaving precariously, his face flabby, his eyes bloodshot, had begun to talk of home, pioneers, democracy, and the American woman. As he had swayed there, hands in his trouser pockets, tie askew, hair dishevelled and damp, eyes watering with homesickness, none of the rather too fastidiously dressed people had interrupted him, or laughed, or objected. They had just sat and watched. Something of the atmosphere must have penetrated into his foggy mind because he had grown aggressive, had challenged one and all to fight him with their bare fists and find out what kind of men Americans were . . .

Pat turned away from the mirror, feeling shame and disgust that were almost as overwhelming as on that night.

The following morning Jean had told him that South Americans were dull, had no sense of humor, and hated Americans because they had an inferiority complex.

"From now on I'll stick with our crowd," she had said. "I want to have fun and not be bored to death by their unintelligible lingo."

He had informed her that it was indeed good-bye to her "crowd," as well as to the "natives." They were going home.

Back in America they had talked of divorce. He had been willing to go ahead, but her cool discussions of friendly separation had always been followed by her casual mention of some project for the future. Then the baby had come.

This son, to whom he had transferred all his emotions and who someday was going to be such great company, had died at eight months. Pat, in reaching out for some moral hold, had found no one except the one person who could entirely share his grief. Little Pat's death had drawn him and Jean together more than his birth. For weeks they had thought and felt in unison, until one evening she had smiled at him, a soft, melancholy smile, but strangely light. "You're so heartbroken, Pat. I didn't know you could be like that. Darling, I'll give you more babies."

This was to be the official end of mourning. She had said it as one would say, "We'll have another automobile." A few months later they had started divorce proceedings.

There was a knock at the door. Pat opened it a crack and said, "another hour." It was after eleven. Maybe von der Heiden was with her and she could not get rid of him. The idea was painful. Von der Heiden in Tony's apartment. Be still, don't think. Or rather, do think of his presence there and the dangers it holds for her, the quick wit, the discernment it requires, and the technical knowledge she doesn't have. You should think less of yourself and more for her. You let her work too independently. She's too inexperienced, you're expecting far too much.

He thought of how well she was handling matters. She had none of Jean's loud, practical efficiency. At least, their strange relationship had given her no occasion to shine in anything except the capacities of mind and heart. There was nothing to keep up their interest in each other—no stimulating entertainments, no beautiful backdrop of nature or social spectacle—except the well of their own personalities in the drab, repulsive surroundings of furtive hotel rooms. He was confident that if so much life and warmth could develop and hold its own in this iron cage of depression and fear, once the door swung open they would step into a sort of paradise. Or maybe, seeing one another in the light of the everyday world, would they find each other different from what they had perceived in this fantastic half-shadow?

"Good evening, Pat. I'm late."

"Yes, Tony, I . . ." But he must not let her know that he had worried, must not rob her of self-assurance, the only foothold of those who had no ground under their feet.

"What?"

"I've been waiting a long time."

"Von der Heiden. When I got home he'd been there for a while, read-ing short stories. Stefan Zweig, of all things."

"Has he a key to your apartment?"

"No, the charwoman let him in. She's coming in the afternoons now. I often sleep late in the mornings," she added ruefully. She perched on the low wooden foot of the bed, sighing. "Couldn't make him talk of anything but Zweig."

"What reading for a good Nazi!" laughed Pat.

"Oh, it isn't that with him at all. His father brought him up to think that such literature was degenerate and not worth reading. He picked it from my shelves and was tremendously impressed, must have met in it his own weak-ness, his own being overpowered by life, his giving himself up to the vortex and giving in to himself . . ."

"You like Zweig, don't you?"

She nodded.

"I don't care for his dissection of the motives of the motives of his char-acters. Even less so because they're all sick, egocentric individuals who can't cope with life and should never have been born into it," he said.

"Most people are torn. And many who weren't born so get to be that way."

"You're no Zweig type, if that's what you mean," he said. "You're in an abnormal situation where you feel extremely uncomfortable and out of place and from which you seek a way out. You're well-balanced, fine, and strong—you're all the good things God thought up for mankind . . ."

He stopped. He had been listening to himself as he did sometimes after several drinks, when all he said rang true—yet through the twinkling veil of intoxication loomed the thought that the return of sobriety would make it seem preposterous.

They looked at each other in surprise.

"I think I love you, Pat."

"I know," he said almost somberly. "God, Tony, the war's going to be long. Let's wait before we speak of it again."

"Yes." Her eyes were downcast, her voice husky. Then she looked up. "Everything went smoothly. He read Nagel's letter and told me to make sure that the ship was really sailing tomorrow night. Yesterday I gave him confirmation," she added with a grin. "And just now he told me the man was ready to do the job."

"Fine. Do you know what's going to happen to him?"

"Oh, Pat, must you do that again?"

He shook his head, laughing. "Nothing of the sort. They won't so much as touch a hair of his head. When they 'catch' him he'll find that he's been invited on a cruise to England and that, if he doesn't want to blow himself up, he'd better take the bomb from where he put it. And then they'll take him along. That will be your prisoner of war, Tony."

"Pat . . ."

"Yes?"

"How much longer can it work? I mean, how much longer will von der Heiden, and mainly his superiors, believe in Nagel's letters?"

"I don't know, Tony."

CHAPTER THIRTEEN

THERE HAD BEEN A GRADUAL CHANGE in Antonio's attitude. The warmth and enthusiastic interest he used to show Tony gave way to cool formality. It was obvious that he avoided her, and looking back she wondered if he had said more than good day and good-bye to her in a long time. She asked herself if it could be a reaction to her curt words on the yacht in Mar del Plata; but the transformation had come much later. She was puzzled and hurt.

Spring had come again and slowly blossomed into summer when Carlota gave a cocktail party in the garden on Avenida Alvear. Tony stood on the lawn, a glass in her hand, looking at the straight back and shoulders of don Antonio who was bantering with a couple of half-flattered, half-bored teenage girls. Her past swept back in the memory of her father, and Antonio's strange coolness stung her heart again. She edged toward him, and as he released the restless girls who fluttered off to a group of wise-cracking youngsters, she spoke to him.

"What a lovely party, Antonio." A foolish, trite thing to say, but the spontaneity between them was gone.

"I'm glad you're enjoying yourself," he said, smiling. "You'll excuse me, I'll have to see about the drinks."

There was no need for him to see about the drinks when a staff of waiters was taking perfect care of it, and she held on pathetically to the fact that he had smiled at her.

Feeling so miserable and slighted, she accepted half an hour later Fernando Belmán's invitation to dine, as he expressed it, *en ville*. She wanted to put off her thoughts for a couple of hours by means of another drink, music, and the kind of banter ordinary people would engage in. For this tour de force there was no better stooge than Fernando.

They dined on the roof of the Alvear Palace and then toured a number of the sultry, smoke-and-perfume-drenched boîtes. His waggishness sounded wonderful at this moment. She felt as if under its stimulus the staleness of her own mind was taking on effervescence again, and the rhythmic contact of dancers on the crowded floor lifted from her the eternal feeling of isolation in a wasteland; so that at three o'clock in the morning they drove homeward in giddy merriment.

As they were nearing the residential district, Fernando said, "Let's take a turn through Palermo Park."

"Yes," she giggled, "and then you run out of gas, Fernandito. Let's stay close to the filling stations."

But he headed back north toward Avenida Alvear. "You're a flippant creature. Don't you know you love me?"

"Thanks for the warning!" she laughed. "Let me go home and dream of you, will you?"

"You're a foolish thing," he replied, continuing with enthusiasm. "We're two young, intelligent people, and in spite of our bickering we're made for each other. Why won't you admit it?"

"Don't be an idiot." She began to feel vaguely uncomfortable.

He headed into the dark park and, driving slowly, turned toward her his small, sallow face, eyes glittering under the black homburg. "You're perfectly warped, my dear Tony. You want me as much as I want you, and you know it." His teeth glistened wet between lips that looked strangely prominent in the thin, white face.

The veil of liquor and excitement tore with a jerk, hung around her in untidy shreds. "Be a gentleman, Fernando. That's enough."

"My dear marble virgin," he stopped the car by the silent lake, his face falling into cool features again, "do you think you must be virtuous to qualify for society?" His tone was sneering.

Tony sat up straight. "If you will please drive back to town, I'll answer that one."

He stepped on the accelerator and said gaily, "If, alas, that's the only way to get the sphinx to unveil her secret, *faute de mieux* I'm willing."

"Well, Fernando, I know little about Argentine society. I happened to be born into another, older one. However," she slipped into jest, "a society that includes and tolerates your type doesn't seem much to aspire to. But let's not fight." She had found the easy touch again, the only way to deal with him, and her irritation was gone.

"I agree, my dear. But why not take what this stingy life has to offer? I don't deny that I'm a disreputable character, but so is just about everybody else, male or female. You can't wait for the ideal man or woman. And, on the other hand, a little immorality doesn't make us any worse. To me, for example, Carlota is perfectly admirable. In every respect."

His voice became charged with emotion. "To my mind, she is almost a saint. And yet, if the powers that be knew what you and I know, she would be ostracized."

He felt Tony's eyes bore into him and turned an eager face toward her, ready to provide any details she might desire. When she spoke, however, her voice was slow and sharp.

"When I first met you, Fernando, I thought I hated you. But then there didn't seem to be enough solid matter about you to make a firm concentration of any feeling on you possible. I see that, after all, there is something solid, and that's your wickedness. I detest you. Now you will, please, let me get out."

There was a beginning of the accustomed cackle. "My dear, you're really quite . . ." but he did not finish. He stopped and, reaching across her, opened the door.

She saw the car speed off, vanish among the trees, and alone in the nocturnal park, she stretched her arms in pride for having taken, after such a long time, the liberty to rebel against something, the joy of having indulged in speaking her mind.

When she told Pat of her moment of euphoria, he said gravely, "You mustn't make enemies in your situation."

"I mustn't make enemies, I mustn't make friends. Pat, no one can live completely without reactions. How do you expect me to exist?"

"I want you to be cool," he replied unemotionally.

Coming out of a store in a street off Florida, she stood before Peter. It struck her as so unreal, so impossible that for a moment she stared without saying a word.

"Hello, Tony. I just came in."

A wave of pleasure carried her up, then dropped her into hollow disenchantment. "Why didn't you let me know? And your luggage?"

After a second's hesitation he said, "It was all so sudden. My suitcase is at the station. But let's go."

They started toward Florida. "Why?" she asked with the definite feeling that something was wrong.

He frowned. "You see, I don't even know if I'm going to spend the night. I just have to see someone at the Sociedad Rural."

"No," she said, linking her arm with his, "now that you're here you'll stay at least until tomorrow. Let's get your suitcase." She was glad but there was an edge to her happiness.

"Look here," he said, his tone urgent, a little upset, "you take a cab home and I'll go get my suitcase."

"But I have nothing else to do. I'll go with you."

He whistled for a cab, almost pushed her into it, and gave the driver her address.

When he reached the apartment she took his suitcase to unpack. As she snapped the lock, she saw him start and turn, but she had already raised the lid on a pair of slept-in pajamas and two sets of used underwear. She looked at him in hurt wonder.

He stood in the middle of the room, scowling. "Don't make this maiden aunt's face. If you have to know, I've been here for a couple of days— at a hotel."

"Peter, why?"

"What a question!" he laughed but his voice was sharp and uneasy.

"That's all right, Peter," she said softly, but she sensed that there was nothing like a love affair behind this. Only she could not imagine what it might be. The one thing she knew was that, for some inexplicable reason, Peter, too, had become a stranger.

After an uncomfortable hour of stilted conversation, during which he tried desperately to be friendly and natural, he left her and returned only at night. She was awake but, to spare him embarrassment, did not stir.

During her long lonely hours she had found an explanation. Peter must have heard of her activities. Maybe the Germans, trying to recruit him, too, had mentioned her. If he had discussed it with him, it would also explain Antonio's attitude. She enumerated with self-tormenting precision: Romero, Peter, Antonio. Who would be next? It no longer mattered any more, for the loss of Peter made all other ties seem unsubstantial.

In the early morning he came into her room to say good-bye. He leaned over her and stroked her head on the pillow with a new shyness. "Take care of yourself, Tony."

She felt that he wanted to say more, so she did not move, did not even lift her head, just looked up at him with grave black eyes. He turned abruptly and left. She heard the entrance door click shut. She hated everybody, even Pat.

She told Pat of the incident with unreasonable reproach, as if he had brought all this upon her head.

"Don't worry about your brother. He probably came to town for a little fun and didn't like to have you minding his business. You're developing a complex."

She looked at him, the stranger. "Mind his business? You don't know us, Pat."

CHAPTER FOURTEEN

A FEW WEEKS LATER PAT SAID, "Guess who was at the embassy yesterday?"

"I can't imagine."

"Someone you know well."

"I don't know."

"Antonio Guerida Paz."

"Why?" An unreasonable fear stirred in her.

Pat laughed. "Not to deliver Mata Hari into our fangs. You know he's a friend of the ambassador. He was giving him information concerning some Nazi firms when he offered his services."

"It's kind of logical, really. And?"

"They were accepted. And it's given us an idea." He threw a soiled cushion off the lilac grosgrain divan and sat down. "We've been guests of these dumps for too long. We've changed as much as possible, but even this city's wealth of such institutions is by now exhausted. We've been too often in the same and," he laughed, "people must begin to wonder why we don't get married or rent a garçonnière."

"And what could Antonio do about it?"

"You could give him your information to pass on."

"You mean, we wouldn't meet at all any more?"

"That's what the embassy wants. Tony, it's not only better for them, but much, much, safer for you. He's your cousin, you're in and out of his house anyhow . . ."

She was close to tears, yet she spoke on as if it were only a practical matter. "But do they want to let Antonio know about me?"

"Yes. Nobody really is more trustworthy than he."

"Why then, only last summer, was I not allowed to tell him, when I was fighting to keep my sanity? Why, if he's so trustworthy, did I have to go through this misery? Because you want me without enemies and without friends?"

"Don't hold me responsible for the decisions of others, Tony," he begged. "That's the way it is."

"I can't . . ." She realized that she was crying, and Pat rose and knelt beside her, taking her hands, not with the gesture of a lover, but of an adult adjusting to the smallness of a child.

"Tony, look up. Look at me . . . look at me, Tony."

She raised her head. "I'm childish. I shouldn't ever have taken on this work. I'm not mature enough. I hardly ever think of the job. I only think of . . ."

"I know," he interrupted quietly. "It was merely an idea. Anyway, you'd have to talk to him first. They want you to put out a feeler."

"Pat, this isn't wishful thinking, but . . ." she hesitated.

"What, Tony? Say it. We must talk everything over as we've always done. We want to look at it from all angles." He sat on the floor, cross-legged, like a classmate trying to solve a study problem with her.

For a moment she gazed at him distrustfully. Was it just another pose? "It's what you just said. We must talk everything over. If Antonio gives me your instructions, I might not be able to carry them out. There are always details we must discuss. You know how we do . . . "

"That's true."

She tried to laugh. "Oh, Pat, it's really only that I feel calmer and surer if, before I go, I can tell you I'm scared."

"No, no, you're right," he said seriously. Then he looked up at her with a bewildered smile. "Say, Tony, are we right or is it wishful thinking?"

On the next day she asked Antonio for an interview. Their relations had become so cool that it was quite a formal affair. Rather than have her come to his home, he asked her to his office at the Sociedad Rural. She did not mind and was happy at the prospect of justifying herself and unburdening her heart of the strange episode with Peter. Her twin's attitude remained a puzzle. He would write regularly for some time, then there would be a long silence. His letters were cordial, even with an occasional tremor of tenderness, which she attributed to pity, as she interpreted the intervals in his writing as an attempt to let the correspondence die down.

Antonio received her in his sober office among pictures of forbidding prize bulls and stately pedigreed horses.

"Antonio," she asked, "do you think I could get translation work from the British Embassy? I'm asking because you're a friend of the ambassador."

"No," he said, categorically.

"Why not?"

He leaned across the heavy quebracho desk. "In the first place, you're of German nationality, and besides . . ." He hesitated.

"Besides, what?"

". . . besides, Antonie, I have something to tell you. I should have talked to you before. Who is the German visiting you?"

"German?" she echoed, playing for time.

"You won't believe me when I tell you how I happened to hear of it. There's a cobbler's shop in your house, isn't there?"

"Yes," she said, puzzled.

"Well, this cobbler works for friends of ours. They got his son a job, and ever since, the old man has been very attached to them, and when he delivers his repairs he always comes in to pay his respects. One night at dinner—fortunately neither María Teresa, nor Carlota were present—they repeated a fantastic story the cobbler had told them about a young German translator in his house who had an affair with a Nazi diplomat, and further elaborations that I can spare you because you know more about them than I do."

"Or the cobbler," she said dryly. "And what makes you think that I'm that girl?"

"Is there another young German translator in your building?"

"What gossip!"

"Yes, but there's something to it, isn't there? Antonie, is it love?"

She shook her head.

"Work?"

"Yes."

Antonio rose. "I feel sorry for you. You must be very unhappy and in a bitter conflict. But I cannot understand you. Don't try to explain, it would be useless. I've tried for months to find an explanation, but there's none that excuses."

"I bet you haven't thought of everything."

"Of blackmail and all kinds of threats, of everything. But you have no family left in Germany."

She sensed that he was waiting for her to rise. "You'd better not mention too often that my parents are dead. And please, Antonio, sit down so I can tell you why I'm here."

The Cadillac raced along the dusty highway. Beneath the livid sky the rows of eucalyptus trees on the plain felt the enticing softness of the coming rain. Here and there cattle grazed and scattered horses chased over the pampa. At long intervals the mud huts of forlorn ranchos would appear, and everywhere was flat land.

"A cigarette, Antonieta?"

"Thanks." Smiling brightly she drew one from the pack Antonio was holding out.

"That's the first genuine smile I've seen in a long time. It's like one of our rides to the estate."

"It is," she exclaimed. "It feels good. I wish we hadn't waited all that time."

"You're a brave girl. All this quiet contentment when you're really on a wicked errand."

"Don't you see it's paradise now?" she laughed. "Flanked by you and Pat, I actually feel snug."

His eyes grazed her then looked back at the road. "Do you call each other by your first names?"

"It's all the name I know."

"He seems like a nice fellow."

"I love him," she said without taking her eyes off the road ahead.

"And he loves you. I could tell. Yet it may not be wise to give in to this kind of thing. What's to become of it? You know it can't be for long. My little country house will be safe for a while. Just as safe as were the hotels. For how long? Your work is dangerous in itself; even if you remain completely cool and cautious, which nobody can when they're in love."

"I know."

"Take care of yourself, Antonie."

She put her hand on his arm. "I will."

The small bungalow was built of palm tree trunks. It stood in an arid garden surrounded by a wooden fence. Antonio dropped her in front and, not to leave the car parked, drove on. She walked through the gate and up to the house in Alice-in-Wonderland anticipation. The door opened while she was still a few steps from it and she ran the short stretch toward it. Then it closed behind her.

The room into which she stepped was different from what she had imagined. There was nothing deliberately rustic about it. Fine colonial pieces stood darkly against white walls bare except for two English hunting scenes. As in all of Antonio's dwellings, like the first time she had entered his magnificent home on Avenida Alvear, she had the sensation that she was coming home.

"I meant to make some tea," said Pat, "to celebrate this improvement, which is somewhat like being transferred from a jail to a mental institution. But there isn't even a grain of salt in the house."

"I don't think they ever use the place. But isn't it beautiful?"

They looked at each other somewhat helplessly. The sordid surroundings in which they had met until now had nevertheless become familiar, the natural frame for their reunions, and their attitude had been molded by them. Now that the defensive detachment was superfluous, there was nothing to take its place. Tony fled into the business at hand. "I remember Hell, Taube, Reisch, and Greiner. They were too many. There are at least forty names on the list."

He was gnawing his lower lip. "If we could see that list. Wouldn't he give it to you?"

"Under what pretext would I ask for it? If I could just see it once more I'd memorize more names. But he wouldn't show it to me again. Why should he?"

"He still has it, you think?"

"I suppose so. He's got a peculiar way of carrying papers around for weeks. Even that kind."

"Couldn't you take it from his pocket?"

"How?"

He laughed. "He doesn't ever take his coat off, does he?"

She shook her head, smiling. "Never."

"Doesn't get tight either?"

"No."

"Why don't you pour something over his sleeve and insist he let you have the coat to take the spot out? But then you'd have to read fast."

A few heavy drops splashed against the diamond panes. Then the wind howled.

"What did you do," he asked, "on rainy days when you were small?"

"We'd play Rummy or Quartett. You know what that is? It's a card game where children learn about painters and sculptors or the classics. Four make a trick. The romantics: Novalis, Byron, Vigny . . ." She screwed up her eyes and nibbled on her index finger. "Who was their fourth?" She shrugged. "Never mind. Anyhow, I'm afraid that's where part of my sketchy general education comes from. But often I'd just press my nose against the window pane and watch it rain. And you?"

"I'd listen to the rain, too, and think that such afternoons weren't made for being alone. Together they're beautiful; alone they're awfully sad."

"I mean, when you were a child."

"Even then. It seemed somehow senseless to have your friends only on sunny days, for a ball game or a hike. On bright days there's so much to do a child hardly needs friends. But on rainy afternoons when they need one another, each sits alone in his room and feels sad—is bored or broods."

"It was always beautiful, though."

"What was?"

"Oh, being little. To be put to bed early and to lie there knowing that it is evening and time for you to sleep while others, who only go to bed at night, still go around as if it were day, doing commonplace little things. To know that out there your governess goes by the door, not sleepy at all, putting away clothes and glueing a toy, while you lie there and listen to the steps and recognize each one: hers light and swift, Mother's hard and high-heeled, father's a silent tread, the shuffling of Mother's old maid, and after her the pup's light tap, the tag tinkling on his collar. And to see the light filter through the lacquered white door and to grow sleepy . . . "

"And to be sick," he carried on. "To have a sore throat and your nose red from blowing. The smell of chicken broth and apple sauce. A thick children's book finished much too soon. And a dozen toys on the night table; and when no one's around to stick your foot out from under the covers."

"Will we have that again?" she asked, discouraged.

He shook his head. "That's childhood."

"I mean, will our children live so peacefully?" She realized that for the first time since her parents' death she was contemplating the possibility of having children and, with a pang of embarrassment, that she associated them with Pat. She hoped he had missed the implication, though it seemed oddly natural in this misty hour of dusk in the solitary country.

He came to sit on the arm of her chair, and they looked through the window at the eucalyptus trees bending in the rainstorm.

"Do you want children?"

"Yes. And a home for them. To remember, to remain around them until the end of their lives. Like a fortress. Even if it had to disappear someday, as has mine. Where they could go back in their hearts if things got really bad. I even," she said almost apologetically, "want them to learn German. So they'll know the poetry I recite for my own benefit when I feel really lost. I'm now always among strangers. Where nothing belongs to me and I belong to nothing. There isn't anything to hold on to, or into which I can withdraw. I sit between two *Parteigenossen* and recite to myself Rainer Maria Rilke."

Their eyes were still turned toward the window. Pat said:

Doch alles, was uns anrührt, dich und mich,
nimmt uns zusammen wie ein Bogenstrich,
der aus zwei Saiten eine Stimme zieht.
Auf welches Instrument sind wir gespannt?
Und welcher Spieler hat uns in der Hand?
Oh süsses Lied.

His accent was strong, but his comprehension seemed total. She was pleasantly surprised.

"I didn't know your German was so good!"

"I had a study grant and went to Heidelberg for a year. Didn't I tell you?"

"No. But I'm glad. I'd like to show you my volumes of poetry."

He bent over her uplifted face and kissed her. They were wrapped in the dim grey of the late hour, covered by the hush of the lonely room, only the rain singing on and on, all the events and demands of their lives far away, as if seen through the wrong side of an opera glass, beyond reach, small, and at an infinite distance. When a horn sounded, they disengaged themselves, leaving in each other's hands their souls as if for safekeeping.

CHAPTER FIFTEEN

"I'm sorry! what have i done!" she exclaimed, reaching for a napkin to wipe his sleeve. "And you're invited out!"

Von der Heiden grimaced. He disliked awkwardness. The vermouth had left a large red stain on his forearm.

For a moment she seemed at a loss. Then she said, "Give me your coat. I'll clean it."

He hesitated, looked at his watch. It was half past eight, too late to go home and change. He rose and took off his coat with a great deal of embarrassment, allowed her to carry it to the kitchen, and sat down again to leaf through a magazine. But he did not grasp what he was reading and put it aside to follow her.

The kitchen door was ajar. He saw her at the faucet waiting for the water to steam, holding a white cloth, his coat over her arm as she had carried it out, one of the sleeves still hanging down.

Now she turned around, smiling. "It'll come off."

"I thought you might need help." He felt embarrassed, shamed by her smiling innocence.

"Not help, but company." She was rubbing at the spot now. After a moment she said, "All right, we'll hang it by the open window. In a few minutes it'll be dry enough for ironing."

She threw the cloth on the drainboard, went to fetch a hanger from the vestibule, and hung the coat on the window knob.

Back in the living room, she shuddered at the thought of what would have happened had it not occurred to her that he might follow. He had never set foot in her kitchen and was not the type to amble into the prosaic dependencies of dwellings where he was a guest, but he was so particular about his apparel.

"Fenloe, the Hungarian, was there," she said, "and the red-haired Canadian . . ."

"Harrond? With whom?" he inquired vaguely. The painful awareness that he was sitting there in shirtsleeves made him unable to concentrate.

"With a young girl. She looked like an Argentine."

"Tall and slender with a very straight nose?"

"I think so."

"That's the Spanish girl. When did they leave?"

"Early." She should have said that it had been late when she had seen them once more in the hotel garden. A mistake in the dark would have been plausible. She realized that her mind was with the coat in the kitchen. She rose. "Do you want to come along?"

He followed her, and she tried to put up the ironing board, which maliciously and persistently kept sliding and collapsing onto her feet. After he came to help her, their combined efforts only led to another collapse, but finally it stood and she plugged in the iron.

It must have been all too obvious that she had never used either before. While she waited for the iron to heat she was silent, hoping he would grow bored. But then he was probably too well-bred simply to get up and return to the drawing room.

He considered the situation ludicrous. Stephan von der Heiden in shirtsleeves on a kitchen chair while a young woman was putting up an ironing board to press his coat. On the other hand, he felt curious, believed that he was discovering an unknown part of her life. "Do you know how to cook?" he asked.

"Soft boiled eggs. And, best of all, canned food."

They were silent again. She leaned against the wall, gazed at the brown trickle that had run from a used coffee filter bag onto the drainboard. From the faucet, drops beat into the sink. The sharp light illuminated a corner where the charwoman had dropped potato peelings; she was becoming slack. But she must think about the list now, not the charwoman.

She took the coat from the hanger and laid it on the board. The breast pocket felt heavy where his wallet was. She began to pass over the sleeve lightly, very lightly, afraid to burn the cloth.

"My father says my mother was a good cook," remarked von der Hei-den, wishing to put her at ease in case she minded his insight into this graceless annex of her existence. "According to my father, she felt that the mistress of a house, like a captain in relation to his troops, should be able to carry out her own commands. I frankly can't imagine my mother express-ing herself that way, but that's what my father says."

Tony did not know what to answer. She was unsympathetic to the whole idea of his Teutonic kin, and at this moment he was getting on her nerves. "My mother ran an exemplary household," she snapped, "without so much as knowing how water boiled."

He blushed. "Frankly, my only boyhood remembrance along those lines is connected with my mother's soup dumplings, which tasted like wood pulp. I couldn't swallow them to save my life. But my father forced me to, and it gave me nightmares. I used to dream that I was in Venice—which at the time I'd never seen. I wanted to paint. But everywhere were soup dumplings, even on my chest. And they grew heavier and heavier . . ."

"Do you paint?" she asked perfunctorily, continuing to iron, though the sleeve was dry, and wondering for how much longer she could keep it up. The figments of his angst were none of her business.

"A little. Later I really wanted to paint in Venice. But by then the palace of the Doges was festooned, column by column, with huge posters of the Duce in a steel helmet. So I skipped it." He laughed.

She put the black leather wallet with the gold corners into his out-stretched hand, thinking, thank God you don't see that I don't know how, that I only make vague pro forma gestures. Pat, who grew up at his mother's side in the kitchen, as you and I by our nannies in the nursery, wouldn't have been fooled for a minute.

"You know, our kitchen walls have no tiles. All that is brick, though re-cently Father's had a gas stove installed," he added, regretfully. "The do-mestics won't use wood any more."

For domestics, he had used the feudal word *Gesinde*. Did his kind of people, when out in the country and away from the enlightened urbanity of the salons, continue to talk like that? She found it hilarious. But after all, she thought, they all cling to their childhoods. Whether they've left it behind and only remember or, like Pat and me, sort of carry it along. To an extent, so does von der Heiden, which makes him seem somehow human, no matter how he acts. I must not let myself be deluded by it.

"Good old German childhood memories," she said. "Speaking of Germany, I don't imagine you still have the list you showed me the other day?"

"Why?"

"I happened to hear a name at the Free Austrian Club that I meant to keep in mind because I thought I'd seen it on the list. Someone supposed to be working for the British. But I've forgotten. I might recognize it, though, if I see it. Could you bring me the list sometime?"

"I think I've got it." He leafed through his wallet, thinking, Would she have searched my pockets if I had not followed her? I must be more careful with my papers.

Tony went over the names again and again. Then she returned the sheet to him and, passing the iron a few more times over the coat, spoke with somewhat flustered emphasis. "I simply cannot remember. But I'm going to find out." She must talk and at the same time not forget ten precariously memorized names.

When he had gone she jotted down eight, two had by then hopelessly slipped her mind. She turned off the ceiling light, and as she sat by the reading lamp her thoughts drifted, dreamlike, back to Pat.

In this mood, which she called the reversed opera glass delusion, it seemed to her that the rain was once more singing around her, that the light was soft and grey, and Pat's voice was saying, *doch alles, was uns anrührt, dich und mich, nimmt uns zusammen wie ein Bogenstrich, der aus zwei Saiten eine Stimme zieht . . .*

As he spoke the German words, she had for the first time heard him use the intimate du. Of the languages she knew, in none but English could one pass so smoothly from friendship into love, arriving by a gentle ascent to find oneself at the summit, surprised by the height.

She had been an adult for some time, like most strongly emotional people desirous of affection. But love had in her imagination assumed the shape of shared verses and landscapes, laughter and tears.

"A normal function," her mother had commented, "like eating and drinking. It is whatever we make of it. A meal, too, can be repulsive if badly performed. But in a lovely setting, artfully prepared, and, rather than an end in itself, enhancing the spiritual rapport of ideal companions, it can be a great enjoyment. You know the difference between *gourmand* and *gourmet*."

A mouthful, punned Tony, who hated puns. Of course, the metaphor was ingenious, but it limited itself to daintily tending the blossom while fastidiously ignoring its root. It had spun off the delusory bobbin of free choice, while she, it seemed to her, had neither tested, nor approved, but found herself in the arms that her nature had inevitably, almost blindly sought.

CHAPTER SIXTEEN

WHEN TONY ENTERED THE CROWDED APARTMENT, her Anglo-Argentine hostess started to introduce her but soon gave up. She drifted from snatch to snatch of conversation, until the host took her arm.

"Let me introduce you to a very interesting chap," he said. "Pat Larson, correspondent for one of the most important American papers. He has spent some time in Germany. Pat, this is Tony Herrnfeld."

"How do you do?" smiled Pat.

"How do you do?"

"I'll get you a drink, Tony," said the host. "You aren't drinking anything. A highball? Soda or water?"

"Water please."

They looked at each other, pain in their eyes. Then Pat smiled gravely. "I'm glad you know. It seems more right now, doesn't it?"

The room swayed, and though she was warm, she felt a strange coldness around her body and face and wondered if she were going to faint. Fighting her dizziness, she gave him an uncertain smile.

"Let's not leave yet, either of us. It would be conspicuous. But let's not stay together either," he said softly.

Their host was back with the drink. A tall blonde was playfully pinching Pat's arm and cooing at him with a throaty Texas accent. "Well, ol' sweetheart, I didn't know you were still in B.A. Tell me all about yourself." With a smile and a wink at Tony, he turned to her, and the group broke up.

Half an hour later Tony left, to spend the rest of the night in misery. The injustice of their situation angered her as though it were inflicted by an individual's arbitrary will. Behind closed lids she kept seeing Pat the way she had tonight, at a normal distance, as she had never seen him before. Dressed other than in tweeds, an extraordinarily handsome man, unknown to her, yet her own. She saw the well-groomed sleeve, the starched cuff over the golden wrist, and the sinewy, rather delicate hand holding the glass.

Excitement born from physical knowledge and a new kind of desire, sparked by the unfamiliar guise, electrified her skin. She wanted others, everyone to know that he was hers, that she belonged in this hand, had made her home in it. She thought grimly that the chances of it becoming reality were slimmer than those of the ever-hopeful Argentine of winning *La Grande,* the grand prize of the lottery.

As if their breaking of the barriers had been a sin, they were punished by being forced apart even more than before their rush into each other's arms. For a few weeks Pat seemed uneasy, as if he had on his mind something he did not wish to tell her. Then, one afternoon he said, "I don't want you to start worrying now. But neither do I want you to be unprepared if it should happen. There's been some talk of sending me somewhere else."

From then on everything was dark, even their moments of happiness were tainted by anguish. No pain, not even fear, had been with her as constantly in waking or sleeping as the thought of Pat's transfer. Having for months shed each day like a burden, she now held on to every hour in panic at seeing it slip by; if earlier she had tried to hurry time between reunions, she now savored it as possibly the last to lead to joy.

"We ought to pull the curtains. One might see light from outside."

"Why, it's dark here."

"Your shoulders shine." She felt his smile. "You shine through the dark like a slender white holy image. If you were a Madonna I would become a Catholic to worship you."

She slipped down to rest her head on his chest where she could hear his heartbeat, loud and even and exact like a hammer.

"Have you heard any more about your transfer?"

He shook his head.

"Really?" Anguish in her voice.

"Really. And you mustn't think about it. We'll always be together. Even after I'm gone, you'd always know I love you."

Her lips pressed against the hollow of his shoulder so her voice sounded muffled and oppressed. "No, Pat, no. I wouldn't know anything at all. I can't be without you. Couldn't I go with you?"

"No, Tony, I don't think so. But it may not even be. There was just some talk. It may not come and yet it may come any day, overnight. And then I must go. So I wanted you to know. So it wouldn't strike you like lightning out of a clear sky."

He buried his mouth in her hair and closed his eyes tightly not to groan. He did not know that he held her so close that his collarbone hurt her forehead. But he felt her fingernails fastening into his arms and her body straining against his for shelter, so that he turned over with her as if she were a part of him.

"I wish we could have a child," she whispered as though she did not really want him to hear. Yet when he did not answer, she continued. "I know it's madness . . . and we mustn't. I know, but . . ." and then her voice grew hot and breathless. "Stay with me, Pat . . . don't let go of me!"

Her words seared him, became unbearable. As he was closing in on those insistent lips, he tasted tears. Pulling back to look into her face under the now rising moon, he saw more than grief. There lies my strength, he thought, mirrored as in a pool, worthless strength, impotent to shield her from unhappiness, at best able to make her feel happy for an unthinking moment, at worst to merely let her forget how unhappy she is. The strength of a bull, not a man.

She was spellbound by the violence pouring down from his eyes, oddly like pain, eyes torn by desire, drowning in love, while his teeth advanced and glistened, oddly as if in hatred. He heard the minute mating call of which she was unaware but that he had come to know and wait for, and thought: But this is a happiness only I can give her, not the aristocratic hothouse plant in whose hands I may have to leave her. The thought made him take her to him like a trophy.

Her head heaved up and down on the waves of his heart, while she listened to its quickened beat, felt it jerk once more and then grow calm, until he breathed quietly as if in sleep. But she knew that he was awake and thinking, like her, that within the hour she would be on her way to town, and he at a windy rural station, waiting for the train to Retiro. And then there would be another evening like this, and perhaps another, or perhaps none. Her tears dropped to his chest and he drew her closer. "Sleep, darling. I'll wake you in time."

"Time's far too precious now. I don't want to sleep another minute while I know you're in Buenos Aires."

"Then you mustn't cry. Since our time is precious we must enjoy it."

They heard the ticking of his watch on the bedside table, ticking away with implacable indifference each second of the remaining hour.

CHAPTER SEVENTEEN

"MR. HEINRICH WOULD LIKE TO SEE YOU, SIR," said the office boy, putting a stack of letters on von der Heiden's desk. Stephan threw a quick glance at the upper one, was about to reach for it, but changed his mind and threw the whole package into a drawer. Following embassy regulations, he locked his office from the outside before he went down the hallway toward the last door. As he knocked he drew himself up, but loosened his shoulders before he turned the knob.

Heinrich sat behind his desk, his head, too big for the small, narrow-shouldered body, thrown back, the tiny white hand resting with fingers spread on the table top.

Von der Heiden nodded and smiled. "Good morning, Mr. Heinrich." Without waiting for an invitation he sat down in the chair facing him. In crossing his long legs he exposed to Heinrich's view a thoroughbred ankle clad in black silk. Heinrich returned von der Heiden's smile, the horizontal furrows on his forehead deepening, forcing out fleshy rolls. It was an unfailing indication that he was not quite sure of himself—which in von der Heiden's presence he rarely was. He did not actually feel inferior. On the contrary, he enjoyed his superiority in rank. But he was aware that this order of rank did not count for von der Heiden, whose father was a general, and landed gentry for good measure. The German *Kleinbürger* had never lost his submissive awe when confronted with the little word "von." Old man Heinrich had been a carpenter.

"Have you ever seen such heat in early summer?" he remarked, passing a hand over his forehead, which was dry.

Stephan took a cigarette from his case and lighted it. "That's bound to change again," he replied, looking indifferently out of the window.

"Well, I hope so." Heinrich was gazing at the clipped, almond-shaped nail of the forefinger that rested on the cigarette, looked at his own long nails and decided to wear them shorter. "Was that a Dunhill?"

"Yes. They're the best."

"You ought to carry a German lighter," he countered sharply.

Von der Heiden laughed and Heinrich sensed that this laugh put him into ridicule. He did not know in what way; felt he was right, and yet he felt embarrassed. This was what irritated him most about von der Heiden: knowing almost always that he had the upper hand and nevertheless almost always feeling ridiculous. He joined in the laugh and asked cordially, "any news from home?"

"I just got a letter from my father." He's read it already, von der Heiden thought, and since he mentions it he must have found something in it. He felt his nerves and forced himself to be calm.

"What's new in your neck of the woods?" the other inquired amiably.

Von der Heiden was glad he had refrained from opening the letter. "I don't know. I haven't read my mail yet."

"Must be nice to receive letters from home," sighed Heinrich. "I've got no brothers or sisters and my parents are dead."

And no friends, thought von der Heiden. How glad you are, dear fellow, that your father died two years ago and the embassy censorship can no longer scoff at his spelling. Now all they've got left to snicker over is your jargon, but that's more Berlin than carpenter.

"Now tell me, dear von der Heiden, what about your friend Herrnfeld?"

"I couldn't tell you any more than you can read in my reports. Her work seems very satisfactory to me."

"Not to me!" he said, suddenly brutal.

"Why not?" Von der Heiden seemed frankly astonished.

"You know that we take the risk of employing Jews only when the results are extremely worthwhile. They aren't."

"Miss Herrnfeld constantly gives us very valuable information," protested von der Heiden.

"That we can't do anything with."

"It's she who links us with Nagel," Stephan replied dryly, his own apprehensions overwhelming him again.

"In Nagel's name she's made us eliminate Schneckenbach and Wurzer, and God knows whether they were really double agents and not our most valuable men."

"Their reports have, after all, been found in the British Embassy, haven't they? And the memo we found on Wurzer was in the handwriting of the British military attaché. One could hardly expect more conclusive evidence."

"Granted. But it doesn't prove anything. At any rate, Nagel's absence has continued for an amazingly long time."

His arguing showed that he had no instructions from above but was working on his own. Then he was vulnerable, and von der Heiden knew how to manage him.

"I thought the ambassador had given instructions for me to handle this case according to my own judgement," he said, raising his narrow eyebrows.

Heinrich was aroused. "You're just an intermediary, Count. The ambassador has left the matter, if anything, in Herrnfeld's hands. For the moment, and under surveillance. For if there's something fishy and Nagel's been done in, we mean to play along a while."

"If the ambassador had been harboring any suspicions, he'd hardly have made us eliminate two men whom he regarded until then as our best agents."

Heinrich stood up, his short body very upright. "The ambassador does not content himself with negative instructions. He occasionally wishes to see positive ones."

Von der Heiden, knowing that he must leave now, rose slowly. "Nagel is no puppet that moves as I pull the strings."

Heinrich laughed. "It looks like it at times."

The laugh seemed to follow him down the hall. After he had shut his own office door he took his father's letter from the desk drawer.

> . . . for your cousins act like rowdies, ravaging the neighbors'
> property, scarring the walls with foul language that no housepainter
> can cover up. I'm too old to keep them in check. I wish you would
> return to do your share, so we won't sink still deeper into disgrace in
> the eyes of the world . . .

Von der Heiden was very pale, the thin lower lip was quivering. Did his father realize that he was pushing both of them into disaster? He must know that what he was doing was murder. But he understood that his father was trying to save, not kill him, not to draw him into ruin but back to life.

Stephan himself had grown used to thinking of life as something he was excluded from, accessible perchance after Germany's victory over the world, when she would finally feel at peace with her fate and secure enough to dispense with warfare. There would no longer be occasion for bribery, blackmail, and assassination. The German Embassies in Paris and London would plot no more, but dictate.

He would be cultural attaché in some civilized capital, in touch only with the world of art he loved and understood, perhaps one day ambassador. He shrank from the thought of the undignified lack of artistic and intellectual freedom that followed the German boot wherever it happened to stomp—the political gimmickry of the concept of so-called "degenerate art," the Teutonic slips of the taste that under the corporal were even more frequent and conspicuous than under the Kaiser. And, anyway, was he so sure that Germany was going to win this war?

He knew how the bubble of imperial greatness had burst and how the mud-caked jackboots of the brown hordes had torn the Junkers' finely spun plan to replace the puppet of heavy industry with the heir to the throne. He knew how, like the sorcerer's apprentice, the general staff had seen the puppet they had called to life flood them with a a torrent of fantastic campaigns.

Even though the preposterous Germanic gods had so far granted them stunning success, they foresaw the catastrophic end without finding the magic formula to dominate their own creature. He had no illusions. Their distress did not spring, like his father's, from a sense of decency; at best from nationalism, at worst from greed. They had no objection to lawlessness, only to losing a war.

The vision of such defeat did not really frighten him now. He longed for an end to the depressing situation, no matter what kind, as if leaning thirstily over a poisoned well, accepting life's termination with that of the torment.

He felt dizzy at his desk, his face in his hands, his brain in a hot whirl, his heart cold and clammy. He thought of Heinrich's words about Antonie Herrnfeld, and a chill voice within him said, *Nagel is dead.* Despair darted through him.

109

He tried to analyze himself, thought, you've come to love her because she's proud and cool and aloof, you love her because she's like your sisters and cousins, fine and out of reach, unlike the wives and daughters of your embassy colleagues. Yet it is only a veneer, all this gentility. She has sold out to the butchers of her people, worse than a harlot.

No, you don't love her, he assured himself, lighting a candle and burning the general's letter. You feel akin to her because she's as gentle and decayed as you. Or isn't she? He refused to think about it or to seek an answer.

While Tony was waiting, she checked a finished translation, made a last correction, put the sheets on the coffee table beside her, and, pulling her feet up onto the davenport, looked at the ceiling. Its nearness weighed on her who had grown up in Potsdam's high stucco-ceilinged rooms. It made her think of Pat's description of his clapboard home, like an outsize cottage with a gabled roof, the front steps and the porch (homely expressions) and the few chickens they kept. It sounded so narrow and small-time that she sometimes wondered how she would adjust to a life, if ever she were to become part of it, where women decorated their kitchens more carefully than their living rooms because they spent far more time in them. But whenever such doubts assailed her she brushed them aside.

Would they even remain together long enough to ever get married? She felt sure that he would not leave her of his own free will; their love was unaffected by jealousy and doubts. But their fears centered on something much more unpredictable and irrevocable, on extraneous events that might separate and then forget about them.

A few moments later she received von der Heiden, felt small and somewhat embarrassed in his long arms, which, singularly enough, had acquired the right to hold her, but she had long since ceased to fear him. He retained her longer than usual, in a strangely ardent, almost commanding embrace, and she had come to know him well enough to realize that he was off balance.

"What's worrying you?" she asked, sympathy in her voice. She walked to an armchair, and he took his seat on the davenport, spoke gently and rationally as if wanting to reason with her. "Antonie, don't you want to tell me where Nagel is and whatever you know about your correspondent?"

"The very idea!"

"Be sensible, Antonie. They're not nearly convinced of your loyalty. They even suspect that the whole thing is a farce. They'll stand by and watch only until they're absolutely sure, because they're a little afraid of Nagel and his connections in Berlin. But by and by, they're beginning to feel a bit foolish."

"Why? They've got all the proof they can ask for. They've seen the messages I've received in writing, they've seen from where they were mailed, and that's all I know about his middleman or his own whereabouts. All tests and investigations have turned out in my favor. I can't do any more."

He did not want to speak and yet he did. "Antonie, I don't believe you. I don't believe any of it. I have all material evidence that you're speaking the truth and very little to the contrary. But you yourself, your personality, all I know of you, gives you the lie."

She looked straight at him. "Have you passed on this impression to your supervisors?"

"No, Antonie, no!"

"Then you're a poor servant to your country. And since you're handling my case so sloppily you probably do the same with others. That's Nagel's principal objection to you: lack of spirit and determination."

She was frightened as she spoke. What if her words incited him to take action? Yet he had been negligent too long to hope for redemption through such a belated act.

"To point to your lack of reliability at the embassy would be carrying owls to Athens," he replied sarcastically, and at the thought of how precarious her position was her heart missed a beat.

When the door bell rang, she put both hands on the seat, sat upright, and listened with bated breath as if she could hear who stood outside. The feverish idea that it might be Pat was ridiculous, Pat in danger, coming to hide.

"You'd better open," said von der Heiden. "After all, the janitor knows you're home."

"How come he knows?" she asked sharply, but he did not even answer her. "And if it's the police?"

He smiled. "Police? Police looking for Germans? Their jails are crowded with Britishers and Frenchmen—and Jews who work for the Allies. So it all boils down to whether or not you feel that you can afford to open."

With a look of hate, she walked into the entrance hall and drew the curtain that separated it from the living room. If it were Pat he would know enough not to speak. She could say, "I'm sorry, you have the wrong apartment," and take him, perhaps unnoticed, into the empty servant's room. When she opened the door she faced Carlota.

"Hello, Tony, I hope I'm not in your way. I was driving by on my way home and . . ." She stepped into the room where she stopped short.

Tony trying to appear unruffled, made the introductions as indistinctly as possible: "Carlota, this is Mr. Hei . . n. My cousin, Miss Guerida Pa . . . "

Carlota had turned pale. "Count von der Heiden," she said very clearly. "There are two persons I've painstakingly avoided, though they're at every official function. The so-called 'French' ambassador and you. It's too bad that my own cousin, of all people, now forces this introduction on me." She turned toward the door.

Tony hurried after her into the vestibule. "Carlota . . . "

Carlota hesitated, then she opened the door. "You wretch, toasting that Nazi boy with your parents' blood."

The door shut, and Tony returned to where von der Heiden still stood on the same spot, pale and rigid.

"I can't come back here," he said huskily.

"Why not?" she sputtered. "There's no risk for anyone except Jews and Allied agents. Besides," she added, somewhat more matter-of-fact, "this visit was an unheard of exception. All Carlota suspects is that we're having an affair."

"That's just as dangerous. We'll have to find another meeting place."

More than by the danger of the incident, though, he was struck by its significance. The fact that a well-bred young woman had not hesitated to abuse him as she had done showed him what an outcast he had become in the eyes of everyone except his fellows. The interview with Heinrich, his father's letter, and now this slap in the face, all in the course of a single day, had tossed up emotions he had held down forcibly for years. He would have to reason them back into submission before the morning. And precisely arguing those things out with himself was what he knew he must avoid at all cost. Only by refusing to think had he so far kept afloat on the murky waters of his own life.

"It would be best," he heard Tony's cooled-down voice, "not to meet any more, if one of your colleagues could take me off your hands."

She intended to clinch their previous argument by this proof that she had a clear conscience and no one to fear. She knew he would not consent afraid that someone else in spite of everything might find a flaw. Besides, and more importantly, she sensed rather than knew that he could no longer get along without her, more accurately, without the fusion of their conflicts.

"We'll see," he said curtly, and she suspected that their next meeting would take place in one of the embassy-held rented garçonnières that delicacy had so far made him shun and opt for the far more conspicuous meetings at her place.

As soon as she was alone, the pain about Carlota flowed over her in a stream of bitterness. She was going to explain, not let herself be robbed again. This time she stood to lose her only woman friend by a sadistic coincidence. But she knew that she must stand by and let it happen.

Of course, there was still Antonio. But, bitter as he had always been about Nazis and Nazi sympathizers, if he now were to take her side, he would cause Carlota to wonder. He could not help her either. No one could. She was alone and all would eventually have to turn away. Pat was still with her. But who could tell? Half an hour ago Carlota had still been her friend. Another freak coincidence, a misunderstanding to make him believe she was, after all, a genuine double agent.

CHAPTER EIGHTEEN

WHEN AT NOON ON THE FOLLOWING DAY she heard Antonio's voice on the telephone, she said, relieved, "I'm glad you called. I must talk to you. Could you come for me an hour early?"

"We're not going tonight. But we'll meet at two at the races."

"At the races" meant by the lake in Palermo, which was close to the track. Tony wondered why she was not to see Pat, and the worry succeeded in moving Carlota into the background. Why was she not going to see Pat?

As she approached the lawn, she saw Antonio walking back and forth under the trees and, as always, the sight of his straight figure, the familiar step, seemed to relieve her of part of her burden.

They wandered slowly through the blossoming of early summer, and Tony asked, "What happened to Pat?"

Antonio kept his eyes on the hoof prints at his feet. "I don't know, Antonie. We'll meet a man who'll explain to you. But you needn't worry. Pat's all right."

They were silent for a while till he said, "I know about last night. I've never understood how he dared come to your apartment."

"A friend of his lives across the hall—that's his alibi and, incidentally, a wonderful control over me. Antonio, I'm so unhappy about Carlota. She was my only girl friend."

"Someday we'll be able to explain."

Tony sighed. "That doesn't make me less lonely now."

"I know, Antonieta. But what's most important, Carlota's knowing won't harm you. She won't tell anyone and will let no stranger know that you're not seeing each other. She respects her friendships even after they're wrecked. Carlota is very fair and very loyal."

"Why did she tell you?"

"We've always been like one person," he said proudly.

"But how can she keep our breach a secret? I mean, María Teresa . . ."

"I'm taking them to Mar del Plata before Christmas. That'll give them only a few more days here. And then there's the whole summer where the situation can't arise. I'm terribly sorry, dear. I imagine you realize I had to play along. We're both condemning you for your love affair—nothing else."

She squeezed his arm, giving him a sad smile, and they crossed the street to a bar where stableboys discussed the coming races over their *vino tinto.*

She remembered the man with the crew cut who had talked to her at the British Embassy. Antonio went with her as far as his table, then made a gesture of farewell.

"Stay and listen," the man said to Antonio. "You can, if need be, do more for her than we could. It might be less awkward." Antonio joined them.

Tony's heart skipped a beat. "Where's Hull?"

The man ordered *cafecitos negros,* and then spoke in a low, rapid voice: "Hull and a man we'll call 'Bill' have a set of orders for tonight. But we understand that someone got wind of it. Bill will be at a café at Riobamba and Sarmiento this afternoon, and I want you to go there. He's all too easily recognizable by a deep scar running from his forehead down to his left nostril. You take a table next to his and light two matches. With the third you light your cigarette. Ten minutes later you leave and walk once around the block. He'll follow. Tell him the night's excursion is off; they'd find an unpleasant surprise in the car awaiting them. Bill's to leave town for a while. That's all."

"Does Hull know?"

"Impossible to contact him. But I imagine he'll check back during the day."

"And if he doesn't?"

The man gave her an astonished look. "We'll take care of him."

"Why did you say," asked Antonio, "I might be able to do something for Miss Herrnfeld? Is she in danger?"

"I wouldn't call it danger, but the police aren't too happy about our people's rendezvous."

He gave Tony the name of the café and asked her to be there at five o'clock sharp. Then Antonio and she walked silently back through the woods and parted beside his car. After what had happened the night before, she should no longer be seen even with Antonio.

She recognized her man, and as she was lighting the second match, surprise and distrust flashed over his disfigured face. Ten minutes later she rose and left. As she was turning the corner, someone caught up with her.

"Follow me," he said, showing an identification. "Police."

She did not know where she was going and no information was volunteered, but she imagined that it was a jail and knew that, without a consulate or embassy to intercede for her, she was from this moment on at the mercy of good or bad luck.

She entered a large cell at the Women's Penitentiary of San Miguel. It was filled with prostitutes picked up for stealing or disorderly conduct, its walls lined with cots covered by nothing but straw mattresses. The matron who had taken her in went to lock the toilet for the night and placed, instead, a large tub in the middle of the cell, eliciting an obviously routine bombardment of scatological jokes she routinely ignored. All the while a couple were fighting over a silver ring that one was said to have won from the other over cards; another was cleaning her fingernails with her teeth, humming a tango.

After the matron left, a group formed around Tony to question why she was there. She stood stiffly in her grey linen suit beside her assigned cot, as if still expecting to get out of here in a few moments. She answered the barrage over and over with a dazed, "I don't know," until they finally turned away to discuss her among themselves.

"I'll tell you what she looks like. Like a shoplifter."

"Or one of those dames the pansies use as bait for the cadets."

This was argued out while Tony thought desperately. What am I going to do? I can't even sit down on this filthy cot. The question of how to get along here physically was more prominent in her mind than of how to get release. Every passing second filled her with panic at the prospect that sometime she would have to sit down, or, nameless terror, perform natural functions.

She went to lean against the wall to be able to stand longer, but even so her feet began to ache in the tight pumps, and her stomach felt queasy. She had the dreadful idea that she might become sick here and, trying not to look at the tub, walked quickly to her cot, sat down on the very edge, head swimming, sight blurred. For a long time, she did not know how long, she was unaware of everything except her struggle against nausea. Then she noticed that it was growing dark and saw the other inmates get ready for the night. She shut her eyes to the picture, feeling tears forcing their way up to her lids, and tried to take refuge in the old device she had described to Pat:

Sein Blick ist vom Vorübergehn der Stäbe
So müd geworden, dass er nichts mehr hält.
Ihm ist, also ob es tausend Stäbe gäbe
Und hinter tausend Stäben keine Welt . . .

Had she forgotten him in her frantic preoccupation with physical discomfort? Now it was night and the automobile was waiting for him somewhere in the gloom. She saw men with guns in it, binding, gagging him . . . thought of his large face, the firm, reliable mouth, and the rough skin on his neck . . . recalled the feel of his chest against her forehead and the grip of his fingers . . . knew that all this strength would be useless against men with guns. He never carried a weapon. Perhaps he had called the embassy after all and had been warned. The man Bill must have been aware that something was wrong, knew perhaps where to find him. But he, too, had probably been arrested. "Perhaps" was poor comfort when it was a matter of dying.

She now felt like screaming and hammering with her fists against the bolted cell door. It was as if she had let him go into a trap and then had to look on at his perdition. She stirred on her cot, oblivious of repugnance, indifferent to her own plight and the fate awaiting her, except in its bearing on Pat's.

At break of dawn she realized that she had dozed upright. Daylight and a natural urge brought back the problems of her own situation. How was she to get through the indefinite time ahead of her? Despair and physical malaise instilled insane thoughts.

The sun was hardly up when the matron brought coffee and bread in tin dishes and unlocked the latrines. She did not touch the food but, after a while, decided to use the toilet. Then she tried to arrange her hair. It was still in place but oddly coarse looking. Her skin appeared porous and thick with powder turned grey and smudgy from perspiration. The dried-up lipstick, worn off except at the edges, was smeared down to her chin. She rubbed at it with her handkerchief, only succeeding in giving the grey grime a pinkish glow. She thought ruefully that she was beginning to resemble the rest of the inmates.

Later the cell door was unlocked again. The matron came toward her, and she braced herself for a quiz with the police. She was almost relieved. It might just possibly put an end to her impossible situation, and she was determined at least to get out of this common cell, quite willing, if need be, to bribe the matron who was telling her to come along.

She followed with precipitous haste and no sooner had they stepped outside, when she heard the incredible words, "You're free," and felt a gentle shove propelling her toward a policeman waiting in the corridor.

She followed him, stunned, into the office of the warden, who apologized for an "unfortunate mistake" and asked if she wished to take a bath before leaving the jail. Tony was sure that at this moment she looked like a trollop even to the warden, but she declined. She wanted to get away.

The same policeman walked her to the gate, smirking, "Well, Negrita, you've been lucky."

Puzzled by the captain's mention of mistaken identity and hoping to learn more, she grinned back. "What happened?"

"Must have taken you for an English spy," he placed a familiar hand under her elbow, "and found you, after they'd brought you in, in the other register."

"What register?"

The *vigilante* colored under his dark Indian skin and let go of her arm. "I mean, the register where they keep the people who're all right."

CHAPTER NINETEEN

AT THE NEXT MEETING WITH ANTONIO, he told her that Pat was safe. Nothing else should have mattered, but to see Pat was too dangerous, and Antonio was about to go to Mar del Plata. Even contact with another agent was, for the time being, risky, but she had to find a way to transmit information.

"What about your mother's jewelry?" he asked. "Why not convey information that way? I mean, you could wear it in public places and, through a code, Pat could gather the news from their arrangement. Something like that."

"It would be rather sketchy collaboration," she objected. "He couldn't give me any instructions or answers that way. Granted, it would be better than nothing."

The embassy thought so, too. Once a month she saw Antonio, and whatever occurred in the intervening weeks was communicated according to plan. She went almost every other day to suburban and neighborhood cafés, sat all alone before a *cafecito negro* at a scratched wooden table, resplendent in diamonds and pearls. At times, under the patrons' curious or jeering eyes, she was afraid that something might happen to her. The whole thing seemed a very poor arrangement. It was, however, the only one, since the more normal one of letting them cross each other in the lobby of a moving picture palace was made doubly impracticable by the twin taboos of crowds and darkened rows of seats.

Pat would walk through, as if looking for someone else, or sit at a table in the distance. Their eyes would smart from not looking at each other. A few times, when he was not quite sure of something or unable to see whether the dial of her watch was on the inside or outside of her wrist, right side up or upside down, he would stop at a nearby pinball machine and play it absentmindedly like any patron. He would cast an impersonal glance at her while she put her arm on the table and turned her earring-bearing profile so no detail could escape him. Often he was so close she could have touched him, yet the gulf was impassable, the moments so fleeting and so out of focus that it never became real that they actually met.

There was nothing but loneliness around her, night after day, day after night. Ironically, Stephan von der Heiden was now the only remaining link with even the most recent past, he and the suffocated moments when she saw Pat and must not recognize him.

She stood by the side table in the living room, ready to go out, putting a compact into her bag, when she heard the mail being slipped under her door. There were few letters now, even from Peter. She put down the compact and went to the vestibule, bracing herself as she stooped in the dark, for another disappointment—a bill or an advertisement.

It was not Peter's square type of envelope she dropped on the table. Though the address was typewritten, it did not look like a business letter, and she picked it up to turn it over, but it bore no return address.

Inside, a neutral sheet carried the words:

NUÑEZ WANTS ZAVALÍA TO PICK UP A PARCEL BEHIND THE BOSTON BAR COUNTER AT 4 O'CLOCK ON FRIDAY, JANUARY 10. TRANSMIT.

For a while she looked at the sheet, tremulous as if it were a bomb. Nagel wants Zechau to pick up a parcel behind the Heidelberg counter. There could be no such letter as she was holding, for Nagel was dead, except in her lies. The messages she had handed the Germans had been written in code, snugly in an office of the British Embassy.

She shook her head as if wanting to free herself from the spell of a ghost story, telling herself that there was no return for a body that months ago had drifted out to sea. The dead did not rise to mock the living.

This was, if anything, worse. It was a plant, the very material and calculated work of humans, complete down to the inevitable flaw any ever-so-clever deceit carried in it. The postmark was of the same obscure village at the foot of the Andes from which her own last letter had been mailed, while the British had been careful to dispatch each message from a different place, skipping from the southernmost territories over the northern frontier with Paraguay, from there to the Atlantic coast, all the way to Uruguay and Brazil, and again to the Pacific, in order to prevent tracing.

They meant to catch her this way. But how? What did they expect her to do with the letter? What if she were innocent, and what if she were not? She sat down on the straight chair beside the table, trying to follow their line of reasoning, but the path was blocked by a wall of terror. This letter was proof that they did not believe the Nagel story and were now ready to do something about it.

She put it back on the table, starting as one corner fluttered in the breeze from the open window. She held the paper down with a reluctant hand, staring into the diamonds at her wrist. What would she do now if she were innocent?

At a twist of her arm, the evening sun released in the stones a shower of sparks and, as if one of them had ignited in her brain, she thought, I would turn the letter in as I have done with all the others. That's what they want to see. They don't know. They don't know! They only suspect and are fumbling for evidence. If I don't pass the letter on, it is because I know that I cannot possibly receive a message from Nagel. Thank God it's so easy! she thought, relieved.

It can't be so simple, though. There must be some trick, something that, were my situation different, I would notice. I mustn't go ahead before I've talked it over. Antonio's in Mar del Plata. I can't call him there, he doesn't have a personal line as he has here. I can't go to the embassy. I can't signal Pat because he's not coming this afternoon; I won't see him for days . . . I'll just have to fight this out alone. It may be better so. I alone bear the consequences of their orders, and as long as it's mainly my safety at stake, they'd be more willing to gamble with it than I am. I've been told more than once that the rescue of one cog is not worth wrecking the machine.

Here she checked herself for she knew that, no matter how small the embassy's personal concern for her, her exposure would damage them no end. She restored the letter to its envelope, put it into her purse, and went to the bedroom, where she slipped a large ruby onto her right hand.

She wore the danger signal for the first time. Pat might be there after all, though he had never broken their schedule before. At any rate, it was most unlikely, and this message must be passed on as promptly as all others. There's no difference, she insisted, between this and the half dozen I've given von der Heiden up to now.

Pat had not come. On the following evening she handed von der Heiden the letter, scanning his face for a flicker of emotion. There was none. Why did it terrify her, since she knew him to be self-possessed enough? Had she come to rely upon him as an eventual rescuer, he who had trapped her and then, with an easy mien, kept up the cynical fraud concerning her parents throughout a full year of increasing intimacy and (at least on his part) growing sentiment? She shuddered at the idea that they were both playing, against each other, the same macabre game of making the dead come alive.

She had grown to believe in the basic truthfulness of his affection. Though he had never spoken of it, she believed his caresses were not prompted solely by desire, being less convincing than the gentleness and respect he showed her and the light that came into his eyes whenever they ventured into general conversation. Yet she knew that any falsehood must be child's play to the man who could, without a wince, tell and unflinchingly maintain the lie about her parents.

On the following morning, however, she received a surprise visit from him. Still in a négligé, her long hair down, she was not prepared in appearance or countenance for this unlikely call.

He remained standing. "I hate to barge in on you like this, Antonie, but I want you to tell me, was there anything wrong with the letter you gave me last night? I want you to tell me the truth."

My "reaction," she thought, was not sufficiently revealing, so now they're sending you to get the whole story by your sweet hangdog method. "No, why do you ask? Anyway, not that I know of. Why?"

He sat down, took her hands to make her sit beside him on the davenport, and looked into her eyes. "They want you to come to Prietzmann's to talk to Heinrich himself. It must have something to do with the letter. Antonie, dear, let me know if you have made a mistake—before it is too late. Please."

It was the first time he used an endearment. So far even his caresses had been mute. Tony did not waver, though, as she had sometimes done when he had sounded so sincere.

"What kind of mistake could I have made, if you please?" she asked calmly, withdrawing her hands. "If there's any mistake in the letter it can only have originated with Nagel's agent, or with himself. Don't you see?"

"No, Antonie, I don't." As she had freed her hands, his had dropped, slack, to his sides. He had not stirred and still sat motionless in a discouraged posture—in sharp contrast to his initial ardor, though his eyes kept holding hers.

She looked away, stood up, and shook back her hair. "Why are you so crestfallen?" She put a hand on his shoulder, bent over him and laughed into his face, without meeting his eyes. "And if there's a mistake, so what? That parcel of billets doux—I hope it isn't a time bomb—whatever there is behind the Heidelberg counter won't get lost. And if it does, it's not going to make the bright boys lose their war." She straightened up. "By the way, what is wrong with the letter?"

"I don't know, Antonie, and that's what frightens me. But if you aren't afraid, I guess it's all right," he added in a colorless voice.

The words, "if you aren't afraid," brought home how very frightened she was indeed. "Why didn't you ask them?" she inquired lamely.

"They wouldn't . . . it hadn't occurred to me . . . that is, I hated to draw even more suspicion upon you by asking any questions."

There we go again, she thought, always aiming at the same point, always trying to make it slip that I'm vulnerable. "What kind of suspicion are you talking about?"

He rose with a sigh. "It's no use, Antonie. I'd better go now." He stopped. "By the way, I don't want them to know that I was here. I'd been asked to telephone. So you don't know why they summoned you. I almost forgot, tomorrow morning at ten o'clock at Prietzmann's. Just walk through the door behind the bar as you've been doing lately."

"How you love your little intrigues. I'm not going to tell on you." She laughed, reached up to pinch his ear and blushed. The gesture was as unnatural to her as the motion of the head when she had thrown back her hair, as unnatural as the roguish bending over and laughing in his face. Still, then she had not touched him. The vulgarity of this touch made her ashamed.

123

He looked at her in wonder and left.

She paced the room repeating embarrassedly, senselessly: what a farce, what a farce, what a farce . . .

When she walked into Prietzmann's backroom, Heinrich sat alone by a round table under a homely, old-fashioned dining room lamp with a silk shade such as one saw in German lower-middle-class homes. It was pulled down low over the table and lighted, for the room was windowless. And with no outlet, she noted for the first time, except the door through which she had come. Heinrich's legs, too thin and short for his small but stocky body, were crossed. His little dimpled hand held a cigarette and the square, oversized head swayed a little in the smoke. He looked like an evil goblin.

He was looking in her direction, yet did not move. Not a muscle stirred in his face, while his wide-open eyes followed her like those in old portraits that held you wherever you went. When she stood close before him, he suddenly rose, an unheard of courtesy that reminded her of the last grace under the gallows.

"Sit down," he said in his high-pitched, metallic voice. When she had done so, he sat down, too and, staring at her without the slightest expression, asked, "What about that letter, Fräulein?"

"What about it?" she echoed.

He played with his watch chain and his yellow eyes bored into hers. She felt them corrode her heart, her courage, her wits.

"That letter didn't come from Lagen."

"Didn't it?" she asked, surprised.

"You ought to know." His thin smile made shreds of her self-confidence and brain power.

"Was there anything in it that should have made me doubt?" she heard herself ask calmly and with a genuine ring of interest. She had rehearsed this very carefully.

"Wasn't there? Or, in other words, would you have needed any indication to inform you that it didn't come from Lagen? Answer me that, Fräulein."

She had counted on an approach either less or more direct. None of her prepared answers would do, and there was no time to consider how an innocent person would understand this cryptic remark. She was terrorized, could not think at all, did not even try to control her face. She suddenly understood the confessions the Gestapo succeeded in drawing from people who otherwise might not break under torture.

Then she heard her voice, smooth and cool, not her own but Pat's, while his unperturbed eyes were looking out of her face into Heinrich's. She had not thought of him but carried him within.

"I was sure it came from him, though for the first time, as you may have noticed, two consecutive letters have been mailed from the same place. Is that what worries you? I'm still convinced it's genuine. Is there no way of checking up?"

"There is. And we may have you help us with it." His voice had turned sweet and the threat in the words became more repulsive in their passage through the licorice.

CHAPTER TWENTY

THE INCIDENT HAD BEEN TOO NOVEL and too intricate to convey by the jewel code. If Antonio had been in town, she would have signaled that a prompt meeting with him was in order. As it was, all she could do was make Pat understand that she wanted operations halted until Antonio's return from the beach in February.

When at last she met with Antonio, she told him what had happened and added that the succeeding month had brought no further complications. The British Embassy decided to release another Nagel message, an inconsequential one, which von der Heiden accepted as calmly as before.

But after a while he asked, "What's come over you, Antonie? You're seen bejeweled and beribboned in the dingiest corner cafés. What's it all about?"

She knew he should not have given his knowledge away, and realized with glad surprise that he was trying to warn her.

"Am I being shadowed so constantly? They could at least permit me a private life."

"And what part of your private life is that?" Though he smiled, his face remained overcast.

"If you must know, it's all the private life I have. What else is left? I've lost all my friends. I'm not allowed to make new ones, except in line of duty. I'd go crazy if I couldn't sometimes identify with things of the past and hide where I can give way to fancy."

It sounded silly, uncharacteristically so, but her voice was so empty of all hope that he had no doubt she meant what she said.

"I wouldn't, though, Antonie. Others don't understand. Why don't you go to some nice places if you need an outlet?"

"Maybe you're right," she said gratefully.

She immediately exchanged the cafés for the lobby of the Alvear Palace, the Plaza Hotel Bar, and French restaurants, wondering all the time if Stephan was just trying to protect, or actually help her. The latter seemed fantastic, tempting and dangerous.

She went out almost every afternoon or evening. Following a movable calendar, Pat averaged about twice a week, so no observer could wonder at the coincidence of seeing both always in the same place at the same hour. After a time, Antonio passed on the additional suggestion that she make a few dates, so as not to be always seen alone.

She had no friends, neither men nor women. Anyway, during the summer months few porteños, except relieved grass widowers, were in town, and she was on dating terms with no one. Once she exchanged a smile from table to table with a young man she had met at a party a long time ago, and through him she subsequently got to know other footloose bachelors. To all appearances, she was letting herself be drawn into the substitute life of the *chica fácil*.

However, since she did not finish the evenings in parked cars or garçon-nières, few dates saw a return engagement and the choices became scant. Soon she was seen ever more often in the company of elderly men, whose patience was a little sturdier.

She lived, eyes averted from her existence, for the minutes she and Pat spent in the same room. While her companion spoke of pre–World War I Europe, or women, or money, without looking at Pat she evoked the warmth of the man who had been—still was—her lover. She followed the pain within like a substitute for physical contact. She thought that they were bound to send him away sometime so that she would no longer have these poor minutes. Even if he stayed, she would never again have anything else.

One evening she met don Federico at the Plaza. With his family away, he was alone at a table, very possibly in pursuit of adventure. Seeing her alone, too, he came over and asked her to dine at the grill. It was one of the dreary, depressed evenings when she knew that Pat was not coming, and she accepted gratefully.

He was pleasant company, this *chevalier vieux jeu,* who knew his vintages and delighted in the finesses of food. Since they were speaking a great deal of her mother and she knew of his early infatuation with her, she told him about her comparison of lovers and gourmets.

"Your mother had a great deal of esprit. I used to be very much in love with her, but I guess it's lucky she didn't marry me. I would have destroyed all those pretty illusions. People don't really think with their heads, you know, but with their bodies. The head thinks what the body relays. You might say, heat rises . . ." He chuckled.

Tony could not help smiling. "I don't imagine she'd ever found that out. Or maybe she wanted me to learn by myself."

"And have you?" The little brown eyes twinkled.

"Answer expected?" she laughed.

"Not that I have any prejudices. A woman without a past has no future."

"That's quite an epigram! But isn't it a bit radical, don Frederico?"

"A woman's business is men," he shrugged, "whether in a paying or honorary position. If she wants to get along, she's got to know her trade."

She did not know why his eyes resting on her, kindly but somehow inquisitively, made her uncomfortable.

"You know," he went on, resting knife and fork on his plate, "I'm not a very smart man and certainly haven't made my own life a success. That's precisely what taught me that we can't afford too many mistakes. The net result of a life is, after all, what's left over, the balance, after subtracting all mistakes and failures. We all must, at one time or another, stoop to an emergency, but we must do it wisely . . . especially a woman."

The *canard à l'orange* was growing cold on their plates. A vacuum-like sensation of being misunderstood invaded Tony. She was flushed and her lips quivered. Don Federico never stopped watching her. "I sound like a cynical old man to you, but I just know that, though a body doesn't wear away like soap, a reputation does. And for a woman, life without a good reputation is tough."

"I don't know why you should be so preoccupied with women's morals," she said, hearing the insincerity in her own voice.

He nibbled perfunctorily at the cold fowl. "Maybe I've put my foot in, Antonie. If I have, I'm sorry. I'm just afraid you're going to suffer. But what are we talking about? I only want you to know that if ever you should need help you wouldn't want to ask anyone else for, you should come to me. I'm not a rich man, but I can help you."

God, thought Tony, he thinks I'm going around with those people for their money. He thinks I've turned into a slut. She could not think of a single word to say, while it dawned on her that this was what everybody thought—that she had jeopardized her entire personal life and, for Buenos Aires, had become an adventuress.

He saw the misery in her face and said gently, "You've got what it takes, Antonie, and I imagine you know what you're doing. In a way, a tough life makes one as hard, but also as brilliant, as a diamond. I've never really known trouble, so I wouldn't know. Only I wish you'd think about what I've said tonight. Don't make any irreparable mistakes.

"After all, you're not a helpless refugee girl. You have the Gueridas and you have me. And even if you count us out—you still have those trinkets." He pointed at her large diamonds. "Why don't you put them to better use? I'm sure your mother would have wanted you to. And now let's order dessert and then look in at a nightclub."

"Don Federico, it isn't as you think. I can't explain just now. But someday I will."

"You needn't explain anything to me, Antonie," he smiled. "If you know your Martín Fierro, you'll remember how old Vizcacha said that if the devil's a devil he's so from age rather than from devilry. I know you're a great girl and I'll always be your friend. Remember that."

She did not see Antonio again before the end of March, but when she told him of this conversation he was enraged at the demands put upon "a young girl just at the doorstep of life," as he expressed it. He was shocked to see her future stamped out in this impersonal, relentless fashion.

"And I passed on that order like a fool. At my age! I should have known."

"Never mind," she said. "My future isn't here, but with Pat," and wondered if it were true, if he would come back to her after the war. She was no longer sure of anything.

"We'll find another arrangement."

"Let's just leave it as it is," she said wearily.

"By no means. There's no need for you to go tomorrow, anyhow. There'll be nothing new between now and then, and whatever there's now, I can tell Pat. Then we'll see."

"Please, let *me* go," she pleaded, and he knew that she would have gone to the stake if Pat had been there.

"But it will be the last time," he said gruffly, "and you'll go alone."

She smiled. "I couldn't very well show up alone at the Plaza after telling my Romeo that I can't keep my date with him."

"To hell with your Romeo!"

"Don't forget, I must by no means make enemies. Enemies rank as a taboo, next to friends."

Pat was at the Plaza Bar in the company of a slick Argentine with disagreeable eyes and a disgusted mouth, when a group of five others came in. One of them recognized the thin old man at Tony's table and hurried over. The two embraced like long lost brothers, thumping each other's backs and talking so loudly that all eyes were drawn to them.

"*Hola, muchacho!*" exclaimed Tony's escort, his sagging cheeks folding into a smile that showed a set of false teeth. "What have you been doing with yourself?"

"*Hola, ché amigo!*" cried the stranger, stepping back spectacularly to eye the other. "Growing younger every day!" And with a side glance at Tony, "Congratulations! Always in good company!"

He turned to her. "Easy with our friend Juancito. He's an old wolf and as clever as they come. *Bueno*, Juancho, I'll be going. I know when I'm de trop. Once more, congratulations. What a conquest!" He slapped his friend on the back and then, touching his fingertips to his lips, threw a connoisseur's kiss into the air.

The old man turned to Tony, his face all pride and glee. "The rascal shouldn't throw stones when most of the time he's sitting in a glass house himself. What with the money he's got, women . . ."

The other stopped short. "*Ché*, I'm quite poor. Don't give the *chica* here any ideas."

He winked and followed his group that had stopped at Pat's table to watch the scene. He made some ironical comment, his forefinger pulling the skin down under one eye with the indigenous gesture of *ojo* (caution) and they all laughed, Pat with them.

She hid her eyes in her pocket mirror, and then, looking up, saw Pat's back disappear through the plate-glass door. The head was bent as if the nape were tired, the neck seemed less vigorous, the shoulders had a discouraged droop.

As they were leaving the hotel through the revolving door, Carlota entered it from the street and gave her a shocked look through the glass. The door swirled too swiftly for even a nod.

On the following day the telephone rang, and when she heard Carlota's voice she hung up. She knew what Carlota would have said: That she had heard rumors without believing them but now had seen them proved with her own eyes. That for past friendship's sake she wanted to warn her, help her, if possible. Tony knew that Carlota was eternally loyal, but she was not allowed to take the extended hand. There was no explanation, except the truth she could not speak.

CHAPTER TWENTY-ONE

VON DER HEIDEN HALF LAY IN HIS CHAIR, his long arms hanging over the sides. His face shone so pallidly through the dusk that it seemed transparent. He kept his eyes on the narrow clothes closet of the studio apartment and spoke in a flat, low voice, swiftly and fluently.

"I don't really know why I'm telling you about this, except that maybe it no longer matters. Also perhaps because you're cold and fearless and determined and could teach me the use of those qualities, which aren't innate with you either. But you're able to apply them like tools whenever you need them. So I've decided to let you know."

He paused as if expecting an answer, and, when none was forthcoming, pursued. "Von Ravensburg, who has been our solicitor for as long as I can remember (I even think it was he who drew up the papers for my parents' marriage), in one word, the faithful factotum, has advised me with pious condolences of my father's passing.

"Oh, I'm so sorry, Stephan," she said with sudden sympathy. "Truly sorry."

"Thank you," he said dryly. "Enclosed was the death certificate made out by the local doctor. Heart failure. Our peasantry had seen and heard nothing; and our pastor had proceeded to make his funeral oration before the little congregation without asking any questions. All those within eyesight and earshot seemed to have turned blind and deaf. Only on the outside people seemed to have remained masters of their five senses. A boyhood friend, who broke with me years ago and is now the director of the self-styled 'Free Germans' in Lisbon, got word to me that my father was executed and that the embassy here had instructions to leave me in the dark.

"I went to see Heinrich," he continued, "who claimed the ambassador was too busy to see me. So I tendered my resignation, which was rejected. They believe that now they have a firmer hold on me, that they can make even better use of me because they think I'm afraid."

He paused, and as Tony did not speak or stir, he continued. "The general was involved in a plot. My father was cautious as a fox, pragmatic, and rather selfish. If he risked his life, the cause must have been worth the sacrifice. And he must have had many important men beside him; he never gambled. Our people want no more of the wild man whose false cards are at last being turned up and who, trapped crook that he is, has reached for the gun."

He paused once more, waited for a reaction. When it did not come, he continued, rather more uncertain. "They've dared to murder my father. They dare to touch our caste, which has seized them, the tiny ones, between two fingers and put them on a pedestal. Those same fingers will sweep them back down with a snap!"

"How?"

He turned his eyes toward the shadows where the short, crackling word had come from, slowly and bewildered. "If you knew how stupid they are, how drunk with force. They underestimate people like me who don't have bull's necks and don't bellow . . . Like the Pied Piper we'll lead those yokels back into the nothing, the darkness where they existed before we made the mistake of believing them useful tools and putting them behind desks."

"And how do you intend to do that?" came the cold voice from the twilight-filled corner.

"You can help me as I once helped you."

"You . . . me?"

"If it had not been for me, your parents . . ." The words had come reluctantly, as if they cost him an effort, and he could not finish.

"That's true," she came to his rescue.

"Antonie, I can get in touch with the Allies. I hate to. But though it is commonly called treason to work against one's own country, in this case I'm not working against my people, rather against the scum that is oppressing them.

"It has ever been the responsibility of my caste to protect them, including against themselves, even when they let down one of our own. I know what you're thinking. We, too, have ruled and, as you would term it, oppressed them for centuries. But don't you see we weren't rabble? We were born to rule and gave our protection in exchange. I know you're laughing. You're thinking, the knight of the woeful countenance . . ." His tone was a question mark, which she left unanswered.

"If we take a stand now," he went on, "the peace treaty will be mild and the reconstruction of Germany a trifle. In ten years' time we'll be strong again, a true world power and . . ."

"Engineer the next war."

There was a moment's silence. Then, with more defiance than conviction, he said, "Maybe. But it will be with the entire Western world against the Bolsheviks, and under real military leadership, not that of a corporal with delusions of grandeur."

"Just now he's not managing so badly, your corporal." Then she hushed again.

Until he asked, "Will you help me?"

"No."

Von der Heiden was stunned. "Why not?"

"Why should I? I'm no traitor. I've given my word. Besides, I don't intend to endanger my parents. I haven't led this inhuman life for nothing."

"Oh, Antonie!" He sat up, pained, yet with sudden energy, as if relieved of a loathsome burden. "And if I tell you that it's all been a cruel farce, that your parents weren't alive when we met for the first time?"

There was no answer. For what seemed to him an eternity, he waited, miserably.

"I would not believe you."

"I can prove it."

"And then, what? I couldn't back out any more. Had you offered your hand sooner, I might have taken it. But once you make a pact with the devil you can't return to life. I've slammed forever the door of decency behind me. Now I want to belong somewhere, anywhere; I can't be all alone."

Von der Heiden heard the firmness in her voice. The clipped syllables crossed out, like the peck of a typewriter, all he had thought he knew about her. He realized suddenly that it had grown black around them; and the fact that even her shadow had become invisible made her words devoid of humanity. The hour was fantastic and uncanny, and he was locked up in it with yet another enemy, more dangerous for being hypnotized, moving forward like a mechanism set in a certain direction. He felt at an unsafe dead end, for he had not anticipated a refusal, let alone after playing his sad trump card.

He rose and walked toward her in the darkness, not seeing, but sensing her. His long, narrow hands seized and drew her to him, lifted her lightly as one would a child, and now that his want of her was hard and throbbing, he feared his own harshness in the taking; for there was now no tenderness, nothing but the will and need to force her open to him, body and soul, to penetrate and make her receive him and hold whatever he wanted to leave of his own in her. He felt her stiff and motionless like a doll from terror. The tenderness, the pity, returned so he would have cradled and consoled her, but she jerked and stood free.

He heard the door shut and it was as if a last card were slipping from his hand. She felt nothing for him, and it crossed his mind that it would have been safer to strangle her when he had surprised her in the dark and held her between his fingers. It was so absurd that he smiled.

Then he covered his face with his hands and cried, cried himself tired and almost peaceful as he had done in childhood. And soon he realized that he was crying for Antonie, who had been the only shred of life he had ever possessed, for the discovery that she would never love him, that she had been machine-tooled into a steely robot, perverse in its inhumanity. Ironically, the final proof, prayed for so long and fervently, that she was not knowingly a double agent, now held nothing but unhappiness.

Then he waited senselessly for someone to come and strangle him, to throttle the confusion and bewilderment within. He thought of his childhood, when he had been ever confused and bewildered while all others had gone through life as securely and naturally as if it had been made especially for them. Each had his place and knew at every hour just what to do and how to carry his head and how to laugh and how to speak. He alone had yearned to be now a knight on the Rhine, now d'Artagnan, now Erasmus, or Vasco da Gama, or else just a wandering minstrel.

He thought of the girl on the neighbor estate whom the lovesick boy had trusted with his iridescent dreams and who, once tired of him, had laughed: "You'd never have made a hero, or even an adventurer, because you're a weakling who won't take a crop to the groom who plays tricks with his tack, but blushes and feels embarrassed instead!"

With that she had run off and spent the autumn riding to hounds with his cousins, who smirkingly took to calling him, after a grotesque old tale, "The Valiant Knight with Bells in His Belly." The vulgar sound of it alone made him hot with shame to this day.

Tony looked about apprehensively. Though there was satisfaction for her in Stephan's plight, it further complicated matters. Her meetings with him had been the only safe ones; now that he, too, must have become suspect, even they had turned into a venture. But no one was following her.

She tried to gauge the import of the change and to plan her next step. Her first, logical idea matched her wishes too closely, and she stopped to allow herself to concentrate, looking up at the rounded corner facade of a strange apartment house. Light fell heavily into her eyes, bright and festive, figures moving between drapes, a party, entertainment a purpose in itself.

She barely remembered when last she had done something without a practical purpose, before even sleep had become part of a regimentation, a certain amount prescribed to keep the nerves steady and the brain clear. Personal things, like pain and worry, had to be cut off at reasonable hours lest they interfere with duty relaxation.

She looked at her watch; if she wanted to get Antonio on the separate line in his study she must hurry. She ran down the sidewalk sloping toward Retiro Station. As she got there, the clock high up in the red-brick Torre de los Ingleses struck eight. Her eyes lifting to its dial hit a hard, blue sky, star-studded as with scattered stones. The air was cold and still and very clear. A grand autumn night, like perfect steel. She shivered and hurried into the electric lights of the railroad station, where a warm, musty-smelling crowd was milling, confused, often angry, impatient, bored, mostly tired. It was ten minutes past eight before a telephone booth was vacated.

"I'll get in touch with him," said the servant who answered. "Is it important?"

"It is," she replied testily, looking with unreasonable contempt at a woman waiting outside, struggling with a suitcase, a baby, a handbag, and a coin. Everything seemed ugly, undesirable, except endless sleep.

CHAPTER TWENTY-TWO

ANTONIO PICKED HER UP AT THE EDGE OF TOWN at ten o'clock on a black night. The sharp, unsteady wind was chasing thick clouds over flickering pinpoint stars.

"It's going to rain," he said. "The roads will be slick. It'll be slow driving home."

"Yes," she smiled, dazed. "An accident would ruin our reputations, wouldn't it?"

Her heart was tight, her nerves ached from elbows to fingertips, the tension of anticipation greater than when first she had driven out to meet Pat, but less joyful. Was it because she had forced this encounter, whose furtiveness was accentuated by the windswept darkness?

The Cadillac's quiet smoothness made the atmosphere more oppressive, as if it were not moving at all through the black, unchanging night unbroken by the headlights of oncoming cars. Then Antonio turned his own headlights off and began to feel his way. They could hear each other breathing as the car glided silently to a stop.

The lantern in the garden gate was unlit. From the whiteness of the arch came a faint gleam like a will-o'-the-wisp. She turned to Antonio, whose face was a shadow but his voice warm and alive. "You know your way. Just walk slowly. And . . . good luck." She reached for the hand that was stroking her cheek and held it a while. When she stepped from the car, her legs trembled from excitement. She paused for control and then took a few cautious steps.

It had seemed that she knew the path to the house so well, but now it was strange and cumbersome. She noticed with relief that Antonio had not driven off. He would wait until she reached the door, but after a few more steps a gulf of darkness separated them. She looked at the now completely overcast sky and then in the direction of the tightly shuttered house, unbetrayed by a ray of light. Of course, it had to be that way, yet an unreasonable fear took hold of her that Pat might not be there and that Antonio, estimating that by now she had arrived, would drive off. She cast another desperate glance back at the highway that revealed nothing and tried to hurry on.

But the path that by light seemed smooth was rugged and hostile. She spread out both hands to feel her way, brushing against bushes that gave way as if receding, then sprang back at her like living creatures. She told herself that she was hysterical, but her terror would not subside. There was a sudden suspicion that this was not the path at all, for never had it been so long.

She stopped, looking back, listening, imagining strange and disquieting noises under the voice of the wind. Then she took another step, stumbled over something hard, and fell forward on her forearms. Her taut nerves snapped and she sobbed without raising herself.

There was a furtive noise, a creaking, a muffled step. She screamed for Antonio, conscious through her terror that the storm was making shreds of her cry, tore it up before it could begin to travel. When she felt a hand on her, panic gave way to weakness.

She must have fainted, for she did not know how she had been carried into the dark house, how the single light had been turned on beside the bed where she lay. Pat stood beside her, looking worried.

"I'm sorry, Pat," she whispered. "I don't know. I was scared alone in the dark." Her voice was shy like that of a child remorseful of a prank.

He took her into his arms. Unbelieving, she touched his hair, his neck, his forehead, a wondering fingertip to his brows and lids. Everything bad was over now, but like to a convalescent knowing himself saved, all still seemed distant and unreal.

"You rest, dear, while I get us tea."

As she half raised herself, she felt a pain on the insides of her hands and wrists and saw that they were badly scraped from the fall on the doorstep. They crudely materialized the foolishness of her agitation.

"How do you feel?" asked Pat, as he returned with the tray.

"I'm all right." She was trying to sound casual. "How on earth did you find your way to the house?"

"With a flashlight. You should have one, too."

"We never thought of that," she laughed. Her hand shook as she poured the tea.

"If you feel up to it, let's tackle the news right away, so we'll have something of an evening left."

She told him about von der Heiden, omitting, she did not know why, the violent end.

"It may not be worth the risk," he said. "At any rate, let's wait for him to approach us. You should stay out of it completely. I'll tell the embassy and they'll decide.

"Now tell me about yourself. They've been beastly months, haven't they, when we met around all the fanciest places? Still I guess I preferred them to the vacuum I've lived in since."

"It was all bad. But it's over now. Pat, how foolishly I've begun this beautiful evening!"

He looked into her feverish eyes with a strangely worried expression, and when he came to sit on the edge of the bed she felt this same residue of anguish in his embrace. "What's the matter, dear?" she whispered.

"Nothing. I love you so."

The shade of despair passed into their passion, and the sense of tragedy that had throttled her in the car engulfed her again until her thoughts fell silent. As they lay side by side in the dark, a sudden downpour drowned out the voice of the wind. Listening, they wondered about Antonio parked off the highway on a deserted country road at midnight. It will stop soon, they thought, such cloudbursts always do. But the barrage went on and on without a sign of exhaustion.

She nestled up to Pat, anxiety gone like a hallucination: "Darling, I'm so happy."

"My sweet." His voice was heavy and cheerless.

"Aren't you?" Disquiet again in hers.

"Yes, sweet. I am, but . . ." She raised her head warily. "They won't let us go on like this. This was an exception, an emergency."

"No!"

"Yes, dear. They very definitely don't want to take any chances. But," he bent over and before he touched her lips, said, "this will last us for a long time, won't it?"

"No! No, Pat! I can't! I won't stand for it! I just can't go on that way!" She sat up belligerently.

"You'll have to," he said sadly.

"Why?" Rage choked her. "Why do I have to? What is it to me? What do I gain by it, while I have already sacrificed everything? I've got nothing left to lose."

He put a steadying hand on her shoulder. "I know, Tony. I know it all. It's too terrible for words. But you know it's worthwhile. You've been very brave."

"Worthwhile!" she sputtered. "What will be in it for me? Will it bring my parents back to life? Give me a home? Give me freedom? It's all for people like you!"

Through the dark he saw the sobs shake her shoulders. They looked thinner, her head heavy, and her arms very long and forceless.

"It will avenge your parents," he said, "though that is poor reward, I know. But it will give you a full womanhood, and a new home, and freedom as Mrs. Larson in the United States."

"A 'damn foreigner' I'll be," she said through her teeth. She lifted her head, the outlines of her face angular, her black eyes hard and wild. "You've told me enough about the freedom for those who don't have the badge of honor of being a certain kind of American. You've told me of 'restricted' hotels and segregated neighborhoods, of the necessity to merge completely— unless one wants to be an outcast—with the 'American Way of Life,' from comic strips to homemaking. What is it to me, this country of personal freedom for all who conform and cry hurrah?"

"You don't know what you're talking about," he said coolly. "You've never lived in a true democracy."

"Democracy!" she repeated, shaking with fury. "Americans carry that word on their lips as constantly as the nouveau riche the word *money*. I . . . I . . ." She burst again into sobs. "Pat, why are we bickering about things that have nothing to do with our trouble? I didn't mean to be nasty. I could have said it calmly."

He took her into his arms and stroked her hair. "Just cry, dear. You've been too brave. You had to crack up once. Just cry it out, darling."

A kind of smugness in his voice, the superiority with which he passed her outburst off as hysteria, without considering its very concrete cause, sympathetic yet detached, only underscored her loneliness. She freed herself. "Cry it out? And then what? Go on, pull, pull, until you break down! I can't . . . I can't . . . I can't . . ."

"Look here, sweet," he said, drawing her back. "Imagine we were married and I had to go away to the war. Wouldn't you want to keep your chin up?"

"You would be mine," she murmured into his shoulder, unconvinced, sniffling like a child after a tantrum.

"I am yours. Shrapnel wouldn't respect a marriage license. But I'll try, honey. I will. Maybe I can put it across. They might let us get together once in a while. You know I want it as badly as you do."

She sat up, feet tucked under, eyes cast down, her fingers stroking his chest, tracing his ribs and, almost shyly, the muscles of his thighs. "I'm sorry, Pat, I was an idiot. I've spoiled the one happy evening we were allowed together. Forgive me."

"I'm glad you burst out the way you did, darling. You were more yourself than if you had pretended cheeriness. It's you I want tonight, not just your company. All of you." He drew her hand closer where, blushing, she could feel his excitement rise. "Now . . ."

The rain had calmed down to a soft patter when they heard a short, muffled honk.

"Good-bye, my love."

He took her into his arms. "Not good-bye. I'll try to fix things."

She shook her head. "No, Pat. Let me be foolish, but not you. We're safe while you keep cool. That's what makes me love you so; you're a man, I don't have to be wise because I have you."

"I'm not going to be foolish," he said, turning off the light in the hall. "Don't you want me to walk to the car with you?"

"No, Pat. I know my way now." She squeezed his hand, rubbed her cheek against his shoulder, and walked out hurriedly, hoping that her steps looked firm, straight ahead into the dark.

Back in the car, she cried again. Antonio looked silently through the streaming windshield, thinking "like rain on a scorched soul." He felt old and empty and a little envious, even of this sad, hopeless kind of love.

Pat went to submit Tony's information to the British Embassy, then to tackle the question of their meetings. He wished she had first gone to the American Embassy instead; but of course America had not been at war, so it would not have occurred to her that his diplomatic mission was a better address for her. If Tom O'Shean had taken her over rather than Lionel Fleming, he now could say, "Don't worry, Tom, I take the responsibility."

And he would have felt a great deal more hopeful about the outcome. The world—its diplomatic surface, as well as its underworld of secret services—was full of wagging heads about this happy-go-lucky mentality that it called American naïveté. But Patrick Larson, stepping across Fleming's threshold, wished himself back on home ground with Tom and the boys.

He now began to expound the situation very carefully, telling about the strain Tony was under and about her apparent nervousness.

"She's almost had a crack-up," he concluded, "mainly because she feels at loose ends. I used to give her very detailed instructions, which she carried out remarkably well. Remember, she's very young. She simply doesn't feel up to being a full-fledged secret agent, and a fake double agent to boot."

Fleming was playing with the brass knuckles serving him as a paper weight. "If she's about to have a nervous breakdown we'd better lay her off. That's almost more dangerous than lack of loyalty, because it can catch you off guard, anytime. At any rate, let her discontinue her work for a couple of months. After that we can decide."

"She can't interrupt, much less quit," protested Pat. "She can't quit the Germans and must keep handing them stuff. Where is she to get it if not from us? If she could just talk things over with me from time to time—I don't mean regularly—she'd be all right."

The man looked up from his brass knuckles. "No. We're not going to take any more chances. Let her go on if she wishes, but the same way she's been doing." Rising, he added, not unkindly, "Don't you upset the applecart, Larson."

CHAPTER TWENTY-THREE

TAKING VON DER HEIDEN'S MOVE FOR A TRAP, the British Embassy, instructed Tony to give him little, if any, encouragement. The German Embassy, on the other hand, had not taken him off "the case Antonie Herrnfeld," while from day to day it became clearer that his intentions toward her had been sincere.

Since then they had tacitly gone back to meeting at her own apartment, as if to escape each other's associations with an incident that they chose to view as a slightly ridiculous accident, to be ignored like an embarrassing fall on slippery parquetry. Cautiously she had begun to test the ground, aware that each step in his direction made her position more unequivocal, although he did not seem to notice anything unusual.

She felt his strange kind of love and hoped that now, his sense of duty shaken, he would hold his eyes forever shut. At times she was plagued by the thought that to turn her over to the Germans would prove his patriotism and help him back into the saddle. His leading her on, rather than the melodramatic fiction of the Nazi in love with the Jewish girl, was the logical, realistic explanation.

He wondered if her hints were tactics to get him into a scrape. He was aware of what she merely sensed, that he would never knowingly betray her, and when he asked himself the reasons he found two. There was his contempt for the Nazis, which, since his father's death, had turned to hatred; but there was also his love of the girl, which he could not keep entirely separate from his hatred and contempt. Before anything else had nourished it, his feelings had drawn on their comparative kinship in an environment equally uncongenial and hostile to both. Their breeding was alike and so was (barring politics and the ethos they sprang from) most of their outlook on life.

Their separate lonelinesses had converged, making him feel less forlorn. He had ceased to drift along, the only foreign body in an element of predators.

After her short rebellion, Tony had calmed down to a practical resignation she did not allow to waver. Antonio, in telling her of Pat's attempt to continue their meetings, had given her the assurance she needed more than his actual presence: that he cared enough to plead with the embassy. She did not expect him to override them, did not want to see him swept off his feet. Though quite competent under coercion, she felt unable to live forever bearing the brunt of responsibility. She was eager to walk and cultivate the ground her lover cleared for her, but not willing or able to clear it herself.

Still, it was a lonely existence. They tried to break the monotony by messages transmitted through Antonio. A couple of evenings, each in his or her own apartment, they listened to an opera broadcast from the Teatro Colón. It gave them no sensation of nearness, and they consoled themselves with the thought that only petty sentiments must and could feed on such devices. It seemed more satisfactory to let the stock of emotion accumulate untouched than to tamper with it in this frustrating fashion.

When she could not sleep and knew that he, too, was "off duty," at home or at a party, she asked herself if he was physically true to her. She did not know whether men really could not live, as it was said, for months on end without some kind of physical outlet. If he had seemed cool enough in the waiting—during the countless hours they had shared alone in hotel rooms, going from friendship to love—once they had left those unpropitious surroundings behind, he had brooked no delay. From then on every hour together had been vibrant with excitement, surcharged with his drive for fulfillment.

She did not really know whether she had given him pleasure as intense and complete in return. It had seemed to her that there must be more in her to give, more than just herself, that it was there, somewhere within her reach, if only he would help her find it. But he seemed to feel rewarded by her mere thrilling to him, the sting of her fingernails, the low moan with which she lost hold at the height of passion.

She had spoken of their waiting for each other; not of renouncing pleasure. Jealousy was an emotion too commonplace for their uncommon lives.

❖ ❖ ❖

Some time ago Tony had pushed away her last friend with her own hand. María Teresa's return from Mar del Plata had brought up the problem of how to explain the estrangement with the rest of the family. In a rather painful discussion with Antonio she had agreed that he would forthwith let his wife in on the rumors concerning her way of life. María Teresa reacted in a conventional manner and tearfully and unhesitatingly turned her back on her little cousin. Tony was a bit disappointed when, unlike her daughter, she made not a single gesture in search of an explanation, in an attempt to save what there might be to save. But when it was accomplished, it left her cool, caused rather a slackening of the tension as the final fragment of her isolation fell into pattern.

She often thought that her life was what a cliff-hanger might accurately describe as "a rapid succession of disasters," following each other with such regularity that no particular one had a chance to get her down before the next made it obsolete. More often than not she was besieged by several worries at once, which afforded her the relief, when one became unbearable, of switching to another.

Peter had written that he was very busy, so busy he hardly found time for his correspondence. She was not to wonder if she were to receive fewer letters for a while. Of course, she thought, this is the beginning of the end.

"Don't be foolish," said Antonio. "The boy is busy." But his smile was insincere.

During the preceding months of total isolation, her thoughts had dwelled more and more on Peter. His letters were friendly enough but showed a conspicuous lack of inquiries into her own life. They were full of glowing descriptions of an estanciero's daughter who, according to him, was a model of perfection. She held on piteously to sentences like, "I know you would love her," which continued to make her part of his world. She wondered if he meant to marry the girl, but he did not tell her his plans. In this, as in everything else, he had changed. He told her of occurrences, not of events in his life; he did not give her a full picture of it or its aims. His letters had once been as descriptive as a diary.

146

Another letter followed and then she heard no more. When a fortnight had passed without a word, she placed a long-distance call. The mayordomo who answered it said, astonished, "The niño is away. He was going to visit with you, Niña. He's been gone for a week."

For a moment there was silence at Tony's end of the line. Then she said, dazed, "He's probably stopped off to see friends. Thank you, McGregor."

After she had hung up she called Antonio. "This is a personal matter, but it can't wait. You must come to see me right away. I don't care what happens."

When he reached her apartment she hardly took the time to shut the door behind him before she asked, "What's the matter with Peter? You must know! You do know. I called the estancia and was told he had left there a week ago en route to me."

Antonio, his back turned, divested himself with deliberate calm of his coat and muffler and walked into the living room. She only saw how disturbed he was when, settling into an armchair, he drew his lips into a smile.

"God knows what the boy is up to. Another escapade . . ."

"Don't be ridiculous, Antonio! An escapade, really! I've had all kinds of foolish ideas—that he's done something to himself on account of me. Of course, that's nonsense. But what is it? Something is wrong. And you know what it is. If you don't, then something has happened to him and I'll notify the police. But I think you know."

She stood before him, dark eyes and pale lips hard and bitter. He looked up at her, legs crossed, fingertips joined to form a gable, calmer than she but no less annoyed.

"Peter does just exactly what you're doing. He's in a very sensitive spot there at the water's edge, as you well know. There's nothing dramatic about it. He started at the outbreak of the war, even before you, and has done good work on that coast, which is full of German-owned estancias. It was he who got me interested to the point where I got in touch with the British Embassy myself. It's also why you met him in town that time and why it embarrassed him. Now calm down and stop putting your foot in, will you?" He added a dissonant smile.

"And why haven't you told me this before? Why leave me in such anguish when one word would have made all the difference in the world?"

"Why haven't I put an end to Carlota's anguish, she who is a piece of my own heart? Why have you hurt Romero Basualdo when you could have spared him the pain? Why wasn't Peter allowed to know whom he was writing to when the first Nagel message was being prepared? You will remember the form of address, 'my dear,' rather than 'Dear Tony,' and your own objections. Provide the answer yourself."

"So that really was Peter's hand. I thought it was forged. And you knew about me all the time. Don't you think you rather overacted, Antonio?" she asked reproachfully.

"No, I didn't know about you. How could I? That was months before my talk with the ambassador. Remember, it was last June and my conversation at the embassy took place in November. Actually, Peter had asked me for a favor then but only told me that he occasionally acted as a sort of 'courier' for the British. Whatever I know about the Nagel letter I heard later. Some of it from Peter, who, however, only knew fragments in spite of the leading role he had played in the matter. And some from Pat. You want to know how it was done, don't you?"

"Absolutely. Although I don't suppose it's any of my business," she added sarcastically.

"Well, you know that one of Peter's neighbors is Juan Heffler, who works for the Nazis. He happened to be one of Nagel's fair-haired boys among the agents. Peter had befriended him for some time and pretended to believe that Heffler was no Nazi because he had a Polish mistress who, Heffler had told him, was Jewish, which was untrue. This friendship had already proved fruitful on several occasions because Heffler's estancia was handling a large proportion of the U-boat activities, such as landing and slipping out people.

"One night Peter broke into his study (he knew the watchdogs well and had prepared them for weeks for such a coup) and sneaked off with his German typewriter.

"There couldn't be any question of taking it home. You know all the estates up there average in size about like mine, and Peter had come on foot. He didn't want the noise or presence of a car, not even his bicycle parked around.

"So he crept with the typewriter and a dim kerosene lamp into a deep ditch beyond earshot of the house and there typed a letter to Nagel in a code he didn't understand himself, the code Nagel was actually using with his agents on the coast. Peter had helped the British get it, but they'd never explained it to him.

"Pat, of course, not Peter, who to this day knows nothing about you, later told me what it said. That an important agent from Germany, on an inspection tour of the Latin American espionage net, would be set ashore at his place to meet with Nagel at eleven o'clock that night. That was the day you went to Burzaco.

"It went on to say that not only von der Heiden, the backfiring of certain operations, and your part in them, but Heinrich, and even the ambassador, would be main topics, so that consequently channeling it through the embassy was unworkable, and Heffler had decided to send it through a neighbor. Thus Peter Herrnfeld, became an interesting if unwitting recruit for keeping an eye on his sister.

"Peter has been playing the retarded relative very successfully. The consensus out there is that he's *un pobre panete*, and the letter went on to say that 'he takes me for a liberal, as he calls it, isn't too bright, and I suppose that's why the family has relegated him to the country.' Something of the sort.

"On the inner envelope he typed, uncoded, 'for personal delivery only,' and smuggled the typewriter back to where he had taken it. Not that his part had ended. He asked me for help in getting an invitation from the Sociedad Rural for Heffler to lecture, during the critical hours, to a group of young farmers on German cattle-raising methods in some godforsaken village without telephone lines. The invitation went out on official stationery, and a Sociedad Rural employee went to fetch Heffler in an official car. All our farm boys were there. Heffler delivered himself of his lecture and was taken home, full of *bife de chorizo, dulce de leche*, and *Barón de Río Negro*. Mission accomplished.

"The plan was perfect—provided no one but Nagel saw the letter and provided he died before he could talk to anyone. If he checked with the German Embassy in the few hours between your call and the meeting, if he refused to let himself be dispatched, if anyone else saw the message, both you and Peter would have been in grave trouble.

"But it worked, and they're still taking Peter for a not-too-smart refugee boy, unpolitical to the point of befriending the German *estancieros* in

149

the region—as long as they say they aren't party members and drop a contemptuous remark about Hitler. He's even taken to his bosom a few Japanese agents who are planted here and there on their estates as *peones*.

"So that's the whole story. Get me a drink, Antonie. I need one."

"Scotch and soda?"

"No need. I'll take it straight. I don't know what Fleming will think of my telling you about Peter. We'd better let him know, though, even if it makes you out a rather impulsive, emotional person."

Tony stopped halfway across the room, glass in hand. "I don't care," she said obstinately. "I've got a right to know that my brother isn't my enemy."

He took the drink from her. "Don't you think you'd better take a few weeks' rest? Why don't you go away for a while to the sierras of Córdoba, or to Llao Llao? Up in Llao Llao it's just like Switzerland. Snow, sun, skiing . . . I'm sure you could arrange that through von der Heiden."

"Don't you trust me?"

"Of course I do. But everyone needs a rest once in a while. You've been under a terrific strain."

"You're talking to me as you would to a mental patient while tactfully maneuvering him into a straightjacket. I'm perfectly levelheaded. After all, it was only natural to worry about Peter. The circumstances are insane, not I."

"You're perfectly all right, dear. But I wish you would consider a vacation."

She put her hands to her temples. Was she really losing her balance? She had heard of people in a nervous breakdown feeling entirely clear and more reasonable than ever. Was she going to pieces? Could she no longer trust herself?

"I'll think it over, Antonio," she said weakly.

CHAPTER TWENTY-FOUR

THE WOODEN SHUTTERS OF THE SLEEPY CHALET were tightly closed. Vacationers in Córdoba went to bed early, but the innkeeper was waiting up for her. He was a stout, middle-aged Italian with a democratic handshake that took her by surprise. Except for the sour phantom at the Hotel Bolívar, she had seen only starched and servile young men caged behind signs reading *Reception*. After he had carried in her bags and shown her the large, bare dining room beside the vestibule, he led her up a narrow staircase to her room.

As she opened the window, winter air rushed in on her, effervescent and aromatic, tempting her to linger until she went to bed for a night of more peaceful sleep than she had had in years. She was grateful for Antonio's suggestion, sure that this trip was going to be good for her.

At breakfast the center table in the dining room was occupied by the owner and his spinster sisters, who seemed to be fulfilling the functions of housekeepers. Prolific families gathered around the large table, the children chattering of pony rides and bus excursions.

Tony finished her oversized roll and went to the desk to arrange for a horse. Her first ride through the wooded hills gave her all she had expected. Alone with trees, earth, and sky, she felt that, after all, she was just another living creature, accepted by the rest of nature without qualifications, her problems no longer insurmountable. Certainly, her present existence was hard and dangerous and there was nothing she could do to change it. But hard also was the life of mountains and trees, which seemed to have the strength to withstand the tyranny of tempest, thunder, and rain.

She had never felt quite as sure of Pat's love or of their power to outlast the ordeal as she did now, when she was farther from him than ever. The horse's motion loosened tense muscles, relaxed contracted nerves, made her aware of her physical reality in contrast to the artifice of her outward existence. Instead of feeling banished, she sensed that her breach with Carlota and María Teresa was not real, that her insincere relations with Peter were steam to be blown away at will, that Pat's and her love was stronger than the temporary circumstances holding them apart. She returned from her ride face aglow, nerves tingling, ready to carry the globe on her shoulders.

She found the same parents and children at lunch; only the table across from hers was now occupied by a single young man of indifferent looks and excellent clothes. She ate hungrily and without relish, much like her horse might consume its ration after hours of exercise. When she passed him on her way out, the young man rose.

"Pardon me, Señorita, I saw you ride out this morning. Could you tell me where you rent horses here?"

"There are several stables around," she smiled at him, a little sleepy with air, motion, and food. "They'll give you all the information at the desk."

"How about your stables? Any good?"

"Oh, it's all right. I guess they're all more or less alike." She gave him another smile and nod, but he insisted.

"I'm making a nuisance of myself, but would you mind telling me the name of yours?"

"El Trébol," she replied civilly enough. "I don't know much about it, though. I've only just arrived."

"Oh, have you? From the capital?"

"Yes," she said, ready to walk on.

"I'm Juan Gálvez," said the stranger. "From Buenos Aires, too. Would you ride out with me again this afternoon? You seem to be an excellent horsewoman. I like your seat. Have you found good trails yet?"

She had already reserved a horse for the afternoon and hated to give up her *paseo* just to avoid the company of this somewhat importunate young man whose gratuitous praise had nevertheless pleased her.

"Thank you," she smiled. "I'm Antonie Herrnfeld. I've got a horse reserved for four o'clock. Just now I'm going to rest my weary bones."

"Will quarter to four suit you then? Down in the lobby? I'll make arrangements to get a nag."

The eager voice, the carefree tone came from a distant past. She was glad at the prospect of something new that bore no threat.

They rode through the winter afternoon and into the lilac dust. Like most Argentines, he was a competent, all-purpose rider, a fast talker, and generous in his boundless admiration. He was uninteresting, but rather pleasant.

As the days passed, she often wondered why he was there. This was certainly no spot for a playboy's vacation, and it crossed her mind that he might be consumptive; but his hard riding scarcely bore out such an hypothesis. She did not ask many questions, not wishing to answer any herself. And his own circumstances were of no real interest to her.

Their apparent romance became the focus of attention for the rather bored hotel guests. The stir they caused for want of more satisfying, less vicarious entertainment amused them so they sometimes acted up for the benefit of the frustrated matrons and their thwarted husbands. It was like a faint, somewhat dull echo of what her mother had termed "the travel laugh," the unrestrained merriment experienced when, temporarily disconnected from past and future, one delighted in undivided attention to the oddities and relationships of strangers.

They ran into each other at the desk where she was receiving her scant mail. Giving each of the three envelopes a casual glance, she noticed his eyes fixed on them. "Would you like to see my mail?" she laughed.

For a moment he seemed terribly put out. Then he, too, laughed. "I'd love to! Would you let me?"

She handed him the letters. "Open them for me. It ought to prove a fascinating experience."

To her consternation he turned the first, looked for the return address, found none, and ripped it open. It was an invitation to a benefit that he read carefully and discarded before he proceeded to open the next, which contained a dentist's bill. The last was a long envelope that bore the printed return address of a bank communication.

"My bank statement, as you can see," she remarked, not trusting her eyes as he began to open it.

He extracted the sheet and, reluctantly, balance side up, handed it back without scrutiny.

"What discretion," she remarked.

"I love to see other people's mail. I'm crazy about the contents of women's handbags, too," he added candidly. "All the jumble of little notes stained with lipstick, ineffectual midget handkerchiefs, compact covers lying crumpled in a corner instead of serving their purpose. It's fascinating!"

"You're very cute," she said dryly.

"I'm sorry. I didn't mean to offend you." He seemed frankly contrite.

"That's all right. Just don't do it again."

"I wish you'd let me. I love to open letters. Even if I'm not allowed to read them."

His eccentricity was unconvincing, his naïveté contrived. "Sometime maybe, if you're good," she replied. "Let's go in to breakfast."

She put her letters on the table they now shared, and after breakfast took them up to her room when she fetched her gloves and hat to join him for the morning ride. On her return she noticed she must have left, or dropped, the bank statement in the dining room; but the waiter assured her that he had not found anything. She wondered if Gálvez had snatched it, anxious to ascertain the financial setup of a potential match. It was unlikely and, at any rate, unimportant.

On an impulse, she wrote a couple of lines, addressed them to herself, and hurried to a nearby mailbox.

When she walked up to the desk the next morning, he was leaning against it, exchanging halfhearted remarks with the houseboy. There was a letter from her charwoman and the one she had mailed to herself on the previous day. She gave him a challenging glance and laughed. "Would you like to open my mail again?"

The houseboy grinned, as Gálvez had already put out his hand. "Very much."

Tony handed it over. "Make yourself comfortable." She sat down on a bench against the wall where he joined her.

First he opened the servant's letter, reading it with a slowness exasperating to Tony who was a very swift reader. "Who's the man from San Miguel?"

"Let me see," she said with mock earnestness and skimmed over the letter. "Don't you know the Tienda San Miguel? I'm having my curtains cleaned."

"You made me jealous!" he exclaimed reproachfully and opened the other letter. Tony knew what he was reading now: *There is a very curious man around, and I don't like it.* No signature. She was watching his face, amazed to see it turn rigid and clouded. For a while he did not lift his eyes from the two lines. Then he asked, his voice quite harsh. "Who wrote that?"

Tony took the sheet from his hands. While she pretended to acquaint herself with its contents he looked at the postmark on the envelope. Then she said, wide-eyed, "I can't imagine. What do you think?"

"So you don't know?" he asked, a thin smile on his lips.

She stared at him in real wonder now, something telling her that the joke was off. She could not imagine what made him take an innocent prank with such bad grace. Forcing a laugh, she said, "I wrote it, of course!"

"Oh, you did," he replied, obviously relieved. Had he really had any doubts? He took the paper back and scrutinized it. "Is that your handwriting?"

"No," she said, quite annoyed by now. "It's ghost writing."

"What a remarkable hand. Do you always write like this?"

"Only on Sundays."

He was warming up. "I'm terribly interested in graphology." He took a notepad and pencil from his pocket. "Here, write your name and the same two sentences under it."

She complied, rather bored. As he was studying what she had written, comparing it with the script on the other sheet, she asked impatiently, "Well, what do you see?"

"Not much offhand. If you'll give me time I'll be able to tell you a lot about yourself, though. You'll be amazed."

"Won't I." She rose to enter the dining room, this time without inviting him to join her. He put the papers into his pocket and followed her.

During the rest of the day he did everything to make her forget his rudeness; but she had grown disturbed at the idea that he had obviously maneuvered to get something in writing from her. She had begun to suspect him of being an adventurer; but what, in that case, should he be seeking in this godforsaken *hostería* and what, moreover, did he believe he had found after examining her rather mediocre checking account? At any rate, she wanted those two slips of paper back.

In the evening he gave her a wayward description of her character ("domineering, eager for adventure, astute, and courageous") as revealed to him by her handwriting. The evidence that he was not anything like a psychologist gave her the comforting assurance that, if an impostor, he could at least not be a very good one. He returned the papers and they soon found the bantering tone again.

CHAPTER TWENTY-FIVE

HAVING BECOME USED TO CHECKING UP on people, Tony looked in the Buenos Aires telephone directory and found that the home and office addresses Gálvez had indicated existed. He had told her that he was a salesman for an insurance company. He lived with his father, infantry Colonel Benjamín Gálvez Muñoz, whose name frequently appeared in the city papers. It made the son's identity easy to check and dispelled any fears that he was some sort of gangster. It also bore out her suspicion that he needed a financial boost, for army officers were notoriously underpaid and oversociable. His questions rather tended to confirm this, for he showed undue interest in her financial situation, the way she earned her living, whatever she had saved from Germany, and whether she hoped ever to retrieve any of what she had left behind and by what means.

She was more amused than disenchanted to discover that her purse held more glamour for him than her eyes, and very curious how he would eventually go about trying to bring his quarry to heel. The climax came when she happened to overhear a telephone conversation. It was during the siesta hour, when the staff retired for a sacred rest that not even an urgent call could desecrate. Coming down the stairs, she recognized Gálvez's voice without at first understanding his words. The panic in his voice made her stop midway, about to turn and discreetly go back to her room. Just then she heard him say into the telephone under the stairs, "I do need it right away, I tell you. I can't go on otherwise!"

She told herself that she ought to walk on or turn back, but she remained where she was. "No, nobody's going to help me out! My father least of all. They're not going to wait. They're hunting me down every minute, and if something drastic should happen, it would certainly kill the business at hand. Yes, it is definitely worthwhile. Much against my expectations. And I assure you it will make me worth a good deal. Not yet. It would be too early in the game. I need time, and without money I can't hold out." Almost whining, "That doesn't do me any good. It isn't only the expenses. I've got to pay off or . . ." Finally, as if he were choking, "All right. I'll try to get along on that. But if something happens it may blow the whole scheme sky high."

Assuming that she had got the gist of the matter, Tony tiptoed up the stairs back to her room. So her assumption had been correct; newsworthy alone was that he was desperate and thus potentially dangerous. Cautioned now, it did not bother her unduly, and she decided it was safest to keep playing along.

The management had organized a dance. The tables had been pushed up to the whitewashed dining room walls, an asthmatic little band played on an improvised dais, and the innkeeper was offering a glass of sweet cider.

For a while they watched the matrons in full regalia dance with their husbands and snatch occasional turns with someone else's—a change, if not an exciting one.

They soon became bored; somehow the former cheer was gone. Since the fateful siesta hour he had grown obviously worried and she more than slightly uneasy. Before midnight they retired.

Through the open window starlight was showering her room. She leaned into the sky. Her hands touched a frosty film on the sill, almost like snow. In the phosphorescent night the pale tree-lined road led into mystery. It seemed she could now make contact with her real self only in unreal situations. The technique was continually refining itself and some day she would be able to superimpose the dreams on the reality.

She put on her coat, saw in the mirror a slender, fashionable young woman in hooded furs, the long forgotten kind of woman who would have been here with Pat, and smiled and turned around. She looked at the empty corner, let her open arms drop to her sides, and went toward the door.

Hands in her pockets, she walked along the wintry road, which led not into mystery but through the village, by the inn, and up into the wooded hills. Her eyes dropped from the splendor overhead and watched her breath form steam clouds in the icy air. She exhaled, blew, and heard her governess say, "Don't, it's bad for your lungs. Keep your mouth shut." She stopped and pretended to be skiing, felt, without altering her step, the movement the earth would assume under one's skis so one had to go with it as one must with a horse—*faire corps avec la terre*. There was something attractive in the idea. *Faire corps avec la terre*. She must remember the expression.

She fancied a movement behind her, not gliding as of skis but furtive, not quite a sound, barely enough to touch the ear. She listened sharply to the very small, blunt noise, as of a toe's accidental contact with a loose stone, followed by a pointed silence, someone stopping in his tracks with bated breath. Turning, she saw him at about six feet, poised (unless the odd starlight made her see what did not exist) for a sprint into the trees. He was coming toward her in a seemingly uninterrupted sequence of steps, but she was sure there had been a shift of weight onto both feet. His smile, as he drew closer, was easy. "I saw you walking out while I was admiring the night from my window and thought how smart you were to plunge right in. May I join you?"

"I was just about to turn back," she said gruffly, but he took her arm while they returned without speaking, her eyes straining for the lights of the inn. Passing a copse, he drew her off the road and, much to her relief, only clasped her in his arms.

"Don't be silly!" she exclaimed, not particularly angry because she had been prepared for a much more unpleasant assault.

"I'm sorry," he said, piqued. "I didn't know I was repulsive to you. It won't happen again."

They walked on in silence. A few steps from the inn he stopped. "Let's forget about it, Antonie. It was a blunder. I'll be patient."

She had hoped that he would truly take offense. Seeing that she could not get rid of him so easily, she decided to set matters straight once and for all. Under the protective nearness of the neon light from the dining room windows, she managed to laugh. "You can be lots of fun, Juan. But when you're serious you're not only a bore, you waste your time. I don't expect you to make passes at me and I'm not going to marry, ever."

He seemed amused. "You're a good sport. That's the foreigner for you. Our girls, a man can't court them without kissing them, or kiss them without marrying them."

He's a good actor, after all, she thought. But she was quite sure that the underlying issue had been adroitly settled. When they re-entered the lobby their faces were bright and friendly.

She spent a couple of days enjoying the relief from her usual worries. Gálvez seemed to have received a check or draft, for he went down to the branch office of the Banco de la Nación, and his spirits rose to the height of a bottle of native *champaña* for dinner.

On the following afternoon she let him ride out by himself and, after an early lunch, walked down for some shopping in the village. In one of the general stores where she was buying toothpaste she noticed a pair of souvenir cuff links, a wooden mate cup linked to a *bombilla*, the gaucho's silver sipping tube. A harmless trinket Pat might have picked up any day in a curio shop on Avenida de Mayo. She enjoyed the impression of a wide-eyed tourist she was giving the clerk, who lunged forward to sell her more. Unwilling to break the spell, she haggled for a considerable while over a poncho. Somewhere else she stopped and bought an ashtray of Córdoba rocks for Antonio. Back in the street she noticed that she had been away for more than two hours.

When she got home at half past four, one of the resident sisters approached her in the lobby. "Would you mind stepping in here for just a moment?" the grey-haired girl requested gently, opening the door to the dining room. Tony followed, quite puzzled, because so far these guardian angels of pantry and linen closet had been benign but retiring.

On the threshold, the spinster said, obviously embarrassed, "You must know, Señorita, that it is against the house rules for ladies to receive gentlemen callers in their rooms."

Tony stopped with one foot still in the lobby. "Gentleman callers! What do you mean?"

The woman lowered her eyes. "You see, Señorita, things are being observed. Especially during the daytime. There are always guests passing through the hallways. It gives our establishment a bad name. This is a family hotel."

Tony was enraged. "I have no gentlemen callers. Do you claim, by any chance, that you saw Mr. Gálvez in my room?"

"I didn't, Señorita. But he was seen entering it." Her voice was now prim and determined.

"When?"

"At about two."

Tony laughed. "I was out shopping, as you can see, and have been since half past one."

"Your key was not at the desk at the time the complaint was made. I don't mean to meddle in your private affairs, but you must surely see . . ."

Tony tried to control her voice. "Has it ever occurred to you that I might have taken it with me? But, as a matter of fact, I didn't. Since no one was in attendance during the siesta hour, I hung it up by the pigeonhole myself. I wish you would repeat your accusation in front of Mr. Gálvez."

As in a stage play, at these words the door to the street opened and Gálvez walked in, not, she noticed, in riding clothes.

"Will you come here for a moment, Juan?" She called.

"Hello there! How'd the shopping go?"

"This lady claims that you were seen entering my room around two o'clock. Would you set her straight?"

"Enter your room? Who saw me?" He laughed down at the spinster with sarcastic mirth.

She colored faintly, avoiding his eyes. "I have no right to disclose the source of our information."

"No need!" He laughed again. "Must have been one of those envious matrons." He fixed her with a black, menacing stare. "You'd better be careful, Señorita, or you'll be sorry."

There was a strange threat in his words, somewhat too sinister for the occasion. It gave Tony an uneasy feeling, made her suspect him rather than appreciate his energy in defending her.

She turned and walked to the desk. Her key was on the hook. "Here's my key."

The spinster blinked as if at an apparition. Gálvez's face was deadpan. "Obviously," he said.

"I'm sorry, Señorita," said the spinster, somewhat dazed. "There must have been a mistake. But, you see, my brother had just taken over the desk when the complaint was made, and then the key was not there. And he stayed until about half an hour ago. I see, though, that you couldn't have replaced it since," she added with an oddly unconvinced glance at Tony's packages. "He must have looked at the wrong pigeonhole. You don't know how sorry I am!"

"Forget it," Tony said coolly. Walking up the stairs she wondered how Gálvez had been able to grasp the issue of the key so promptly without having heard the argument about it. She raced down the corridor to her room, checked her jewelry, every drawer, her suitcases, a handbag. Nothing seemed disturbed.

But when she came down to dinner, Gálvez had departed. Comfortably alone at her table, she congratulated herself for having escaped with only a black eye from a danger into which, after having received the severest training in caution, she had ambled like a fool. It showed how fallacious was her assimilation to her existence, for she was one person on the job and another in private life.

The next afternoon the innkeeper handed her a telegram. Her hand trembled as she took it, ripping it open before she was halfway up the stairs.

Take the first train back it read, signed, Henriette Paquin.

It came from Antonio; Henriette Paquin was a combination of the names of Carlota's and María Teresa's fashion houses.

She was still standing on the same step, her heart hammering loudly. This was no message of joy; all she could think of was that harm had come to Pat.

CHAPTER TWENTY-SIX

IT WAS A SOMBER, DRIZZLY NIGHT when she got off the train. Half hidden behind a pillar she saw a man in a black overcoat, his face concealed by an upturned collar and a wide-brimmed hat, but she would have known Antonio's carriage had he worn a false beard and dark glasses.

He took her two suitcases from the porter and hustled her out into the dark street and to his car.

"What happened, Antonio?" she asked as soon as they started.

"Pat is leaving in the morning," he replied huskily.

"Why, for God's sake?"

"They're transferring him, Antonie. I don't know what to say . . ."

"Where's he going?"

"I don't know. Maybe he'll tell you. I . . . I don't think anything has ever struck me as hard. If I could only help."

Her voice came from the dark beside him, small and tormented. "I can't bear the pain. It will kill me."

"I know. We're driving out to the house. Pat is waiting for you."

"Is he?" The joy was crazy. It was nothing but the ultimate misery.

A shutter must have been ajar, for a ray of light came from the direction of the house, but she would have blindly made her way without it along the black path, hard as asphalt after two winter months. She ran against the yielding door into his arms, her ear against his heart.

"How small you are," he said. She was very still. There was nothing to say. Often the pain of her past years had been greater than herself, had weighed on her, seized and shaken her, and she had given battle or tried to free herself from it. Not now. The pain was she, and it seemed to her that as long as she breathed it would breathe with her, disappear but with her disappearance.

In the light of the living room he smiled. "You're tan. I didn't know you could look like this—like a little gypsy girl."

"Pat," she said, stunned, realizing that there was no more to say. "Pat."

"It has come, Tony. And there's nothing we can do about it, except remain true to each other and take care of ourselves so we can be together again after the war."

"Where are you going, Pat?"

"I can't tell you. It wouldn't make any difference."

"You must."

He shook his head and took her in his arms, and she looked up into his clear, mellow eyes, eyes old but not with age.

"You must. How are we ever going to find each other again? You may be moved around no end before it is over. I may have to disappear. How am I going to trace your steps if I don't even know the first? I want to know."

"Yes, Tony," he said dejectedly. A fog rolled over the blue eyes, making them seem grey, and the name fell away from him as if he had tired of holding it back.

"To France," she repeated, her eyes wide. "Take me with you. I can join the maquis as well as you."

He did not answer, only stroked the hair off her forehead, incessantly and firmly, as if to increase the tingling it caused in his palm. She put her head on his shoulder. "Why don't they send me with you? I could be useful . . . and so glad to do it."

"They wouldn't think of it. And I wouldn't permit it. You're German, and partly Jewish. Over there, to be found out would mean certain death for you. But you ought to go to Montevideo or Río de Janeiro. Someplace where you could wait for me in relative safety."

"The Germans are everywhere. There I'd die uselessly, while in France I could at least . . ."

"Shhh . . ." He held her a little tighter, resting his cheek on her hair, and they remained huddled together like children in a tempest. "Tony, don't you think von der Heiden can protect you? I mean, whatever you do so someday we can be together again is well done. Do you understand me?"

164

She nodded, managing a smile. "I've brought you a souvenir from Córdoba, but it's in my luggage. So now you won't ever get it."

He pulled her head back gently and smiled. "I'll come back for it. Is it a surprise or may I know what it is?"

She clasped her fingers around his wrists. "They're those little mate cuff links," and added, tightening her hold, "they'll be handcuffs when I get a chance to put them on you."

He put his arms around her without her loosening her grip on his wrists. "We're handcuffed to each other, Tony, no matter how far apart. Till death us do part."

The night held its breath around the lonely house on the plain where two people were saying farewell, must say so much and listen so avidly, look so deeply into the other's face and feel so intensely if they were to keep one another in their ears and eyes and fingertips. They must do it all at once and with such concentration, for there was now only this one time. They clung to each other as if the storm would this way have to carry them off together instead of hurling them apart; passion sharpened by the relentless knowledge that this was the last time, that right after it came the giving up, the turning away, the end.

CHAPTER TWENTY-SEVEN

STEPHAN VON DER HEIDEN, IN A DRESSING GOWN, was reading a book when the telephone rang.

"Hola," he said. "Oh, how are you?" At the recognition a trace of weariness had crept into his voice and now became accentuated. "Why don't you come by the office in the morning?—Well, I don't see—After all, there's nothing we couldn't discuss right now." He played nervously with an enameled snuff box he had picked up from the telephone table. "Well, if you insist, come right over. All right. Good-bye."

With a sigh he went to change into a smoking jacket and to fix a tray for drinks. Whenever he had to receive on his manservant's day off, he felt the lack of a hostess. And yet the thought of the convenience married life would hold was not what haunted him in his beautiful apartment with none of the perfunctory look of a bachelor's flat. It was the stark solitude, incongruous with the warm traces his family had imprinted on the Baroque furniture that had aged with its generations. However, he was no man about town, neither by taste nor by constitution; and so he spent most of his free evenings at home, facing the associations each object held with his reproachful past, gazing from it into the dismal present, and escaping the challenge of the future by concentration on a book that, regardless of subject, pressed parallels upon his obsessed mind. It had never occurred to him to conquer the loneliness of his apartment by bringing into it any of his fleeting adventures, as unthinkable as bringing them into his father's house.

He carried the tray into the living room, unable to say why he prepared to receive as a guest a wretch who would want cash, not courtesy. He knew that the embassy was not going to let him have any more, and he had no desire, let alone the means, to make any substantial loan or gift—which more likely it would turn out to be. He decided to make the fellow understand that he had no right to intervene for him or do anything else, when the door bell gave a timid ring.

He wiped the weariness off his face before he opened the door and said pleasantly, "Good evening. Come right in."

The young Argentine hung his custom-made overcoat on the rack in the vestibule, and Stephan stood aside, far taller than he, to let him pass into the living room. There was a flicker of envy in the visitor's eyes as they took in the mellow oak, the bronze chandelier, the heavy drapes that dropped to the oriental rug. More affected by the habit of wealth they conveyed than by their beauty, he could not help feeling small and embarrassed.

"You must resent my bothering you at this hour," he said meekly, though he had proposed to speak with determination from the start.

"Let's be comfortable," Stephan smiled. Nicety of speech and gesture came natural to him, no matter how he felt about his company. "I'm always glad to see you. Would you care for a whisky?"

"Thank you very much!" exclaimed the guest emphatically, putting up a restraining hand. "*No se moleste!*"

"I want one myself. Water or soda?"

"Soda, please," he said gratefully.

Stephan poured the drinks and handing the nervous young man a heavy Baccarat tumbler, raised his. "*Salud.*"

"*Salud,*" smiled the other, the corners of his mouth twitching.

Stephan settled into an easy chair facing him. "Now tell me what's on your mind."

The young man roused himself from the soft somnolence into which he was being rocked and seemed to recapitulate inwardly the speech he had prepared. He swallowed so his Adam's apple jerked and, passing a finger along the inside of his collar, sat up. "I must tell you, Señor Vonderreiden, that your embassy is defeating its own purposes by technicalities. As you surely know, they sent me on an assignment without giving me the necessary means to complete it."

"As I understand it," Stephan interposed gently, "the embassy has so far at all times paid your expenses, plus an adequate remuneration for your efforts."

"They've paid my expenses all right. But what do you call adequate re-muneration? That depends entirely on what each person needs in order to be able to do the job!"

"And how much would you need, if I may ask?" Stephan inquired, slightly amused, joining the fingertips of both hands.

"You know!" replied the young man, flustered. "You will recall that I told Señor Einrritch what my obligations were, and that he asked me rather sarcastically if those six thousand had anything to do with my interest in the German cause. It hurt my feelings, but on leaving the office you were kind enough to assure me that Señor Einrritch always made it a point to seem un-pleasant. Your remark gave me much confidence in you, and that's why I'm turning to you at this moment."

"And what do you think I could do for you?" Stephan asked mildly.

"Well, Señor Vonderreiden, I simply can't go on. My creditors won't wait! If my father should find out how much I really owe and how serious it is, there's no telling what he might do. At any rate, I wouldn't be any good to you after that. And, after all, you can't deny a certain obligation toward me—had I not been working for you I could have given my time to settling my affairs."

"What would you have done?" Stephan smiled.

"I could have worked."

"I didn't know," he chuckled. But then he leaned forward and put a hand on the carved arm of the other's chair. "Look here, my friend, the issue is, you need money, more than the embassy is willing to give. I have no right to suggest they draw more from their funds than is justified. Your work for us isn't worth more than what we're paying for it. I would gladly help you out a little from my own pocket, but you probably know that we have noth-ing here but our rather small salaries and that foreign exchange laws forbid us to draw funds from Germany at a time when she needs all her resources. I'm sorry I can't be more helpful, but I'd rather make you see the situation as it is, so you can get busy and try some other way of straightening out your affairs."

"You say my work isn't worth more than what you're paying for it. It could be worth a whole lot more if I had the money to do it right. It's a vicious circle. That's what I've tried to explain to Señor Einrritch on the telephone, but he wouldn't listen. He's sent me 500 pesos. What was I to do with 500 pesos?"

"He sent you . . . why did he send it? When was that?"

"Just a little over a week ago. To Córdoba. I had received a letter from a creditor—they always find you, they'd follow you straight to hell—and I got scared. So I called Einrritch long distance."

"What have you been doing in Córdoba?"

"What I was told to do—check up on the girl I got you an invitation for almost two years ago when you wanted her to go to an art show."

"Antonie Herrnfeld?" Stephan said casually.

"That's right. Antonie Errnfeld. At the time I wasn't even working for you. You hadn't introduced me at the embassy yet. You remember the trouble I had getting it?" He beamed proudly, refreshing von der Heiden's memory on services rendered.

"Go on," said Stephan quietly.

"Go on, what?"

"Well, you were sent up there to check up on her. What happened?"

"Nothing happened because I couldn't finish the job. I'd made friends with her—by the way, a peach of a girl—we were together from breakfast to midnight. She had begun to open up a bit when that letter came! Then, just after Señor Einrritch had refused to help me out, she took to leaving the hotel in the dead of night, or to disappearing during the siesta hour to return only after dark, had mysterious telephone calls, and . . . well, it doesn't matter now. At any rate, I couldn't get any quick results since Señor Einrritch had told me to do anything but give myself away. He said expressly, 'I'd rather you come back ignorant than have the woman made wise.' As I couldn't go on without sufficient funds I returned and told him frankly, man to man, that I'd had to abandon the case, promising as it had been, because I couldn't risk a scandal. No more in your interest than in mine. Isn't that logical?"

"Logical enough. And what did Heinrich say?"

"He threw me out on my ear! Told me I wasn't worth a centavo to him, and if the lions were to get me, a good appetite to them." He winced. "*Buen provecho!*" he said in his hideous German accent. "But I . . . I . . . I can't. You see, one doesn't just get eaten by the lions in one gulp. There's

169

so much more to it. Is it fair to expose me to such humiliation after the services I have rendered?"

"Calm down, Gálvez," said von der Heiden, pouring fresh drinks. "Tell me the truth, the whole truth, and maybe I can help you. What have you actually achieved in your investigation of Miss Herrnfeld?"

"Very much," the other said obstinately. "But you won't get another shred of information from me without what I call adequate payment. I'm no fool."

"Yes, you are, because if you want money you must rely on my assistance. You might as well help me with it."

"Tell them to give me what I ask for and I'll tell them what I know."

"May I make a guess, Gálvez?"

"Go ahead," said the other, sullenly.

"You haven't found out anything."

"How . . . why . . . how can you say such a thing?"

"Because," Stephan said slowly, "we know that Miss Herrnfeld is all right."

The man flushed and jumped up, trembling with anger. "But why have you sent me on a fool's errand then?"

"To see just how much of a fool you are," countered Stephan.

Gálvez remained standing, one hand on the back of the chair, staring into a void, remembering the girl's unconcern at his curiosity, the letter she had written to mock him. "Has she reported on the course of our relations?" he asked lamely.

"Naturally."

"What did she say?"

"I'm as reticent as you are," Stephan smiled.

"Has she told you I searched her room?"

"Rest assured that her information has been most accurate."

"But what else could I do?" Gálvez gesticulated. "I had no time to wait for the one slip she might make, or not make, the one contact she might meet, or never meet! Anyhow, I left immediately after it blew up. After all, there was no open scandal. No one knows anything about it."

"No, but if Miss Herrnfeld had been a double agent, as you were made to believe, there would have been others to hear of it."

"I know," said Gálvez, despondently, sitting down on the arm of his chair, his eyes cast on his hands that lay clasped on his knee. "I know. I'm quite finished. And yet I wouldn't be useless if they'd give me the means to carry on."

Stephan was silent, and for a while the room was quiet except for the ticking of the rococo clock on the mantle. The man did not raise his eyes from his hands, and Stephan, holding his glass on the arm of his chair, contemplated him.

"Panic solves nothing, Gálvez. Sit down comfortably and let me fix you a fresh drink. Yours has turned to water."

There was a glint of hope and a question in Gálvez's black eyes. "Sit down," commanded Stephan gently, and he obeyed, getting off the arm of his chair, while Stephan went to the bar for a fresh glass. He mixed the drink slowly and silently while Gálvez sat down without relaxing, in tense expectation.

Stephan put the glass beside him and resumed his seat. "I feel at this moment something we've been taught to ignore at all cost, namely sympathy. It isn't a condescending feeling like pity, but understanding. Unlike Mr. Heinrich, I don't judge people only by the results they turn in. In a way, I know that you're not worthless, even to us. We would never have hired you had you been stupid. You're not. You're hampered by the fact that you can't keep your mind on your business.

"I, on my part, also feel hampered sometimes—by strict adherence to rules. I see much that should be done, or omitted, but can't do or omit it because we're subject to this iron discipline that works well enough for the one, two, three, *march* of the army but handicaps organizations as intricate and subject to fluctuations as diplomacy and intelligence. I often feel that I could do much better if I could occasionally dodge the one-track minds of my colleagues. I'm a career man, you see, a career diplomat, the way my father was a career soldier. Men like Heinrich carry their diplomatic passports temporarily and by the grace of war, like civilians their uniforms."

He looked with tranquil grey eyes at the man who returned his glance darkly, pacified by the show of sympathy but without conviction or relief. "You said you trust me," continued Stephan. "And I trust you. Not because I believe in your friendship, but because you need my help. You must hold on to me, and you know that if you were to drag me down you would sink with me. Is that right?"

Gálvez nodded, expectancy kindling to a warm glow in his black eyes.

"All right. You want money. I want the good of my country. We're an ill-matched team. Still we can pull in the same direction, though from different impulses. I don't ask you to live for the cause of a country that isn't yours. I only ask you to earn the money you're going to make. And as I understand that at times your work will be troublesome, I set a high price on it. But, vice versa, as the profit is great, so is the responsibility. If you fail—through incompetence or disloyalty—you will have to repay with interest. You get nothing in this world without high interest, material or otherwise."

Gálvez said nothing, but his eyes were aflame in his flushed face and the knuckles of his interlocked fingers showed white.

"Do you want me to go on?"

Gálvez nodded, his lips parted to speak, but his mouth was dry. As he reached for his drink, Stephan continued. "There's nothing illicit from the point of view of the embassy in what I'm going to propose. It's all in the regular course of my work. Rather small errands that to my colleagues would seem inconsequential, not worth my time or the government's money, but that to my rather more trained eyes might turn out to be highly rewarding. If I could get results and, maybe, at war's end were to mention who had worked with me, there would probably not only be gratitude but profit for you."

The young man made a gesture of impatience, and Stephan raised a restraining hand. "I don't mean for you to work and wait. Reward in the future is no good to you. In Germany we say, quick help is double help. Alas, as you know, I can't just say, 'here my dear Gálvez, take these 6,000 pesos and forget about your troubles.' But I think we can work out a scheme that will relieve you of your worries.

"I suggest that I pay you 500 pesos each month, whether you actually have any work to do or not. For there may be something one month and nothing the next. Now, knowing that you will have that much for sure, you can work out a settlement with your creditors by which you pay them off in the course of one year. Does that sound acceptable to you?"

The young man swallowed and moved in his chair. "Well, I said that at the time I started to work for you I owed six thousand. Naturally, my debts have increased."

"How much do you owe now?"

"Ten thousand."

"In that case," said Stephan, blandly, "your creditors will have to wait for twenty months instead of twelve. They'll rather do that than make trouble and lose their money."

Gálvez unclasped his hands and took another swallow of whisky. "It won't work that way, Señor Vonderreiden, I simply need a few thousand right away."

Stephan relaxed and leaned back with a sigh. "That's a pity. I would have liked to help you. But I understand. Don't you have any relative who would help you out?"

Gálvez's face fell when he heard Stephan discard the plan without further ado. He leaned toward him, pale now. "All right, Señor Vonderreiden, I'll try to settle my affairs the way you suggest. But what do you expect from me? Without the engineering of the German Embassy I have no connections that would do any good." He was obviously worried.

"You have nothing to do for the present," Stephan smiled. "Nothing except keep our agreement to yourself. I'm not worried about the embassy finding out, except that they might ask me not to go ahead, which would be a minor disappointment for me and a catastrophe for you—as your income would be cut off."

He rose and went to the secretary, taking out a checkbook of the Banco de Londres y América del Sur. While he was writing he watched Gálvez, who had risen, his face tumultuous with excitement and doubt, a mirror of his uncertainty whether this turn of events was a blessing or a curse.

Holding the check, von der Heiden went over to Gálvez and put a hand on his shoulder. "Before you take this check payable to the bearer on an account that, though not mine, is for my use in line of duty, I want you to reflect very clearly because, as a friend of mine used to say, once you make a pact with the devil you slam a door that will not reopen. Not that what you're embarking on is in any way dishonorable, but deceit—even well-intentioned deceit—was certainly not invented by an archangel. As long as you worked through the embassy you were backed by them and only threw the fish into our net. Now, working through me and, while not against the embassy, nevertheless behind its back, you're in the net yourself. You understand?"

Gálvez nodded, his eyes riveted on the check that, now so near, became very real and tempting. Stephan kept it at the same distance. "This time I'm giving you a check because I know you need the money quickly and I won't be able to see you tomorrow or the day after. But as a practice we prefer to hand out cash. Now, are you sure you want to go through with it?"

"I am," he gasped. "I don't know what I wouldn't do for money! I mean, to get out of trouble."

He had blushed at his slip, and Stephan smiled. "I don't know what I wouldn't do in the service of my country. Only that Germany will survive." He handed him at last the check while his other hand on the shoulder exerted a gentle pressure in the direction of the door.

Gálvez obeyed while still putting the check away, and in the vestibule got into his overcoat, silent and embarrassed. Stephan offered his hand, the left already on the door knob. "Whenever there's a call for you from Pepe, call my apartment an hour later, calling yourself Pérez. Good-bye and good luck."

When he had closed the door he returned to the drawing room and plugged the telephone back in. Had Antonie understood his veiled warnings that telephones could be microphone carriers? He gazed at the empty chair, as if he could still look into Gálvez's young face there.

I could have asked you if she'd slept with you. You would have told me. Why didn't I? Someday I might. No, I won't. I know I won't.

CHAPTER TWENTY-EIGHT

AT SIX O'CLOCK ON A SUNDAY AFTERNOON in spring Tony answered the bell. She had hardly opened the door when a man in grey sidled through, closing it with an imperceptible motion of his shoulder. He set down an old-fashioned traveling bag and, taking off his grey fedora, said in German, "I bring a message."

His voice was as foggy as that of persons suffering from laryngitis. He was a thin man of uncertain age, grey of clothes, skin, eyes, lips, and hair, colorless as an animal whose safety depended on perfect assimilation.

"Who are you?"

"Never mind," he smiled, and she realized that she had never seen anyone's expression so little altered by a smile. "I have a message for you from Edmund Nagel. Please show me in."

She motioned to him to go ahead, thinking that in her desk lay a little .22 pistol Pat had given her on their last night. She had assured him that she knew how to use it. Her father had taught her the sport, but not, she now realized in dismay, how to reach for it in an emergency.

She expected him to give her room an inquisitional glance, but he walked straight to a particular chair as if it had been awaiting him, as if he knew every nook and corner here, seated himself, the bag between his pointed knees, and looked at her without urgency, as if he had all the time in the world, obviously waiting for her to sit down. She meant to remain standing, yet the empty chair beside him pulled on her because, she presumed, her knees were too weak to hold her up. When she had yielded he said, always in that voiceless tone that made his person even more opaque, "Mr. Nagel is returning tomorrow at midnight. He will come in a small craft, through the Riachuelo. You will meet him there."

He reached into his breast pocket, looking at her with his empty grey eyes, expressionless, but evidently without missing the twitch of a nerve in her face. She felt sucked into the void of these eyes and struggled to turn her gaze away, but only succeeded when he dropped his own onto a home-made map he was unfolding on his knee. "See the two warehouses here? This stretch between them isn't built up. You see it runs right along the water's edge. At this end, where it is marked with a cross, are some large lumber piles. He'll land there."

"Why do you want me to go?" She heard her voice quaver. "That deserted port area can't be safe for a woman."

"I don't know," he said without a shadow of sympathy. "He may want to go to your apartment. But it's useless to question me. I'm a messenger. Keep this bag for him and notify the embassy. Have another look at the map."

She noticed that the hands holding it were thin and ashen, even the oval nails almost uninterruptedly grey without perceptible division of half moon, center, and edge. Reassuring herself that she was not going to be where the finger pointed, she engraved on her mind the spot where, she was certain of it, her death sentence was to be carried out. Then she looked up. "May I keep the map?"

"No," he breathed, withdrawing it. He restored it to his pocket and, rising, unaccountably put a lifeless hand into hers. "You will be there."

Although it was a dead weight without grip, cool and rubbery, it was hard to disengage from it, the pull away like the jolting separation from a suction cup. As he turned around, she wiped her palm on her skirt, and the door clicked shut.

The grey man had vanished, the grey whisper that had steamed the atmosphere with fog was gone. Now the stagnant blood suddenly rushed to her temples and inflamed her vision. Her heart knocking in her throat, she took a few violent strides that led her to the wall.

I'm not going, she thought. I must call Antonio. She glanced at the telephone across the room. Strangely, she did not feel alone, unobserved. With fluttering heartbeat she tiptoed to the door, peered through the lookout. The hall was empty. Yet still on tiptoe, as she returned to the room, she felt a strange eye and mind on every one of her moves. The visitor's foggy quality, having failed to make his presence tangible, now rendered his absence less material.

He is gone and the door is locked, I am alone, she told herself and moved toward the telephone. She sat down beside it, where she had sat before, reflecting that tomorrow night she was intended to die, probably the way Nagel had died, and that she had only thirty hours to escape. Escape where? She was not shackled yet, but the world was one great prison with guards in every passageway, at every door. She could try but, trying, would plead guilty. And if they did not get her that night, they would get her the next, or in the middle of some sunny morning.

As she stared at the metal lock on the bar fastening the shabby leather bag at her feet, the keyhole's winking eye and the drawn-up grin of the snap came to form a human face. Again she felt the magnetic pull. Again coming from an inanimate object. Within and under her, like an evil current. She reached out and pulled it open with frightened hands, looking over her shoulder with the ever-present sensation of being watched, that someone knew what she was doing and was following her motions.

The bag contained men's clothing. Its touch made her want to vomit. Yet she could not keep her hands off. They were obviously Nagel's clothes. There was even a bottle of *Uralt Lavendel*, the scent that had always hung about him; the sheer silk shirts through which his undershirt had shown; a pair of shoes, very pointed at the toes. Their creases had been made by walking feet whose heel imprints remained inside. Feet that had ceased to exist. And yet these shoes were uncannily alive. Molded to the motion of living feet, the laces rounded by the grasp and pull of fingers, they stood on the rug, facing her, one set forward and outward in a human gesture of approach. With a queasy fingertip she pushed them into a more inanimate position, turning away from her.

She found no papers. Only a vial containing one pill, marked CYANIDE. She had heard that the more melodramatic Nazi bigwigs carried poison, like the "knights of yore." Why this painstaking detail when they did not mean to deceive anyone?

She replaced everything in the order she had found it, though she, no more than they, had no one to fool; there was pitifully little need for caution. The touch of each object as she replaced it caused physical revulsion, and once she had shut the bag (it wheezed with the sound of sucking in air), she hurried to wash her hands.

By the time she was turning the dial of the telephone, the feeling that she was being watched had not subsided, and as if this magnetic figment were more perilous than the probably actual surveillance of her telephone, she prepared to speak in a low voice. There was no answer to her call.

She tried the Gueridas' listed telephone. No answer either. For more than an hour she remained where she was, doggedly dialing the same number. On a beautiful Sunday like this they sometimes let the entire household staff off and went to the estate or cruising on Tigre River.

A beautiful Sunday. Antonio might be saying the same words at this moment. How insular each being was in relation to even those who were closest. A lover laughing while miles away his beloved died in an accident. The laughter did not cause the day to be beautiful and the death did not spoil it, not for others commenting on the weather. She had a vision of Antonio on the yacht, of Carlota and María Teresa . . . She must not throw her shadow over them. And so she could expect nothing from the time left her, the appointed hour had in reality already come, there was no more to do. Why wait? The thought of the .22 made her see that, rather than another stage effect, the vial was the crucial contents of the bag. She was handed her final assignment. "Young refugee with society connections takes own life. Unrequited love? Financial difficulties?"

In a way it was mercy, but she recoiled from taking the road they were pointing out to her, preferred to go her own way. Pat's way, she thought, not without bitterness, who must have guessed in which direction the gun might have to be turned. It would be easier to swallow the pill. It took less willpower. Get a glass of water, she prodded herself, swallow it. In a few minutes, maybe seconds, you'll be asleep, well out of it . . . Her hands on the edge of the chair were pushing her up and holding her down as in a struggle between the two. If it were my own pill, not theirs. I'm afraid to take what they urge on me, as if they could harm me even within death. What do I fear? Death is always the same. The pill they push on me could not bring a different, more redoubtable extinction.

But I do not want their kind of death. I'll take ours, the one Pat has chosen for me. Pat gave me the gun to fight, not to give up . . . He must have known that this impasse was bound to come, and took his chances. He can't have cared so much. He told me that a Mr. O'Shean at the American embassy knew about me and would be able to help if things got really bad. How am I going to reach him on a Sunday? The protection Pat had given her while he was near had become as abstract as their love, dwindled to an impersonal, halfhearted assistance.

But she would set her face against this death that was ready for her, even now, where the Costanera ran into the Riachuelo, where the dingy piers with their smoke-blackened warehouses and factories, their ragged barges, forgot by daylight what they saw at night when the riggings of the ships were only shadowy skeletons. Their crews would be ashore in the noisy dance halls of Avenida Leandro Além, and indifferent freighters of foreign nations would close their eyes in the distance, their stacks cloaked in darkness. The Riachuelo, haven of artists and rogues, the far end of the same Avenida Costanera where at one time, how long ago, she had stood with Romero Basualdo, discussing dreamily the melancholy of life.

Why was I sad then, she wondered. Why are the living ever sad? It's good to be alive, no matter how, good even without Pat, even if we never meet again. I want to live, sick, poor, in distress, what does it matter? We all live together, each in our own fashion, within reach of one another. The dead are not dead together.

We live together, affected by others and affecting them . . . So then as long as one has an identity, one can't be as completely cut off as I think I am . . . There's the British embassy . . . But will they help? I'm neither one of their citizens, nor a very valuable foreigner. A code name known to only a few. Fleming is on leave and I wouldn't know who else knows me . . .

She found a Thomas B. O'Shean listed in the telephone directory, rang his number (let them hear if they had bugged her line!) and was told that he was away for the weekend. She could call the British ambassador . . . The notion that she was a nameless subordinate, at least formally unknown to any of the machine except the small wheel of which she was a cog, had been drilled into her so thoroughly that even in her present situation it seemed scandalously indiscreet to demand acknowledgment. She rebelled against her own timidity, but it brought home how hopeless the attempt would be.

She racked her brain for someone who could help. Neither of the two embassies was accessible to her before morning; and it would be reckless to waste twelve hours when one supposedly had only twenty-four to live. There was one other person. Stephan. Why, for the first time, do I think of him by his Christian name when I'm still having difficulty calling him by it? He's the bailiff, if not the hangman.

But there is a small chance that he'd try to save me. And if he doesn't? She shrugged. I've got nothing to lose.

It had grown dark. She turned the light on and looked at her watch. It had stopped. My God, she thought hysterically, has time already stopped for me? She dialed the time service. It was almost ten. There was a slight chance that he was at his apartment, and its slightness gave her courage. She was going to try and let fate decide; and even then she would not give herself away, only tell him that she had a message. She had orders to transmit it to the embassy, hadn't she? But should she do anything at all they told her now? She could not unravel the problem, aware that one wrong step could undercut any other solution that might occur to her. But inactivity would automatically be fatal, while the presence of the pill encouraged her to think that they did not go without a certain reluctance about her forceful elimination.

In her address book she had written down, though never used, Pepe 72-9144. She dialed it backward, 44-1927. A signal and two and three . . . He was out. She should have felt relief, but the slackening of her heart was rather that of disappointment. Four . . . Fi . . . About to replace the receiver, she heard a distant "hola . . . hola . . ." and, nerves twitching excitedly, put it hastily back to her ear.

"Mr. von der Heiden?" she asked timidly.

"Speaking."

"This is Tony." Her voice was uncertain and low.

"Who?"

"Antonie."

"Oh, Antonie!" He seemed pleased. "I didn't understand you. How are you?" Then a little worried. "Is anything the matter?"

"Just a message for the embassy." She controlled her voice. "Could I see you right away?"

"Of course you can. I'll be right over."

"No, I . . . I'd rather come to see you. Would that be all right?"

"Yes, Antonie, naturally. But . . . hadn't you rather I came to you?" He was astonished.

"No. I want to come to you," she said firmly. But then, against her will, her voice turned small again. "Please, let me."

"You know my address, don't you?"

"Yes."

"I'll be waiting." She heard the emotion in his tone, was troubled when she realized how he had interpreted her spontaneous call, and wished for even this unsavory predicament to be true.

While she walked down the stairs and stepped into the dark street, the vague sensation of being watched was supplanted by the very concrete knowledge that someone she did not see would surely follow her, and she was unwilling to walk with a malignant shadow behind her. So she waited in the doorway for a taxi, without looking too closely into the shadows, like a child who hides its head under the covers not to see the nursery spook.

No caution had prompted her decision to go to von der Heiden's apartment. His visit to her would have been natural, hers was unusual and therefore suspicious. No reasoning had furthermore led to it, only the instinct to free herself from the room that had turned magnetic with the coming of a grey man who had left there his dreadful message and the shabby traveling bag of the dead. She whistled sharply, afraid to have the lonely cab pass by, starting at her own whistle, looking about, expecting to see something stir in the dark. All was still.

"Posadas 1322," she told the driver as urgently as if headed for a haven. She reminded herself sharply that it was nothing of the sort, that von der Heiden must know and, if not actually approved, most likely acquiesced. Yet each day had made her surer that he had broken away from the *Vaterland* spell. No matter how weak he was, she could not believe that he would knowingly send her to her destruction, but when skirting a precipice, optimistic speculations were treacherous ground to tread on. She knew only too well that she yearned to throw off the straightjacket of caution and that her own mood was an additional hazard. She sobered up with an effort, and it was like the hung-over temperance after a fanciful, excited night in which nothing had been accomplished, where one had merely whirled in an unrecognized impasse.

It seemed as if no coarse spook of deserted piers could penetrate the walls into the parchment glow illuminating these fine woods and mellow colors, into the urbane, almost courtly atmosphere that flowered only from centuries of well-spent hours. However, it was Stephan von der Heiden's culture, his taste, and what he had grown from. It was reassuring in appearance, yet as sapless as he himself; good to look at, yet rotten and threatening to crumble if touched.

He stood facing her, fine and gentle, looking clean and pure in beige gabardine. She took stiffly the offered high-backed chair by the candelabrum, her hands in her lap, her eyes rigid and black.

"Edmund Nagel is to meet me tomorrow at midnight on a Riachuelo pier."

"No, Antonie!" Terror jumped into his eyes. "Edmund Nagel is dead! Why do you repeat such a wild lie when you know they're mocking you?"

Her eyes narrowed, and sensing her resistance he sat down on the footstool before her. "What has happened, Antonie? Don't playact, don't try to cover up anything. It had to come one day. Had you never lied to me, we could have kept it from happening. Let us try to save what we can now."

She saw how pale he was, saw the lines from his nostrils to the corners of his mouth deepen and quiver, the first moment's terror in his eyes mingle with despair. He was ignorant of what was being done to her. But the old caution raised its head. Then derisive, silent laughter stamped it out; there was nothing more to hide. They knew all about her, and Pat was beyond their reach.

Looking down at him she felt like slipping off her chair against his chest, giving herself up to whatever real or illusory comfort he could give. If he did not know what had happened, only he could help; and if he knew, or approved, it seemed easier to leave herself in his handling than in that of his fellows. But she did not move and said with the same rigidness of eyes, "And what am I to do then, except carry their own word back to them and follow their instructions?"

He touched her hand. "Antonie, pull yourself together. Don't help them in your destruction by letting them drive you to hysteria. Because that's what they want. Plain, unsophisticated murder of a defenseless girl would be so easy, so there must be more behind it. You must tell me everything, quite in detail. I swear to you that I know nothing of what has happened. I'm your friend."

"All my defenses are down," she said, dazed. "You see I've stopped pretending. If you can help me, help. But don't play cat and mouse with me now that you have me. I'm not trying to escape."

"I've never played cat and mouse with you. At least not since I've got to know you," he added sadly. "I've tried to make you understand, but you were unwilling to believe. I have known for a long time that the letters you gave me were fake. They contained too many mistakes. They worked for a while, but not over such a long period of time . . ."

"Why did they leave me alone if they knew?" She was still probing him as if she had not committed herself beyond retreat.

"Because last January, after they became restless, I began to correct the mistakes before I turned the letters in," he said without pride. "Because I haven't even passed on those that couldn't be fixed. I tried to warn you, once more on the day your cousin broke in on us. But you wouldn't listen. I had to work alone, not even sure whether I was working with or against you. But they've never been sure either. And I don't think they're sure yet, unless what you will tell me proves differently."

Tony recounted laboriously the incident of the afternoon. Although the door of the trap remained shut, it was good to know that someone outside knew she was in it.

While she talked she was also absorbing the discovery that Stephan von der Heiden had swerved away from the Nazis. Be it only for her sake, before his personal disappointment, she wondered how things would be now had she dared to believe him. She saw his face darken at every word, and when she had finished, she asked, "They know now, don't they?"

He shook his head. "No, I'm sure they don't. They wouldn't have given you a warning, a chance to . . . to what? But as I said, if their minds were quite made up, it would be so easy just to . . . ." He broke off. "You see, they've known since early in the year that Nagel couldn't be alive. But they still have a doubt whether you're actually deceiving them or are deceived by the British—they know it's their work—into mailing those letters. As long as they're not absolutely positive, they're reluctant to do anything to you because you're dangerously well connected with society here. You're not only a half-Jewish refugee, you're also the Catholic member of a great Argentine family. Your disappearance would cause a stir."

"But they're sure about Nagel?"

"Of course! However, they believe that he originally disappeared of his own free will, following the message you took to him at Burzaco and that presumably called him away. They've never stopped believing in the authenticity of that one. But then they think that very possibly he was killed by a British agent and that since then you've been passing on fake messages, unwittingly or otherwise. You see, they almost caught the man they suspected. But he disappeared overnight without a trace."

Thank God he left, she thought. How often have I thought that if he'd cared enough he could have refused to go, or put it off . . . he had no time, couldn't stop for me, not even a moment. And he did wait, longer than a day . . .

Stephan misunderstood the light in her eyes. "Antonie, they don't know, but they must have decided that you're not worth the risk. It's almost as bad as if they knew it all. We must think, and think fast."

The present came back and its doom made all other successes or failures null and void. She looked at him, not with hostility but bitterness. "Why did you draw me into this? Why did you?"

"Because I served my country, Antonie. We're at war. Don't the English, the Canadians, the French of the resistance, don't they all kill and maim and betray for the sake of their homelands? I was prepared to do the same as long as I believed, if not in the justice of our cause, at least in its justification. Anyway," he added reluctantly, "until I began to understand you and what you stand for; until you brought back the things I had been made to forget." He paused as if to consider the validity of his own statement. Then he went on. "I haven't been any good to my country, or you; have not been able to serve oppression or liberty. Now I must be some good to you before it is too late. And yet, again, I doubt if I can. First of all, you must tell me very accurately what has happened since we met at the art show."

"There's nothing to tell, except what you know: that I have worked for the British since the morning after you spoke to me."

184

"I didn't know it was so soon. But who are your contacts? I want to know, because it's the only way I can tell who might be able to help."

"No one," she said quietly, "except the agent you spoke of. And he's gone."

"You must be in contact with someone now. You must tell me, Antonie, because every detail may be important. Isn't there anyone who could hide you if we were able to reach him?"

Again she thought of Antonio and shook her head with an effort. "No. There's nobody. Except the embassy. But what could they do? No matter where I hide, your people will catch up with my life as they've caught up with Nagel's death."

Stephan rose, saying desperately. "Defeatism doesn't help, Antonie. We mustn't dramatize, we must seek a solution. You see, my people, as you call them, have a harder time spotting anyone than the British. Though there are fewer British than Germans in the country, they own the railroads, their banks have branch offices everywhere, and the population is sufficiently sympathetic to the Allied cause to answer their questions. That's why one hasn't found any definite proof of Nagel's death. So let's take things as calmly as we can. I'll fix us a drink, and we'll talk it over."

He took a decanter and two slender-stemmed glasses from the bar and set them on the table. "This comes from my father's cellar. He thought a great deal of this particular port. It's been ages since I touched it. As in all these years I wouldn't have had the moral courage to talk to him eye to eye. Until now when it's too late."

He poured the drinks and handed her a glass. "Antonie, do you love me?"

"No," she said. "No, I don't. But I don't detest you. I've never detested you, much as I reproach myself for it."

They drank the aged wine in silence, and finally he said, "I can't help you as I wish I could. You see, what I know of the embassy's information and reactions has not come to me directly. I've had to spy for it. They trust me almost as little as they trust you. A word, even an inquiry, from me could be fatal. I'm no bridge for you, only a companion in arms.

"But I have a scheme, though it is still very vague in my own mind. As I see it, our only foothold is their doubt whether or not you're a double

185

agent. If we could convince them you're not, they might refrain from immediate action. But we've got very little time to do it in."

He fell silent and looked into her eyes. Behind the milky, blue-veined forehead she could almost see his mind working to unravel the balled-up thread that might lead to the core. Then he stared into the golden liquid in his glass, bronzed and dull with the patina of years, until he spoke again, more rapidly. "If by some means the British could convince them that you're considered an enemy . . ." He broke off and frowned. "They'd have to catch you, the German agent, before tomorrow night."

"Yes," said Tony slowly, distrustful of a salvation outlined so hazily that at close inspection it might prove impossible to carry out. "I guess I could meet someone early in the morning. But I'd have to call the embassy."

"No. You mustn't. You'll be watched all day tomorrow. If you make a single suspect gesture they might move before it is too late."

"How're they going to know then?" she asked in a sinking voice.

"Through me. I've got someone in touch with the man who has replaced your contact."

Tony looked at him as if she were seeing him for the first time. Even on the occasions when she had believed in his good will he had been to her the incarnation of helpless passivity. He saw the surprise in her eyes. "I've been giving them information for several months, through a fellow who believes he's a double agent passing on plants to the British."

For a moment she was silent, then she said softly. "You think I didn't want to help you, don't you? When you spoke of working with us, I suggested it to the British Embassy. They didn't want to take a chance then. And, you see, I didn't value your decision very highly because I thought it was born from resentment. I didn't know you'd been helping us with the messages before."

"Not really helping you, if you put it in the plural. At the time I did it for you alone."

"But since when have you been in direct touch?"

"Since your return from Córdoba."

"I can't imagine why they didn't tell me." Her link with the British Embassy seemed ever more frail, less and less likely to lend her support.

"Because they don't know who supplies the information."

"But they know it comes from the German Embassy, don't they? And that's my sector. Who's your contact?"

"You mean, the middleman? Mr. Juan Gálvez, who's in dire need of money . . ."

"Gálvez! Why, the man I . . . "

"Yes, Antonie. They sent him up to watch you. Didn't you realize? They'd kept me ignorant of that, too. They must have suspected, and rightly so, that I would have warned you. When he told me, I knew we needed help. But we'll discuss your beau another time," he smiled. "Right now we'd better concentrate on the matter at hand. My scheme may not work and it will require courage on your part. But if it does work it makes you safe, and I know you don't lack courage. I'll try to get hold of your friend Gálvez during the night, and get in touch with you in the morning.

"You'd better go home now and stay there. Don't answer the doorbell, and the telephone only when you hear three rings and no more and again three rings and silence. When the three rings have come again you may answer. I'll call you, but you know we can't really talk on the phone."

"How are you going to work it?'

"I don't know yet, Antonie. I don't have the slightest idea," he replied, discouraged. "I wish the British knew about me. Don't you have anything that identifies you to them, that I could send along?"

"I could give you my ruby ring. But it's at my apartment."

"I'll go with you." He rose and she followed suit. "I want to have a look at the bag, anyway. Even if they're tailing us, at this hour it's only natural for me to take you home."

They looked at the clock over the fireplace.

"Midnight," said Tony.

"Yes, Antonie," he answered, aware of the implication. "It will be difficult waiting alone. I wish I could spare you that. But do think hard all that time. Maybe you can find a better solution. If necessary, I'll talk to your cousin, Carlota. Don't you think they would hide you if they knew the truth?"

"I don't want them in this. Promise you won't talk to them without my consent."

"Not without your consent. But I should persuade you."

She rode with him for the first time in a German car since coming to Argentina. It was a Mercedes convertible, the same pre-war model her mother had driven, her last before racial legislation had extended to the possession of automobiles. She sat tautly, her elbows close to her body, her hands in her lap, as if to avoid unnecessary touch with it.

Von der Heiden examined the bag with revulsion equal to hers at contact with what was left of Edmund Nagel. He removed the vial and, smashing it against the incinerator door in the kitchen, threw it and its contents down the chute. "Do you remember," he asked, "how you ironed my sleeve here? I think of your hands every time I touch that suit."

"I needed the list in your coat."

There was a flicker of pain in his face; he took her arm and led her to the door. "Let's not talk about it."

Back in the drawing room, he took her hand, his lips grazed her cheek tentatively as if they had never touched her before. He found her mouth with closed eyes and held her firmly, without the former balancing between reluctant hands, without the strenuous listening into her soul.

"Now there's no barrier of distrust between us. If you'll only trust me. I don't ask for love."

CHAPTER TWENTY-NINE

HE STOPPED BEFORE THE DOOR and turned to the entrance niche of the cobbler's shop beside it. "It's all right now. She won't go out any more."

"I've got orders to stay all night."

"At what time is the replacement coming?"

"At six."

"Very well. Good night."

He drove off. When he had left the car before his door and ascertained that no shadow lurked in the various doorways, he walked to Retiro where he stepped into a telephone booth.

"I'd like to speak to Señor Gálvez," he said with the throaty *R* and French stress on the final syllables that came to him more easily than the native accent.

"Who's speaking?" asked a disgruntled manservant.

"Tell him it's Pepe. He'll know." He chuckled like a midnight drunk who had taken it into his head to call his friends.

"Everybody's asleep," chided the servant, "and the niño's out. Call back after ten. He'll sleep late."

He hung up, sorry he had given his alias before making sure that Gálvez, who had instructions to call him within the hour after such a call, was home. He had never reckoned with a time like this and circumstances quite like these, and the notion that his own line was tapped was ever present in his mind. He would wait a while and then brave the servant's discomfiture again.

He walked up to Plaza San Martín. A few late lights winked from the Kavanagh skyscraper which, in splendid isolation, blocked the view of the harbor and dwarfed everything in its neighborhood. He wished for such a citadel to interpose itself between Antonie and the fate awaiting her on the piers behind it. He entered the wooded plaza and sat on a bench, watching the automobiles amidst the sensuous smell of earth asleep in a spring night and the caress of air in its youth. But Stephan was not given to dreaming. At the end of his fight for Antonie's life he was secretly convinced that only her distrust had gagged her feelings. Now that she might begin to breathe in freedom, he was filled with anticipation.

Yet there was an instinctive belief in him that ever since his birth he had walked inexorably toward his own destruction, had carried it within, completing it step by step. It had given him his thirst for life and his unconcern where it would take him, as all paths seemed to lead to annihilation.

The lack of preoccupation with the survival of his personality and an indifference that since his father's death extended to his physical existence, made his mind cool and clear, as again and again he went over his scheme until it was almost perfect.

When no more limousines entered and left the Plaza Hotel's driveway and the Kavanagh had fallen asleep before the harbor like an overpowered giant watchman, he returned to the station. Gálvez had not come in. When he tried again he received no answer. Discouraged, he regained his apartment, uncomfortable at the idea that Antonie was waiting, inactive, for results that he had not attained.

But she was not so trustingly expecting him to solve her problem for her. At first every fiber of her had ached with fear. It was the kind of anguish she remembered in childhood before a session at the dentist's. She wondered if it was any greater, or rather if the child's terror had been less pungent. And as in time she had outgrown her childhood fear, she now was outgrowing this terror.

When first von der Heiden had turned to leave, she had had a strong impulse to hold him back or beg him to take her along, not leave her alone with the ghost in her house. She had been afraid it would start to pull and whisper again as soon as his presence was out of the way. His light, sure step in the apartment had seemed to exorcise it, the disgusted touch of his hands had driven the black magic from the bag that now stood, tamed and shamed, in the farthest corner to where he had relegated it. And the dry,

170

efficient, no-nonsense crack that had broken the poison vial on a garbage chute had contemptuously disposed of that. But wouldn't it all come back to life as soon as she was alone? Only she had been too proud, or perhaps too vain, to ask him to take her home with him.

And then she was glad, since now she was certain that the exorcised ghosts had been figments of her overwrought nerves. Yes, she was sure she had outgrown the terror, was able to review her life and what it would have had to offer. The glaring impact of the part Pat had in her life. He was gone, in all probability forever, as if he had never existed. He was a hero dreamed up or read about in an absorbing novel whose characters, however alive and stirring, became substanceless after the last word had been read.

There was no one that would be hard to leave. Antonio, though a friend, had other bonds that took precedence; Peter now led his own life. From recent letters it had become evident that he would marry the girl he loved, that he, too, would soon have a family to whom she would be *la Tía Antonia*. If there was no one to leave, there was nothing to leave. Only humans made the world for each other and she was alone. Though she wondered if her listlessness was genuine or just induced by physical and mental attrition, she felt lighter without the fear.

There must be something people should do when they know they are about to die, but she could not think of anything. It was pathetically obvious how little there was to her. Once she was gone, her scant possessions would go to Peter, and nothing would be left of Antonie Herrnfeld. She began to gather up some books for Antonio, her volumes of Rilke and the cuff links from Córdoba for Pat, like a lovesick teenager toying with the idea of death without believing in it.

Once more she considered taking a shortcut out of her misery; but she knew that her hand would refuse the trigger. In her present stupor she might have swallowed the cyanide, which, anticipating this mood, Stephan von der Heiden had destroyed. No doubt, he was fighting for her life.

It was three o'clock. By now he might have made progress, found a different solution requiring instant readiness. So she bathed and dressed, all doors open to the telephone, but it did not ring. Now that she was sitting, ready and quite aimlessly, the night became endless.

Four hours later Stephan, who had not gone to bed, walked back to Retiro. The servant refused to wake the sleeping niño, and he was afraid to insist. All he could do now was go to the office, for his absence would be suspect. But it was almost equally suspect not to pass on Antonie's message. Luckily Heinrich was tied up in conference with the ambassador, and there was no occasion to inform anyone except those two.

He watched the clock advance with irritating slowness toward ten, fearful at each tick that Heinrich might finish his conference before he had made a respectable pretense of waiting and eventually leaving. He tried to look busy to the inert walls and began to doubt the efficiency of his plan.

They were to meet in a secluded clearing in Palermo Park where benches surrounded a sandpile. As he waited for Gálvez, Stephan wondered if he had not grown wary of his nocturnal calls. Until now he had avoided any show of urgency or excessive caution because a wise Gálvez might be dangerous. Stephan knew too well that by denouncing him to the embassy he could get his ten thousand in a lump sum, instead of painfully laboring on installments. He only hoped that Gálvez did not know it.

As time went by he grew nervous but told himself that the fellow was merely intolerably lazy. To keep his nerves from rubbing themselves sore against anxiety, he focused his attention on two little boys digging in the sand. The sunny peace pervaded him with an assurance that while two children could be at play in a park, even if it did not counterbalance all the terror in the world, there must be a part of it that was not lost.

One of the youngsters got to his feet and hit the other over the back of the head with his shovel. Infuriated screams from the victim, an air of sullen triumph on the face of the aggressor. Into the midst of this tempest in a sandbox that Stephan was watching, utterly shocked, ambled Juan Gálvez.

"This is an important assignment. And if you do well I'll see to it that you get two thousand extra right away. If it works, I'll tell the ambassador that on this particular job you've been helping me. When can you contact your man?"

"Sometime today, *me imagino*," answered Gálvez with exasperating indifference.

"It will have to be immediately. Can you do it?" Stephan asked impatiently.

"*Me imagino.*"

"All right. You tell him that at midnight a certain person they've been wanting to catch for a long time is going to be at a place indicated on a map I'm sending along."

He sat down on an empty bench where Gálvez joined him. Offering his cigarette case, he continued jovially. "It's a ticklish business, and that's why I want you to know what it's all about. Of course, the person, our agent, won't be there. But they're going to send just the people we've been wanting to get hold of for years. You understand?"

Gálvez nodded, a little worried and, it seemed to Stephan, not quite convinced. He repeated: "At midnight a person they want will be at this place on the map."

Stephan put a small sealed box into his hand. "Besides the map, there's only a sort of decoy in this box. Don't lose it, though. Give it to your man. I don't have time to explain its purpose, but it's immaterial for you. Just follow my directions."

Gálvez repeated once more. "At midnight, person they want, at place on map, deliver box."

"That's it. Make it plain to them—very plain—that they must get hold of the person at that time, or that it will be too late."

"Okay. Anything else?" Gálvez asked wearily.

"Nothing else. Of course, they'll never even have time to look around that place," chuckled Stephan, as though self-satisfied. "I'll meet you at No. 2 at . . . at what time do you think you'll be through?"

"Before lunch, *me imagino*," was the noncommittal reply.

"I'll see you at one o'clock at No. 2 then. And keep in mind that if you do a good job, I'll have two thousand for you the day after tomorrow. Goodbye and thank you for coming."

He walked off, and Gálvez, his eyes following the slender, gentlemanly figure, was puzzled and uneasy. Again a suspicion crept over him, but he slid over the uncomfortable insight the picture of two 1,000-peso bills.

193

On his way through the park Stephan took his glasses from his pocket and knocked them against the stone basin of a drinking fountain. They splintered at one blow. He left them at an optician's shop on Florida and walked to the embassy where he went straight to Heinrich's office.

"Good morning, von der Heiden." Heinrich was stretching lazily in his armchair. "It's a dull life. Where've you been all morning?"

Stephan took the chair opposite the desk that in his mind had taken on the characteristics of the defendant's dock. "I was very anxious to see you as soon as I came in, but you were tied up. And then I broke my glasses and had to take them to an optician."

"Who does your repairs?" Heinrich asked pleasantly.

"Di-Si."

"I didn't know you couldn't get along without glasses."

"Hardly. Anyway, I'd rather not."

"Well, what's new?"

"Miss Herrnfeld came to see me last night, very excited, to tell me that a messenger had brought her news that Nagel will be returning tonight through the Riachuelo and that she's to meet him there. At first she was a little doubtful, but when I went to examine the bag he'd left her and saw that it actually contained Nagel's belongings, I was quite sure there was nothing wrong."

"What's the bag for?"

"The man indicated that he wants her to put him up. By the way, do you have any idea who he could have been? She said he was very pale and seemed to suffer from laryngitis."

"Haven't the palest notion." He laughed heartily at his pun.

"Do you wish to see her?"

"No. What for? Good, good," he added with a deep satisfaction that chilled Stephan to the bones. "But why did she come to see you? Has she done that before?"

"Sometimes," said Stephan, casually.

"So you've finally made her!" Heinrich laughed, dropping his pudgy little hands on the desk top. "Hot stuff, isn't she? Or not?"

And when he received no answer, "I'd always wondered, wouldn't you or couldn't you? After all, there's no *Rassenschande* for good officials abroad!"

Stephan had colored. He was watching Heinrich, who was all quiet contentment. Did he fancy it, or was the man really for the first time completely at ease in his presence? No fleshy rolls appeared on his forehead, no hesitation had at any moment crept into his speech.

"So she's going? At what time did you say?"

"At midnight. Any orders for her?"

"No, nothing." There was again the deep satisfaction. "Life'll be easier after this."

"Why?" The smug words had jolted his heart.

"Well, wasn't it easier with the wise guy around?" Heinrich asked candidly.

Stephan forced a grin. "Not so much. I've often wished he'd gone back to his misguided Creator, as we suspected for a while. Remember the beastly reports he used to send to Berlin about everyone? He'll do it again."

Heinrich leaned across the desk with a confiding smile. "You know, I can't believe it yet that he's really alive and kicking. I've got so used to praying for his soul. So the girl wasn't a fool, after all."

Stephan left the office with the sinking feeling that he had painted himself into a corner. He had not dared to put off the interview until after receiving Gálvez's confirmation that his message had been understood and accepted. If anything went wrong now, this first step might block any other maneuver.

In the meantime Antonie would be waiting, getting desperate at seeing the morning slip by. Against his better judgment he went to a movie house on Corrientes and called her.

By the time the telephone signal came, there was not a drop of courage left in Tony. She had come to the point where, even if this maneuver should lead to salvation, she dreaded going through it almost more than quietly giving up. She longed to hide and wait like a child for someone stronger than she to fight it out and then take her away to safety without any intervention of her own.

"Nothing yet," said Stephan. "But I got it started. Don't worry. I'll call back." He had hung up. His voice had sounded tense and so empty it was hard to believe he had achieved anything at all. She went back to her chair, faint with exhaustion, and for a time there was only semi-wakefulness.

At one o'clock Stephan and Gálvez met at "No. 2" behind the Torre de los Ingleses in Retiro Park. Gálvez, still pale from lack of sleep and rather disgruntled, made von der Heiden feel that he was going to a good deal of trouble for him.

"They want you to be at eleven where it says on the map." As he handed him an envelope, there was a spark of glee in Gálvez's eyes at the idea that now von der Heiden, too, was to take his share in the adventure. He resented doing all the work, like a servant for his pay, without the gentleman so much as scorching his fingertips.

"Have you told them that I . . . ?" Stephan asked, annoyed, less about his revealed identity than the man's indiscretion.

"No." Gálvez flipped his cigarette to the ground with a smug gesture. "But they want to see face to face the mysterious gentleman who has insisted on being so helpful."

"Very well."

"Are you going?" Suspicious curiosity in his voice.

"Of course not. I'll send someone."

The suspicion in the other's tone had not escaped him, nor had the mischievous glint in his eyes on giving the message. While so far polite as to an equal and collaborator, von der Heiden now said tersely, "I'll call you back when you can come for your money. Stay home until then. I might still want to use you."

He walked off without another word, and Gálvez, taking his curtness for discomfiture, smiled dryly after him.

Stephan went to a pay phone. "I'll be with you in a few minutes," he said. "I'll ring three times."

This time there had been more assurance in his voice. Tony still believed that in the end flight would be the only solution, and it seemed good to escape the nightmare instead of working oneself through it. So she was miserable when Stephan told her that at the appointed hour she would have to go to the Riachuelo.

"I got a message through. I'll meet the British at eleven o'clock at a spot close to yours. I've conveyed the gist of the matter, and right there I'll arrange for them to catch you and whoever is expecting you. If my plan prevails, they'll cross-examine you in front of him and let him get away to tell his tale and thereby convince the German Embassy that, for one, you're not a British agent. Do you understand?"

Tony saw the lack of confidence in his fatigued face. "I see. I hope they'll be on time."

"I'll be with them."

"And if you're seen?"

"If all goes according to plan, I won't."

"But if anything goes wrong?"

"Then we're done for anyway, aren't we, Tony? That's what your friends call you, isn't it?"

She nodded, embarrassed.

"I'm not going to call you that. Antonie is a beautiful name. After you hung up last night, I realized it was what you'd first said. To use it would be like taking advantage of knowledge received from a letter to someone else."

"I'm sorry. You see, it had never come up."

"I know. Now, I told Heinrich that you had given me the message and would be there tonight, and he acted as if he were expecting Nagel, all his trust in you restored."

He rose and kissed her wrist. "Good-bye, dear, and good luck to us."

From then on the minutes crept and the hours rushed. Almost less apprehensive of death than of the hectic struggle to ward it off, she went back to the gun, looked at it . . . but no, she would go through with it. There was an off-chance making it worthwhile, an off-chance that their man had orders to retreat at the slightest hint of trouble. And no matter how dark the night, she had never been quite alone in it. First there had been Pat. Now von der Heiden. She was, at bottom, less afraid of the danger than of facing it alone.

But by eleven o'clock the fear of extinction had reawakened. She sat in a corner whimpering for help, for her past to resurrect and stand around her, for a father and a mother, a quiet child's room, and a nurse to fuss over a little girl.

CHAPTER THIRTY

THE TWO WAITING BEHIND THE WAREHOUSE were surprised to see the mystery informer actually turn up. "It's that embassy secretary, von der Heiden," muttered one of them. And now also Stephan recognized the American, a man of medium height, powerfully built, with the bald skull, hard jaw, and cold eye of the Hollywood Nazi officer. His name was Tom O'Shean.

Von der Heiden approached and said, without taking the time for any form of greeting, "She was told that Nagel would land over there at midnight," indicating the spot with a gesture of his head. "I think they mean to kill her, though they're not sure that she's not only been an unsuspecting tool. But they'll be more comfortable without her."

"And what do you think we could do?" inquired O'Shean, surprisingly soft-spoken.

"If they were quite sure that she has no connection with you people, they might not want to risk a public scandal. I imagine you know her mother was a Guerida. The way I figured it, if she'd tried to run it would have amounted to a confession. But if you were to seize her now, before an eyewitness, you would convince them, I'm sure, that she's not working for you. Neither for you, nor the British," he added with a glance at O'Shean's silent partner. "It would have to be made plain by what you say or do. Does that appear sound?"

Saying these things to the burly American and his British triggerman on this dark pier seemed utterly fantastic. He had the sensation that he could not possibly be sincere, that if he shook himself out of the spell he would realize that he was actually working for his own embassy and laying a trap for them.

O'Shean looked straight at him, not unfriendly and not trustingly either. He was studying him like the printed material in a report, acknowledging and reserving his judgment. Now he nodded. "It sounds all right. But why did you get mixed up in this?"

"I'll stay with you," said Stephan as if he had not heard the question. "There may be more than one waiting for her. I've got a dagger. And you?"

The two sized him up without a word. The mute man's glance was his first participation in the scene. Then O'Shean spoke again, not impolitely, a cool statement. "No we'd better not take a chance on having that dagger in our ribs." He smiled, an ugly, bucktoothed smile, but not sly and vulpine like Heinrich's.

"I see," said Stephan bitterly. He understood them only too well. "Would you like to put someone to watch over me? I'm at your disposal."

"That's all right." The scrutinizing rigidness of the other's eyes relaxed ever so little. "But I would be obliged for the dagger."

As soon as Stephan relinquished it, the mute man's hands were all over him, searching him with swift motions.

"Thank you," said O'Shean. "Stay around if you care."

"What are you planning to do?"

"Never mind. We might not do anything. First we'll see to what degree she's threatened. Come on," he said to his silent companion, and the three turned and walked off together.

The maritime police waved the cab through the harbor entrance. It was now driving past the dock where Tony had once arrived believing herself freed.

A minute or so later, after several vain attempts, she made herself say, jerkily, "Just let me off here."

The driver stopped and turned about, astonished. "Madre mía, Niña, aren't you afraid to walk around here alone? You look like a nice sort."

He was a ruddy-cheeked family man, with a Basque beret and a toothpick in his mouth. Desperately tempted to ask him to wait around, she pressed a bill into his hand and hurried off, remembering the coarse face and blunt eyes with curious affection.

As she penetrated into the port, it occurred to her that Stephan had failed to agree upon a password, and she wondered how she was to know whether her aggressor was make-believe or real. She was feeling for the gun in her coat pocket; it was hard and cold, but she held onto it as to someone's hand. She had seldom been in the port, which now in the darkness had become completely strange. All looked alike, a jumble of stone and riggings and water, all black. She entertained a wild hope that she might lose her way, but it was mixed with the fear that she would stumble, unaware, on the very spot, where would death spring out at her without giving her a chance. Nevertheless, she walked straight to the lumber piles as if someone were drawing her there.

Nothing stirred. For a while she waited, her heart in her throat, staring at the stacked wood. Minutes passed. No sound except the soft lapping of the water. There was a faint hope that no one would come, that she was at the wrong place.

A quarter of an hour. She began to feel dizzy, her limbs ached. She rather sensed than heard a silent tread and, jumping with terror, strained her eyes in its direction. But the night was black and foggy and the gentle lap-lip, lap-lip of the water against the pier made all other sounds uncertain. There was nothing.

And yet, as the day before, after the grey man had vanished, she felt watched. Jesus, let it be the eyes of von der Heiden's man, on the spot, ready to play his part. She wanted a cigarette very badly. It would soothe her and make her motions look more relaxed; but she would not release the gun, ridiculous though it was to rely on it against a professional assassin, when Nagel had let himself be killed by a newspaperman with only a few months' training at a Miami spy school.

Though she had been staring straight ahead, she had seen nothing coming toward her and did not clearly discern it now. It was a husky vapor, at one with the fog. "You did come, as I knew you would."

She had heard this voice thirty hours earlier in her apartment, so disembodied she could not tell whether it was threatening or deadpan. Her fingers sore from clutching the gun, she tried to make out his expression, but as her eyes pierced the mist, if there was indeed a face it was like another shred of fog.

"Where is Nagel?" she asked. She had instinctively taken a step back. But the foggy face had not receded, hovered at the same distance, sockets of

200

moistureless, lifeless eyes hollow in the shadows. She had not noticed, but it must have shifted with her. "He's down in the water," it breathed, "with a cut throat."

The back of her left hand flew against her cheek as if she had been hit and she looked about. What were her rescuers, if there were any, waiting for? Did they want to play it so safe? Intervene only when the knife was at her throat?

The phantom had observed her move and seemed to snicker soundlessly and to have raised two fingers, pointing at her eyes. Two fingers with glowing tips, or the eyes of a werewolf.

"You're lying," she faltered. "I know he's alive."

Futile to talk back to a werewolf. He could do things to one but one could do nothing to him.

She gathered all her strength to take one step aside, but still the face, or what she took for one, and the eyes of the werewolf, hung in the air at the same angle.

"You know Larson killed him."

She felt herself gasp before she could pull her voice down to level. "Who's he?"

"Shush," said the voice, confidentially close now, the werewolf eyes dizzyingly near. "You've lost the game, dove, and you're tired. Come now . . . Come . . ."

"Where?" she interrupted, the single syllable giving her shaken voice no room to vibrate in, the lonely word sounding unexpectedly harsh and level.

"Where . . . where . . . where . . . where," it beat out of the fog like a hammer, an echo of her own heartbeat. The wolfish eyes fading backward left in their place something like a fluorescent hand swinging slowly like a pendulum, right . . . left . . . right . . . left. . . . She watched it, her fingers slackening on the gun, right . . . left . . . right . . . left. . . . Slowly it pulled her along, forward . . . forward . . . the ground sloped down steeper, so steeply she lost her foothold in the pull, almost stumbled after the will-o'-the-wisp toward the water's edge. How does the slope get here, she asked herself and then thought confusedly, down in the water, deep, black, sleepy water. . . .

She roused herself as one does *in extremis* before drifting into a nightmare, and said cuttingly, "Don't try to hypnotize me. It won't work."

Her hand closed again around the gun. "You're the Allied agent who murdered him. I've had a message from him since," she lied. "Mailed, if so, just before his death. It said nothing about coming here."

She talked hectically, gradually backing away, her gun pointing in his direction, though the glow was gone and she did not even know where he was and trembled in anticipation of his laughter. Anyway, she must not shoot, not silence the witness. Witness of what?

But there was only stillness, during which she expected him to lay hands on her. She was walking backward step by step, not knowing whether he kept up with her as before or had long since dissolved into mist, until she could no longer stand it and turned, knowing it was wrong, expecting a blow, or a stab, or two hands closing around her throat. But all was silent as if no one had ever been there.

She pulled loose with the same corklike jolt with which her hand had freed itself the day before, and ran. Racing along, she felt from behind the silent approach of a blacked-out automobile.

Her heart gave a final leap. Now it was to happen! The fools, to give murder a second chance instead of rescuing her while there was time. She staggered another step with the nightmarish sensation of being nailed to the ground. When the car door opened beside her she gave up. Nothing pulled at her, but a window swung open from within, wide and stark. Why had she feared the trembling of her hand, her own regret? It was easy, a joy, a home-coming!

"Antonie." The gun slid, as if in disappointment, from her fingers as she stumbled into the backseat. Antonio's head was over the wheel, and Stephan was pressing her temple to his shoulder.

"What happened, child?" asked Antonio. "They gave us the signal to approach. But we heard no scuffle and it was so quick."

"There was nothing to hear," she rasped, "since nobody came to my assistance. All they did was alarm you. And I didn't want you to know." She disengaged herself from von der Heiden.

"But the British Embassy wanted it," said Antonio. "I meant to call you but they wouldn't let me. And I obeyed."

CHAPTER THIRTY-ONE

"LOOK WHAT I FOUND IN THE BACK OF THE CAR this morning. It's yours, isn't it?"

She took the gun back wearily. "I'm so tired, Antonio. I can't go through with it any more. I had to go to Prietzmann's again and tell Heinrich. He acted as if he believed everything."

Antonio offered her a cigarette she did not seem to see. "He probably does."

"Actually, I think he believes in my good faith. But it's more than I can stand. I can't bear the strain anymore. What did it all mean? Why do they play cat and mouse? I'm not important enough to spare, even if they're not sure where I stand."

"You are. Aside from the Nagel affair, your information has been of value to them. And for your protection, our side is determined to make it appear even more so."

"They must take me for a moron if they believe me."

"Not a moron, but a girl whom they've forced into a métier for which she had neither taste nor talent. The image is perfect."

"Perhaps so, but I can't go on. I'm so terrified I'd only make blunders."

"No, you won't," said Antonio. "In fact, you've been very smart. Since they apparently are so reluctant to touch you, they first wanted to see if it was absolutely necessary and, if so, if they couldn't make you do the distasteful job for them. They tried to terrorize you into confession. What else would suicide have been? It didn't work, so they thought you might confess by trying to placate their man on the pier or to make a deal with him. You've done nothing of the kind. You've reacted the only way you could have, had you been innocent. Was it presence of mind, or had you worked it out before?"

"Neither," she said. "It happened to be the only thing that occurred to me at the moment. How could I have been prepared for what actually happened? It isn't as simple as we all thought and as you still seem to be thinking."

She reached nervously for the cigarettes he had left on the table. "That man isn't just a good honest assassin but a hypnotist. Ask our all-too-innocent bystanders, our all-too-diplomatic observers. I don't think he was even supposed to touch me, just to make sure I'd go into the drink all by myself like a good girl. If nothing else, last night must have convinced them that it will take more than hypnotism to get rid of me," her laugh a wry comment on the way her allies had failed her.

"Don't be so bitter, child." Antonio reached into his pocket. "Here's the Nagel message you told him about. They concocted it during the night. Von der Heiden thinks they'll leave you alone for the time being, but I've told my people, anyway. You can reach me or leave a message at any hour of the day or night. We're not going away this summer either."

"You shouldn't have," Tony objected without conviction.

"I think we've played fair enough till now," he said. "And we're not going to deceive the embassy, believe me. I'll tell them. Tell them that you're entitled to a minimum of security. Besides, you impressed them by sparing them the inconvenience of exposing themselves in the process of protecting you."

Tony shrugged. "They didn't exactly fall all over themselves to spare me the inconvenience of protecting myself. With half of me already caught in the spell. Another few seconds and I would have gone under. He only would have had to whisper, for example, 'Shoot yourself through the temple,' and the gallant knights wouldn't have heard a word, only the shot. But forget it. What, by the way, did Maria Teresa and Carlota say?"

"Carlota was, of course, enthusiastic and quixotically ready to burn at the stake for you," he smiled, "and María Teresa was in gentle tears, planning to whisk you off to the South Pole if necessary, chaperoned and all."

"I wish she could," mumbled Tony. She was quite empty, experiencing little joy at having been spared death, only apprehension at how to go on living. There was something ominous in the past night's anticlimax, more threatening in its opacity than violence.

"Von der Heiden says one of the two was an American," said Antonio. "Tom O'Shean. You remember Pat talked to us about him? It looks like the

Yankees are finally getting more watchful and active. It won't be long now before they come in."

Where would it blow Pat? Into intelligence, battlefield reporting? They might send him anywhere . . . "Yeah," she said, "the British wouldn't even stick their own necks out." She could not get over her bitterness.

"Who is that grey man, Antonia?"

She shrugged. "Von der Heiden says they never mentioned the man to him. There had been rumors that a submarine brought in an agent from Germany. Stephan thinks he's to take Nagel's place. And to me of course Heinrich said that they were 'going to find the scoundrel of a British agent and string him up.' He called himself an 'ox' for being fooled and letting me walk into the trap. It makes me sick. He even confessed coyly that he was worried what the ambassador was going to think of him."

"He doesn't even begin to know how much he's got to worry about," said Antonio, smiling. "So the grey man's a big shot?"

"It seems so. Come to think of it," she said thoughtfully, "the British could have caught him last night if they had not wanted him to whitewash me. Imagine how easy it would have been. It should have been more important to kill him than to keep me alive. They could even have made it appear that I killed him, with no involvement on their part." She hesitated. "I take back what I said."

"You're becoming a crack agent, Antonieta," he teased, "ready to sacrifice everything for king and country."

"King and country," she repeated, her face brittle.

"I'm sorry," he said contritely. "Let's make it dignity and justice."

She was no longer listening. "Now I've seen a concrete example of what Fleming called 'a limited degree of protection.' The British made the concession of letting the grey man live so he could submit my certificate of good conduct, but stopped short of exposing themselves in order to give this certificate credibility. That's about it, isn't it?" She pocketed the letter and stood up.

While brushing her hair on the same evening, she remembered don Federico's epigram, "a tough life makes one as hard and brilliant as a diamond." Why could she not use, for conquest, the same weapons this tough life had taught her to wield for defense?

But conquer what? Happiness? She had felt truly happy in the harbor, when for a second she had believed herself on the way home. Where else was there to go, what else was there to find? At best, sleep. Beside Pat. And later perhaps, but only after a long, long sleep, listen to him, look at him, feel him again. She closed her eyes. To feel as she had felt beside him.

She or someone else who no longer existed. Or was the same girl still there, waiting?

She opened her eyes and gazed at the white face in the mirror as one would look at an old friend whom one had not seen for years. The slanting eyes were still pensive, though not as soft, rigid in the emaciated face that had lengthened beyond an oval. The mouth of a stranger, thin and tight-lipped, not quite embittered but frustrated and aloof. Above it all, her father's large, lucid forehead and, beneath, his pointed chin, more than pointed now, sharp, almost hooked.

The eyes said no, the struggle is too hard, the sacrifice too great, the outcome too uncertain, though the forehead dreamed and the chin was defiant. How would her father have felt about her present face? She remembered a misty November afternoon in the library at Potsdam when he had read to her from Schleiermacher's *Catechism of Reason for Noble Women*. "Observe the Sabbath of your heart so you celebrate it. And if they restrain you, free yourself, or perish."

She thought of Stephan von der Heiden, the love he gave her, the friendship now joining them, and grew afraid.

"And if they restrain you, free yourself, or perish," she quoted to Antonio when they met the next day.

"'To observe the Sabbath of one's heart' means to be loyal to oneself, to remain whole and to not give oneself up," countered Antonio. "To observe the Sabbath of one's heart does not mean to shirk the demands of daily existence. Besides, it's impossible. How are you going to get a visa? Why, you don't even have a passport."

"Everything has its price."

"And so?"

She looked at him for a long moment. "And so . . . Pat said that whatever I did so we could see each other again was well done. It might work."

"No matter what to keep alive, that's what he had in mind," said Antonio. "But what is it that might work, Antonieta? You scare me."

"Von der Heiden wants to help me."

"But would he help you to join Pat? He's in love with you. That's the basis of his helpfulness. He would have to be a saint to help you *malgré tout*. And he isn't. What then?"

"I don't know, Antonio." She sighed heavily. "I don't know. But I must try. I think he will."

"And not seek vengeance or destroy you and himself in despair?"

"He may not," she said. "He isn't like other people that you can judge. He's got two souls."

The British Embassy had worked it out very carefully. A few weeks after the message she had invented at the spur of that dreadful moment with the grey man, Tony handed von der Heiden another.

When von der Heiden gave it to Heinrich, the man's chuckle was genuine. "So they're keeping us posted." He leaned forward, confidentially. "You know that I'd never really stopped worrying about that woman? Those fellows have done us a favor by sending along their 'gray man,' as you call him."

Stephan said nothing.

Heinrich blinked, then went on. "There are a few things that puzzle me. How did the British know we suspected Larson? How did they get hold of Nagel's junk? But," he shrugged, "no matter how smart they think they are, we'll catch the guy and he'll tell before he swings."

The fleshy rolls were there again and also the unconscious giggle interpolated between his lies.

CHAPTER THIRTY-TWO

SUMMER SUN FELL FROM BETWEEN THE CANVAS curtains onto the dry, tinsel-covered branches of Tony's spindly Christmas tree. The light made it look garish, like an old hag ball-gowned in broad daylight. Yet it was evening, and she remembered the icy black Christmas Eves in Potsdam. Christmas in midsummer seemed in bad taste and Holy Night with von der Heiden in worse taste, but she was determined to banish childhood memories for a scheme that had shaped up so slowly it lost much of its sense.

With America in the war since the seventh of the month, it was unlikely that Pat would long remain in Europe. If he went back to the States the door would shut her out until war's end. But he was still in France; she was doggedly sure that he would have sent her a signal through Antonio, O'Shean, or his newspaper if he had moved. So she was pursuing her immediate goal to join him as if, once attained, everything would take care of itself.

She let down the heavy blinds against the day. She and Pat should have been trimming a spruce together somewhere in a cold, snow-muffled winter night. But she must not think of him, nor, for that matter, of this evening's guest. She must attune her mood to an imaginary man, as she had at sixteen, expectant and almost in love, not knowing with whom.

When the doorbell rang, she drank a hurried glass of champagne. Stephan stopped in the bay from the vestibule. His style and distinction, as had happened before, touched an unwilling chord in her and exacted a grudging mental tribute. A glow of more than candlelight fell over his pale face as he noticed the tree.

"Merry Christmas," he said, and she, her cheeks flushed from the hasty drink, furtively slid the glass behind the rose basket he had sent.

"Merry Christmas."

He kissed her in a new way, different from the early reluctant probings, from the self-conscious fondling that had followed the stormy afternoon in the garçonnière, different too from the solemn kiss of the fear-shaken spring night that had conveyed a pledge of loyalty and protection. There was a new element of devotion and groping for affection. She found it easy to respond because it demanded tenderness, not passion. The pitch of his mood suited her to perfection.

They watched the candles burn down, the sweet, heavy smoke of Turkish cigarettes mingling with the scent of singed, glowing pine needles, and listened to Praetorius' Noël drenched in the clamor of church bells.

"Antonie," he said, "I don't know about you, only that you feel my love. I do love you."

She felt as though she had lived through this before and that whatever in those submerged times had followed had been full of anguish. She did not answer.

"It's natural, and then again it is not," he went on, as if unmindful of her silence. "If origins matter, you might say that we are worlds apart. In you, courage blends with the weary wisdom of a sorely tried people. On my side, my mother's Rhenish insouciance should have infused a bit of warmth into my father's rigid Junker stock. Though it seems," he laughed, "that in my particular case something went wrong. I'm some sort of moral changeling."

She liked his young, inconspicuous laugh. It was one of his good points. She smiled, at a loss for an answer as always when he touched on anything personal.

"But it seems," he continued, "as if a capricious sculptor had carved us both from the same block. He's given us different forms and dedicated us to different idols. But we spring from the same rock."

Oh my God, she thought impatiently, the German *Gefühlsduselei,* the sentimentalism, the schoolboy romanticism. It's phony or embarrassing or both. The sense of déjà vu had disintegrated, only the frustration remained and the gêne she felt for him.

He saw the irony in her face, lit a cigarette, and said nervously, "I know what you think of me: I've debased myself, have made myself vile, have soiled my hands. The rabble around me has cut scars into me. They cannot be polished off, I know, but believe me, they don't go deep."

He looked at her, excited, tense, desperate. "I love you with all that's good and fine in me. I love you as the part of myself that I have lost."

The last words seemed to carry his soul to the surface of his eyes, and touched her despite herself.

Still without an answer, he looked at her in consternation before the words rushed on. "I'm weak and there lies my strength, my ability to survive. Any hand can shape me." He laughed sarcastically. "They used to say I was a gentle child, soft and yielding, clay in any potter's hand. Well, I let myself bend, and so I don't break. With the stronger, I am good or vile; one can push me and drag me, and I cannot resist."

She knew that he wanted to hear from her "be good with me." He had given her a cue, handed her a line that by herself she would have been hard put to find and afraid to use. Her moment had come, easier than she had dared to hope. But her spirit resisted the breach of trust against one, the fraud against another.

Refilling their cups, he now seemed calmer, sounded more matter-of-fact. "Antonie, if you . . . " he paused, "if you love me—after all I did to you, you wouldn't share your Christmas with me if it weren't so—if you love me, stay with me. Someday we will maneuver ourselves out of this swamp."

Though to him her face was cryptic, she knew exactly what she should now say to win, but could not get it across her lips.

"I know, I'm lower for you than a worm. I know." At last he fell silent, as if he had ejected all the mire that had accumulated within him and did not feel any cleaner for it.

Wax from burnt-down candles was dropping in large blotches onto the branches, their twitching little fire-heads throwing a honey-colored glow over walls and furniture. She felt very intensely his physical nearness, a temptation to stretch out her hand and touch him, a tingling, sweet, unalloyed eroticism. Oh no, she thought. Then, go ahead now, you'll never feel like this again.

"I'm no more of one piece than you," she said in a tremulous voice, "in a way, I'm attached to you, too. We've both given ourselves up. We live all alone. No one resembles us. I suppose we belong together. But I'm tired. I can't struggle any more. Fight it out for me, Stephan."

The vibration of her voice sounded helpless, exhausted, tender. Through the hum of the champagne in her head she was listening to herself.

It was as fitting, as natural, and seemingly genuine as if she were watching a stage performance—or as if she were really feeling it.

He leaned his forehead against her shoulder. "What do you want me to do?"

"I don't know. But let me go away from here. As long as I'm here there's only one way out. I can't go on living. But if I could go away . . . "

The ground slipped from under his feet. "Antonie, why?" he asked in dismay. "I cannot live without you."

"And I cannot live with you, not here," she said. "I have friends in Switzerland I could stay with while I find the way back to myself. Then we could meet anew. Then it won't be a continuation of our shameful experience. Stephan, I want to free myself, to be clean and . . . " She knew that the truth she was about to speak would strike a chord in Stephan von der Heiden, whose Antonie had been a fearless, self-sufficient girl, ". . . and not be afraid any more. Always afraid."

Maybe he did not fully believe her, but if she only wanted freedom without him, he would give it to her. With it he freed a part of his own, the part he loved in himself, like the memory of someone long since dead.

And when the candles had burnt down, he lay awake. The girl in his arms had wound herself around him in sleep like a slender bright flag come to rest. She had not poured herself out joyfully—as he felt she might have, to another, at another time and in another place—nor passively bound herself over to his will. She had given herself into his hands with the vibrant resonance of an accordant lute.

She sighed and raised her head. The thin ray of a lantern filtering through the blinds fell on her face. A child, he thought. Her hard, flat thigh lying across his body rendered the scent of excitement and perfume. This and the premonition that he would not hold her long, reignited his appeased desire. Under its urge, still in her sleep, she slowly stirred. He knew that this sharp want would dominate him inexorably, at every hour and with equal vehemence, as if each embrace were to be the last.

CHAPTER THIRTY-THREE

TONY'S WORK HAD BEEN REORGANIZED. Antonio's initiative to inform his family had met with only qualified approval from the British Embassy and had prompted doubled precautions. She was put in touch with another, more impersonal agent, which made her reunions with Antonio very rare. The crisscross bus and subway rides, the hurried words in front of a show window, the perilous meetings in out-of-the-way cafés began once more.

She had followed Pat's advice unquestioningly, trusting his judgment and knowing that he would not expose her to undue risks. She had derived an even greater sense of security from the simple knowledge that he was there. She had little confidence in his successor and Antonio's presence did not give her the moral support Pat's had.

Yet Pat had vanished as if he had never existed. At times she wondered if she had only dreamed him and their time together. She was convinced that he still cared. A love too mute and intangible to be of help. Not wanting to hang on to illusions, she told herself that Pat belonged to the past, that she would never see him again. If not a dream, he was equally substanceless.

Obviously, it was not she, but Pat, who had withdrawn from their life. But in trying to regain her hold, hadn't she shut him out for good? Not because of von der Heiden—Pat would have understood—but by reacting to Stephan as a lover would. Their bodies had flowered from the débris of their souls in a few ardent nights, taking the place of all they would never have in common. They now tended what they shared with all the emotion lavished on a single possession.

But when she had a love dream, she dreamed of Pat. The more she realized that they had been shunted onto relentlessly divergent roads, the more she rebelled, the more obsessive became her purpose to force a cantankerous fate to rescind.

For New Year's Eve, Stephan had sent her Heidsieck and Bordeaux, of which there was plenty only at the German Embassy.

The evening passed silently. Stephan was depressed and restless; Tony was waiting for news. They did not allude to this pending matter, but the hours dragged until finally they heard the church bells and Stephan refilled their cups for an uncertain toast. When the bells fell silent, he set his glass down. "A new year. A better one for you, I hope."

"And for you."

"I don't know, Antonie. You do love me, don't you?"

"Yes, Stephan, I guess I do. Why do you ask?"

"I just want to be reassured, again and again. I know it. You're beautiful and loveable and could have escaped this nightmare by marrying one of those influential Argentine society men. Nobody would have dared to touch you then. But you didn't. It may be presumptuous, but I badly want to believe that I know why."

Tony remembered Romero Basualdo and how close she had come to taking that shortcut out of her troubles when they had only just begun. At the time, betrayal of someone loved and trusted had seemed dishonorable, and even the idea of having to practice it on her enemies had bothered her. Since then it had become her only friend and aid.

Her eyes turned to him but went past and beyond. "Yes, I wanted to wait." She was writing aloud the letter to Pat she had never sent, had never been allowed to set on paper, full of the countless small things of which her kind of belonging was made up. "I wanted a home for us . . . friends who would be ours . . . to live at your side, my head by your shoulder, freely and a little proudly . . . to go to the theater . . . and then you'd unlock our door . . . and your wardrobe would not be strange to me . . . Do you know the peculiar feeling when one sees someone's open wardrobe for the first time? It's like throwing a glance into his personality, as if suddenly one had gained access to something very intimate."

Stephan smiled a small, sad smile. His forehead was tense, one eyebrow raised as happened when he was in pain. "We're going to have all that, Antonie. I have good news for you."

She was startled out of her reverie, back to him. "What, Stephan?"

"After the holidays you will receive a visa for Portugal."

When he saw the tears the nervous shock had driven into her eyes, he put an arm around her shoulder and waited.

"How?" she asked, incredulous.

"I know a Jew here, a very rich man who has a way of getting visas for such countries."

"But for you?"

"For anyone who can pay for them. There's so much filth in the world, Antonie. He thinks you're going for us, or he might have been too scared."

"A Jew—Stephan, that's impossible!"

He smiled. "There are Jews here who administer Goering's and Himmler's money, another works for the Gestapo . . . but that's only natural. All people have their traitors."

"How much does he ask?"

He hesitated. "That's the trouble. I don't have enough, Antonie. He wants twenty thousand."

"That's all right. I've got it."

"I hate to ask you for it. But Gálvez has all but drained my resources, and I couldn't bring in any from abroad now without causing suspicion. Do you understand?"

"Of course. I wouldn't let you, anyway."

He passed over the embarrassing point swiftly and emphatically. "As soon as he gets your passport visaed you can leave. The same man takes care of your transportation. Once you're gone, I'll get myself a safe and very 'undiplomatic' passport. But I can't while it might endanger you."

She thought of what would become of him once he realized that she had only used him, that he was once more alone, with no hold, no friend, no raison d'être. There was no shutting her eyes to the fact that he had unhesitantly decided to barter his life away for her escape and that his staying behind made him a hostage.

For the love of one woman, she argued, for the impact of seven burning nights he does this, while a whole humanity bleeding to death, year in and year out, had been impotent to shake him into action. And yet, she did not want anything to happen to him.

He put his hand on hers. "Antonie, I cannot go with you. You understand that, don't you? Are you now afraid of the journey?" He came, like her, from a world where women were afraid, even of travel. She shook her head, the room blurred by tears.

He had never seen her cry, not even on the night when her life had hung in the balance. The thought that tonight she was crying for him took wings, tore the pain up by its roots, carried it whole and unmitigated upward into jubilant agony. The ultimate pulse beat of Iseult; had he died at this instant he would have considered himself well served.

When he was gone she went to stand by the open window. But there was no breeze to cool her. The summer hung outside, hot and heavy, under an overcast sky, smelling of dust. She looked into the darkness. Here and there exploded a belated firecracker. A tipsy company passed by her house singing *La Cumparsita*. Then laughter again, a drunken shout, and once more silence.

She tried to think of how it would be when Argentina was far away, when she would see Pat. But her brain was whirling.

Shortly after toasting the New Year, most of the younger people escaped the Yacht Club's formal atmosphere. Carlota and Fernando went to the Gong and then drove out for a nightcap to La Tour d'Argent.

Fernando laughed as they stepped into the garden. "I wish you'd go and powder your nose, my dear. I'd hate to propose to a beacon."

"Don't be an idiot," she drawled. "If you're sure you won't propose to a shiny nose, let's sit down and be comfortable."

When she saw herself in her pocket mirror, she only thought drowsily, who isn't disheveled on New Year's Day, at two o'clock in the morning? I don't want to dazzle anyone. After the sultry night in town, she felt comfortable in the breeze, and her dance-weary feet rested gratefully and slipperless on the soft lawn. With a contented smile, she ordered a crème de menthe frappé.

"Crème de menthe!" Fernando winced. "What a hideous anticlimax. You might as well drink Chanel No. 5."

"Except that you couldn't pay for it," she teased.

Fernando's limited means had become a constant subject for quips between them. When, in a sarcastic mood, she had told him that his indigence was at the bottom of his ardor for her, he had picked up the cue with glee and ever since kept reassuring her that there was nothing more to it.

Now he laughed his cackling laugh. "Just wait till we have a joint account. You'll bathe in Chanel. Because, as I was heard to remark before, I want to marry you. I love you, Madam, and I am determined to become the prince consort."

When the waiter had left the drinks, he turned his face to her fully. It looked even more sallow than usual in the beam of a floodlight streaming from between the black branches of a giant pine. "I'm serious, Carlota, I want you for my wife."

She tipped her chair back wearily. "Oh, Fernandito, why must you be such a bore when I'm having a good time? Let's skip it. I've given you my answer often enough."

"I know you don't love me," he said lightly. "So I'm just what the doctor ordered for you. I love you, but not enough to tyrannize you. I have enough money to keep you from being ashamed of your match, yet not so much as to make you hesitate to jilt me when you're fed up with me, or to brave my masterful wrath when you fancy a minor escapade. Besides, Carlota Guerida Paz Dorrego Macín de Belmán Iriguren would sound splendid."

"With the drawback," said Carlota slowly, "that my children would be just as likely to turn out little Belmán Irigurens as little Guerida Pazes. No, dear, I'm not going to take a chance on that."

"There are some pretty respectable people in my family, you know? They might take after a mutual great-uncle of ours, don Horacio Guerida Belmán, who never possessed a woman, including his own wife, and died of acute indigestion at eighty."

"I'm most anxious to produce a replica," she said mildly, "but those admirable traits can come down through the Gueridas without the kind assistance of the Belmáns."

His face had turned into an incongruously mournful mask. "We're fooling—and fooling ourselves out of our happiness. Promise, on this first day of the year, that you will give it some serious thought for once."

"All right, Fernandito. But the more you insist, the less I feel like putting up with your inane chatter all my life—or even part of it. Let's go."

As they drove past the spot in Palermo Park where more than a year ago the Herrnfeld girl had stepped out of his car, he grimaced.

"May I make a guess why you've stopped seeing Tony Herrnfeld?" he asked.

"But I do see her!" she protested. "What makes you think I don't?"

"The fact that you don't. And it's because I was right and she's a Nazi spy."

"You're crazy."

"I'm not," he countered emphatically. "And I will tell you why. There's a fellow who used to go to school with me. He's nothing but the son of an upstart colonel, but as a former classmate I grace him with my condescension. One evening this spring I met him at the Pancho bar, and he promised me such a splendid dinner as my destitute stomach had not known in quite a while.

"So my gluttonous disposition—inherited along with a few debts from Uncle Guerida Belmán who, poor gentleman, died of it—could not resist. Good old Gálvez seems to be in the money all of a sudden. Where he gets it no one knows, but you can never tell when you might need a touch . . . for instance, to buy an engagement ring worthy of a Guerida Paz. He got himself tight and began to boast of his friendship with a secretary of the German Embassy, and of his affair with a beautiful Jewess who works for the Germans. He said very clearly, Antonie Errrnfeld. Now, frankly, I believe that Juancito Gálvez is working for them himself—come to think of it, that's where the lobster and champagne are coming from. But I'm not one to mind other people's business," he concluded with coy candor.

"But you do mind Tony's," Carlota said tartly. "Besides, you're sadly off track. There's nothing to it."

"If you don't believe me, ask Gálvez himself." Belmán was strangely anxious to discredit Tony in her eyes.

"Of course, she wouldn't tell you. She's the greatest hypocrite. She wouldn't say to your face either what she's said to me about you."

So that's it, thought Carlota, her drowsiness swept away by Belmán's account. You've gossiped to her about me and are deadly afraid she might have told. "If you ever talk about Tony to me again—or to anyone else, we're through. Do you hear me?"

He, too, was aroused now. It was the first time that she saw him in a genuine temper, like a snake poised for attack. "You won't hear another word from me about her. But others will! This frustrated Gretchen isn't going to get away with it in society. Soon enough everyone will know."

Carlota was struggling, one argument shouting down another. If only she were not feeling so giddy. Why did Belmán have to talk about it tonight, after all those drinks? Why did he have a tongue at all? People who could not control their tongues should not have any. She thought of the medieval practice of depriving tongue-waggers of theirs as the simplest way out at this moment.

Finally she said heavily, "Look here, Fenandito, I promise that I will consider you for a husband—consider, mind you, not accept—if for once you will keep from gossiping. You think you can?"

"If I must," he tittered, all his temper gone.

"All right," she sighed, "because if you don't, you only help the Germans." As soon as she had said this, she felt cold. The dregs of her intoxication dissolved, and she looked back upon the words uttered a second ago as if upon something done a long time ago, in a mood now incomprehensible.

She continued frantically. "Now, Fernando, I'm very serious about this. Tony's person is sacred to me. Swear that you're not going to talk about her to anyone! Swear by . . ." She reflected who was the most treasured person in his life. "Swear by your life!"

"I swear by my life, which is yours," he said gravely. His face was stunned. For the first time he had stumbled on something too tall to be laughed down upon.

CHAPTER THIRTY-FOUR

THE TELEPHONE RANG EARLY on New Year's morning. Tony, sitting up in bed, heard Carlota's voice. "Tony? I must see you! How can we arrange that?"

"Happy New Year. Glad you remember an old friend on this day. Would you like to have breakfast with me?"

"Happy New Year to you," echoed Carlota, abashed by Tony's stiff reaction. "I'll be right over."

She knew Carlota's impulsiveness, but even so this call was puzzling. When she arrived, they embraced and then just stood and looked at each other, laughed a little, and embraced again. "Oh, Carlota, how glad I am! I said those things on the telephone because my line may be tapped."

"Tapped? Oh, you mean, watched. So that's why! I thought you were still resentful. What an ass I've been to set myself up in judgment. If I'd been sensible and talked it over with you, we'd never have been separated. You would have explained."

"I don't think I would have," smiled Tony. "It would always have been the same."

"Too bad we can't act, even now, as if nothing had happened. I shouldn't have called you, I suppose. Oh, what an idiot I am."

"You're all right, dear. Sit down. I've made some coffee. Have a cigarette." She handed her the case, and Carlota whistled. "Blond tortoiseshell and gold! Christmas present?"

"Yeah. I'll tell you about that later. Let me get the coffee." When she returned with the tray and was pouring the coffee, she asked, "What's on your mind, Carlota?"

Her cousin's face fell. After a slight hesitation she said, "I don't know how to tell you. I've failed you again. I'm a wretch."

When she had finished her confession, Tony tried unsuccessfully not to show how shocked she was, "Why did you tell him, Carlota? I know you meant well, but it was very foolish."

"I know. What am I to do, Tony? I'll do anything to fix it."

"Nothing, dear, just keep your fingers crossed." Tony smiled briefly, but then, against her will, she put her hand over her eyes. "It's terrible . . . "

When she looked up, Carlota was crying. "Never, as long as I live, am I going to touch another drop of liquor! But it wasn't the drinks alone. I would never have breathed a word, drunk or asleep, had he not started all that talk and sounded so damned determined to make trouble. I thought, at the moment, I was doing the right thing. But, I guess, my mind was all muddled." She sighed helplessly.

"Maybe it won't matter," said Tony soothingly. "Danger never comes from where you see it. It always pops up at unexpected places."

"You're great, Tony." Carlota lifted a tear-stained face. "How I hate that damned little snake now." She took a hearty swallow of hot coffee, sniffling a little and wiping her eyes and nose with the back of her hand.

"Haven't you always? Tell me, Carlota, you haven't become interested in Fernandito?"

"Interested?" repeated Carlota, astonished at such an assumption. "What's interesting about him? He wants to marry me, though, and that will shut him up."

"No, Carlota, you're not going to marry him."

"Are you afraid I might get hurt? By the kind of well-meaning impulsiveness by which I usually only hurt my friends?" She laughed bitterly.

"Don't be silly. Will you or won't you?"

"You'd better tell me about your beau," Carlota said. "Let me see that cigarette case again."

While she was examining it, Tony thought, I'm not going to tell her, after this. I'm not going to tell her anything. "Have you told your father about last night?"

Carlota's eyes were worried. "No, I haven't. Should I?"

"It's quite unnecessary." She was going to spare her that, her and Antonio. She thought of how proud he had been of her for protecting a friend even after love and respect were gone. She would only ask him not to speak to Carlota of her current plans.

"What a life you have, Tony. I didn't even know that telephones could be—what did you call it?—tapped and all those things."

"It's just a question of getting used to it," said Tony wearily. "Once you're used to it, half the danger is eliminated."

January passed without definite news about the papers. One difficulty followed another. By February Stephan's agent produced a forged Paraguayan passport, made her sign it, and took it back with the promise to return it, complete with the Portuguese visas. He worked slowly, putting them off from day to day, from week to week, and Stephan himself seemed to be losing confidence in him. During the middle of February the man asked for more money to pay another bribe, and still the visa was only a mirage, making them doubt the validity of the passport itself. However, she made her preparations as if all were certain and true. Once she held those dangerous papers in her hand like a lighted fuse she would have to use them immediately.

Into this confusion there came Peter's announcement of his engagement. He seemed too young to marry, his bride was eighteen, and in normal circumstances she would have asked him in a long, careful letter to think it over. Now she was glad that he at least had thrown roots and belonged somewhere. A little later he wrote that his prospective family would call on her in the first days of March. At about the same time Antonio brought the news that Carlota had accepted Fernando Belmán's proposal.

The two girls met on one of Tony's secret visits at the estanzuela and rode down to the same spot by the river where three years earlier they had experienced their first moment of mutual understanding. Carlota gazed across the Paraná which was grey, as it had been then. "I'll always have this."

"Yes, you will. You're not alone. So you can wait," Tony hesitated, "wait for the man who'll be your peer. Someone you love."

Without turning her eyes from the river, Carlota shrugged and quoted: "Yet each man kills the thing he loves. It's safer not to love at all."

"Why Portugal?" asked Antonio. "Didn't you tell him you wanted to go to Switzerland?"

"Yes, but the Portuguese visa can be had with a Paraguayan passport. Mainly with a little Axis influence. The Swiss are a suspicious race. Besides, Portugal's not bad. If I can get into Spain, with my South American passport and accent I should have less trouble getting across the French border than I would from Switzerland."

"You scare me, Antonieta. Aren't you worried?"

"Sure I am. But I can't stay here. You know better than I that the British can't really use me any longer. Over there it'll be different."

"Don't be silly, Antonie," he pleaded. "Come to the house, live with us. They're not going to send their goons into my home, are they?"

"Why do you pretend not to understand, Antonio?" she said impatiently. "You know very well that I must—you hear me?—must be near Pat."

She stood with her back to him, looking through the window into the sun-scorched garden, the same window that more than two years ago had streamed with the rain of a tepid grey spring afternoon. *Doch alles, was uns anrührt, dich und mich, nimmt uns zusammen wie ein Bogenstrich, der aus zwei Saiten eine Stimme zieht . . .*

She had held herself out to this love, had submissively and joyfully, almost gratefully, received Pat like a dedicated vessel, while Stephan had taught her the pleasure of giving, guided her hand, her whole being, as one would teach a young girl to choose and bind and dispose flowers. She knew that probably no one else could have opened the door for her in just such a way into just such a garden, where she was losing herself every evening, aware that her wandering led her farther away from the life she should have lived. But then it did not seem to matter, it was far, so far away.

"I must go," she said and wondered if Antonio really understood why.

Peter's engagement was to be made official at Carlota's engagement party in March. To be with them, Tony was determined to brave the British Embassy's possible annoyance. On the preceding day she would receive his bride and her family; her own problem thus momentarily pushed into the background when the unexpected happened. She received her papers.

For an instant it seemed one of her fancy daydreams had come true. Then she reminded herself that anything was still liable to interfere before or during that very night when her plane was to cross the Brazilian border. Until that second she must remain prepared for a catastrophe. Told of her intention, Stephan thought it was good; if any suspicions should be alive anywhere, nothing could look more innocent than being at an engagement party.

So on the day of Peter's arrival she found herself in a whirl of preparations of the most incongruous kind, very nervous and hardly conscious of herself. She felt that this call of her in-laws was very important for her brother, regretted being but his twin, not an old maid sister of forty, providing a better background for him.

Placing chocolates on two small silver trays, she thought about the four hundred grams—one fork, one knife, two spoons—that emigrants could take along from Germany. Imagined Peter bringing his bride to Potsdam, along the poplar-lined drive across the esplanade, into the drawing room to sit by the fireplace facing the French windows that fronted wide lawns. Their parents coming through the two-leafed door from the library, their gentle voices self-assured. Tea poured from silver into Dresden china cups. Peter's family welcoming his bride.

With a sigh, a glare at the yellow canvas curtains, and a shake of her head at her own snobbery, she went to get the chipped Limoges cups she had once bought at auction from the municipal pawn shop.

She was glad when Peter and his fiancée arrived alone. Her parents, held up, would join them later. She was small, childlike, and extremely pretty. What impressed Tony most was her gentleness and evident adoration of Peter. There was nothing pretentious or artificial about her. Her reddish brown hair was combed out in a long pageboy, the hazel eyes were wide awake but without shrewdness, her mouth friendly and clearly outlined.

Tony's eyes kept wandering from her to Peter and back. She was struck by his resemblance to their father in physical appearance as well as in his choice of a child-bride. After all, nothing was destroyed entirely; creating a man like Peter, their parents had laid the foundation of their own continuance. Hugo's son would again seek a woman like Dolores, and maybe relive with her the happiness his elders had not known how to retain.

But when his future parents-in-law arrived, it was only too evident that the past could never be resurrected. They were pleasant people of an easy warmth that removed all barriers of strangeness. But they sat down in her chairs as if in a hotel lobby and patronized her in her own home. They called the twins "children," and invited Tony to come and live on their estate with them. They offered her protection and gave her to understand that they intended to be a new, loving family to them who had no country, no home, no family of their own.

She would have liked to know if they had an inkling of Peter's secret activities. It was unimaginable, as unimaginable as the fact that she could not ask him if they knew, and that he, by the same token, knew nothing of her.

CHAPTER THIRTY-FIVE

STEPHAN CAME TO SAY GOOD-BYE. Tony was ready to go to the party, he was on his way to a white tie reception, wearing formal attire with the easy elegance of those who have lived in it half of their waking hours. She could not repress a twinge of pain at the thought that he found himself in a hopeless shipwreck. It could not be otherwise, because he had come to her with the unclean hands of an unclean people. She had given him, not knowing whether from strength or weakness, whatever her heart was able to give. She had left in these final nights in his arms a tormented part of it, but now she was dropping strange moorings, her sails were set for home.

She wondered whether he felt it, because his eyes reached for and imprisoned her. Agitated as she was, they added to the restlessness that showed in her own eyes, making them wider, more vivacious.

He watched her move about, in mauve lace, her first ball gown yet, so long ago; her slender arms and thin, faintly veined hands moving, it seemed to him, with unusual lightness under the weight of her mother's bracelets. Shackles on white wings, he thought. When she takes them off tonight, she'll be free.

They had little time left and he was brimming with countless things he felt he must say before it was too late, things of no material value, their content inexpressible. So, his voice filled with them, he merely repeated his directives.

"As soon as you arrive, you get in touch with Konrad von Landen. You've memorized the address, haven't you?" She nodded. "Again, don't write it down. If you forget, you'll surely find it in the telephone directory, since it's the mail slot for the European Free German Movement he heads. I told you that he doesn't think too highly of me just now, but he's a childhood friend. The one who told me of the circumstances of my father's death.

And I know you'll be able to explain to him. Through him you'll also hear from me. Antonie, it will be soon, believe me."

There was a tense pause that he broke in a matter-of-fact tone. "If there's a change in schedule, I'll send you a message. But I don't think it will be necessary."

When they said good-bye, he put his hands on her shoulders. "You love me, don't you? I'm no fool, it is all true?" The bareness of her skin transmitted his touch to her entire body, making her melt into him, into the prison around which she had so agitatedly fluttered all evening.

She endured his eyes, put her arms around him and hid her face on his shoulder. "I do, Stephan, I do. You must believe me." Only if he did would he want to live.

Although she had long since realized the superfluity of deceit, she had shunned the cruelty of confession, and now she sometimes tormented herself asking to what degree it would still be valid. She would go to Konrad von Landen and ask him to help, even if it meant finessing his actions prior to 1941. More she could not give.

He took her head in both hands. A long, almost possessive, surely desperate, kiss, a final supplication for love and loyalty. Then he turned and left quickly, a little stooped, like one who shuts his eyes to walk into the water.

Tony bit her knuckles not to cry. She tried to remember her childhood, her parents, her miserable life of the past years. She told herself of the newspaper accounts of deportation, ghettos, and massacres. It made no difference. She would always be like this, give to everyone she knew a piece of her heart, weep with and cling to everyone who clung to her.

The spacious garden on Avenida Alvear was astir with billowy dresses. White tuxedoes shone from among broad-limbed *plátanos* and *gomeros* where Chinese lanterns swung gently in the night breeze. After the last of a tango series, the Típica band was being replaced by an international one. Most of the guests had already left the buffet on the terrace, and were sitting scattered across the wide lawns. A few couples had begun to use the marble dance floor.

Doña María Teresa and her husband stood on the almost deserted terrace, listening to a slow Mexican waltz, watching Tony's mauve silhouette turn and turn among brighter ones.

"She's much more beautiful than her mother," he said.

"She has more distinction. Do you think she gets it from her father?"

Don Antonio nodded. "Yes. I once saw him, in Paris. He was impressive."

After the first round, they saw Federico Dorrego Macín walk up to Tony, who then seemed to be making an apology to her partner. The young man bowed and walked away.

"He can't leave it alone, can he?" María Teresa smiled somewhat acidly.

With the introductory bars, Tony put her hand on don Federico's shoulder, aware that her contemporaries were smiling, but that the waltz belonged more truly to his generation than to theirs.

"You look more and more like your mother," he said. Something in his voice startled her. She had missed the usual light irony and, aware of her surprise, he smiled. "You don't believe I really loved her, do you? You think I've always been a cynical old man. But I wasn't quite thirty when I met her in Vienna. She was barely fifteen. She told me she loved me, too, and permitted me to kiss the tip of her nose."

Tony laughed. "That was a greater mark of affection than you would think! She always kissed us on the nose."

"I courted her for several years, and I think she rather liked it. But I don't believe she's ever really had more than affection for me. Frankly, I'm afraid I made her laugh."

"Haven't you ever talked to her in earnest?" Tony asked curiously.

"She was such a child. It would have seemed monstrous to speak to her of marriage. But she was my only true love. When she married, I simply couldn't picture her as a wife."

"She's been the best wife in the world," Tony said, a little piqued.

"I know. I met your father, too. I realized then that he was the man she needed. She required a big brother, not only a husband. She was so eager to live, happy only in carefreeness. And, Lord, how she's suffered."

When the music stopped, they wandered toward the trees, along the narrow, groomed garden paths to the Andalusian patio. Inside its low walls of multicolored tile, a fountain feathered skyward. Tony sat down on the edge of the basin and let her hand trail in the water.

"Have you ever heard Mother sing?" she asked, the cascade bubbling through her quiet, somewhat smoky voice.

"Yes," he said. "Does the fountain make you think of it?"

"I guess so."

"Do you sing, too?"

"A little. Not like Mother. She taught us all her songs, though, and Peter's voice is clear like hers. Mine's husky. But she learned Lieder from us, too, and folk ballads."

He came to sit beside her. "Sing something," he said.

While she sang softly to him in her weightless, shadowy voice, Potsdam's sunny mornings, longing dusks, and its woods and lakes seemed to blot out the Andalusian patio.

> Es waren zwei Königskinder,
> Die hatten einander so lieb,
> Sie konnten zueinander nicht kommen,
> Das Wasser war viel zu tief . . .

She smiled at him. "Our Nordic ballads are always hopelessly gloomy. This one tells about a lovelorn young prince who must swim across a lake to reach his lady."

"That's not sad," he chuckled. "Young sportsmen have done more than that for a bit of loving."

"But they don't have to cope with wicked lake creatures leading them astray and making them drown."

"No, I guess not." His white hair shone in the moonlight. No longer like the gentle schoolteacher, she thought. The night has a peculiar magic; he looks like a Biblical king.

"*Con permiso.*" A waiter bowed. "There's been a message for the señorita from her apartment."

The moonbeam magic vanished without a trace, though the stars remained overhead and she was still sitting on the edge of a dancing fountain, holding a fan, wearing the satin slippers that had waltzed to the music that kept coming from far away. It was all there as before, as meaningless as the beauty of a dead face.

"But why?" asked don Federico, disappointed. "Who would call you at this hour?"

"I've been expecting a wire," she said casually. "The janitor was to call me if it arrived."

They made their way back to the party in silence, but before they stepped out from among the trees, he stopped her. "Still the same troubles, Antonieta? Why won't you let me help you? Your mother would have wanted you to."

"We'll see what the news is," she said in a callous tone. "Maybe I'll call you tomorrow." Then her voice softened. "Good-bye, don Federico. And thanks for this hour." She kissed his cheek and, after a moment's hesitation, the tip of his nose. Then she went in search of Antonio.

He was drinking champagne with Carlota and some others at one of the many "Parisian café tables" placed throughout the garden for the occasion.

"I came to say good-bye," she said more abruptly than she intended.

Antonio drew his watch in surprise. "It's only a little after eleven, Antonieta!"

"I know. But I'd better go, much as I hate to. I'm not feeling too well."

Carlota jumped up. "I'll take you home in the car!"

"No, please, don't. I'm just a little tired. I guess the excitement was too much. I want to thank you, in Peter's and my name, for this splendid party. I've enjoyed myself so much."

"Stay overnight," insisted Carlota. "Come on, I'll have them get a room ready."

"No, I'd really rather go home," Tony said unhappily.

"All right, but I'll take you."

"You can't leave your party, Carlota," said Antonio with unaccustomed sternness. "Don't make a scene."

"A scene? I don't get it." She turned away from him. "I'll take you to the gate, anyway."

"Where is María Teresa?" asked Tony relieved.

"She must be around somewhere. We'll find her on the way out." It was not long before they saw her at another table beside Peter and his fiancée.

"Good night, María Teresa. It was a lovely party. You've given Peter a home tonight."

Doña María Teresa embraced her. "We couldn't give you what is yours. But you're leaving so early? Don't forget there's only one engagement party. Until your own."

Tony smiled at her and turned to Peter. "Good night, old man." She tried to keep her voice steady. "Take care of yourself."

He patted her shoulder. "Now sister dear, no emoting. We all know that the women who cry at engagements and weddings are the same who grin hysterically at funerals."

"Don't spoil my act." She threw one arm around him and took his bride's hand, her voice easy. "Don't ever be overwhelmed by him. Always use your own judgment. Our mother—and you are very much like her—lived under Father's spell. Peter is, no matter how different their ideas, his exact replica. Good night, dear." She kissed the cool, round cheek that smelled like a baby's and, taking Carlota's arm, drew her off rather hastily.

"I was hoping you'd stay until everybody else left," said her cousin as they were walking toward the gate. "I wanted to ask you something. Couldn't I work for the British? I'm in such a rut, Tony. I need something worth living for."

Tony stopped short. The message had jerked her back to reality. She was trembling under its impact and the anticipation of the events it so abruptly brought close. But she realized how important, maybe decisive, her answer would be for Carlota.

"There is no need for you, having a country of your own, to fight oppression in others. There's enough that's wrong right here, and plenty of work to be done. Once you make up your mind to do it, people like Fernando won't even have standing room in your life."

They had reached the gate. "Good night, Carlota. I love you very much."

"Ave María! We forgot to call a cab. Let me drive you home, please."

"No, Carlota. I'd rather walk a bit. To say the truth, I have a date."

Carlota was curious. "The tortoise of the cigarette case?"

"Yes. And I'm already late."

After a short stretch down the avenue, she turned back to wait for Antonio, and when she saw him coming she slipped once more through the gate.

"What happened?" he asked, worried.

"A change in schedule, I suppose. Von der Heiden said there was a chance. We had agreed on the message."

"Are you sure it's that?"

"It can't be anything else."

Don Antonio took her in his arms. "God bless you."

"Thanks, Antonio, for all that's beyond gratitude. We'll see each other again."

"We will. Let me hear from you if you can."

"Yes, Antonio. And about Carlota—an engagement is only half a wedding."

Walking away, she felt him looking after her from the garden gate through which she was leaving their world, his and hers, and entering into another. She wanted to stay in Antonio's garden, be bridesmaid at Peter's wedding, talk to Carlota, sing to don Federico. Her brother had not blindly fluttered out of some open cage door into uncertainty like some impulsive, panicked bird, but had found a way to combine the abnormality of their present existence with a normal life.

She thought of the light that would rise in Stephan's eyes were she to tell him that she wanted to stay. She thought, Forgive me, Pat, but I'm not brave . . . although you said so. I don't want to be brave.

CHAPTER THIRTY-SIX

A FOOTMAN AT THE CASA ROSADA, the Government Palace, made his way toward Count von der Heiden and whispered that someone had called for him but then hung up. Stephan looked around apprehensively for his ambassador who, to his relief, he saw was busy trumpeting into the deaf ear of the vice president. Ramón Castillo, who had taken the reins from the hands of an ailing president only to veer sharply and immediately to the far right, was a spidery little gentleman with snow-white hair and mustache whose grandfatherly senility and haughty narrow-mindedness reminded Stephan of Pétain. As Castillo smiled he accompanied the ambassador's words with rhythmic nods so regular and uninterrupted that it was doubtful if he grasped their content.

Stephan slipped away without being caught leaving, in flagrant breach of protocol, in advance of his chief of mission. He could not imagine what mishap had caused Antonie to do such a thing.

He drove to her apartment just slowly enough to avoid an accident. When he peered through the plate glass into the dark lobby, Antonie was not there, though she knew that he could not ring for the janitor. Pushing tentatively against the heavy door, he felt it yield and noticed a small stone placed on the threshold to keep it from shutting. He raced up the steps two at a time.

His ring was answered by a call, clearly the first syllable of his name "Ste . . ." Then quiet steps, as if she were in slippers. Was she sick? He swerved around the opening door and stared, while it shut behind him, into the face of a giant.

He stepped past him without a second glance into the living room. Antonie sat between the luggage and the side table, her cloak still over her bare shoulders, her face chalky, her eyes wide with fear. On the edge of an armchair facing her, rigid and grey, sat a thin man with an empty face who looked at him without a sign of recognition, but as unsurprised as if he had been expecting him.

"What do you want here?" Stephan rasped, as if at a loiterer on his property.

"We've been waiting for you, Count," said the grey man voicelessly and with no tinge of irony. Then he turned to Tony who sat, speechless, her black eyes riveted on von der Heiden.

"I imagine this will get us ahead at last. I shall repeat for the gentleman what I told you. If you turn over all your information, all your contacts, and the names of all other Allied agents known to you, including the whereabouts of Patrick Larson, you'll be allowed to leave the country tonight, as intended."

Tony's gaze never left Stephan whose pallor had turned livid. In his eyes she saw for the first time the flame of violence. They locked with hers, and he spoke to her as if they were alone, without a glance at the grey man or heed to the thug towering behind him pressing a pistol into his back.

"Don't believe them. Watch each word."

Tony did not intend to utter any words. After wild verbal fencing against an adversary who, lifeless and stony, parried with unfailing precision, she saw no salvation in discourse.

The grey man continued as if he had not heard the interjection. "We also expect you to give us every bit of information you have about the treasonable activities of Count von der Heiden. If you refuse to speak, you will share his fate. There's no purpose in shielding him. Having stolen from his country, he'll die like a thief, by the rope. You can't save him. He is going to hang in your apartment as soon as you go, leaving a suicide note confessing his crime and the additional one of having been the lover of a Jewess. It only depends on the value of your confession whether it'll be a double suicide or not."

With this he reached into a musette bag he had placed behind him on the chair, while she thought madly, if only he weren't saying all these things in such a blank voice, it makes it even grislier. He leaned forward and placidly laid a hangman's rope on the table. She started as if at an electric

233

prod and heard Stephan, urgent, almost hysterical. "Tell them about me, Antonie! Tell them!" And turning to the grey man, "Will you let her go if she tells you that much?"

"It depends . . . ," the grey man whispered noncommittally.

"I wouldn't believe them even if they swore on the Bible. But you must try."

She only stared at him.

"Try, Antonie. You can't save me. Don't make a foolish sacrifice!"

Again he met only with silence. "I must be able to give you more information about myself than she. Would that do?"

The sarcasm slipped off the grey man, who whispered, "go ahead."

"I've been passing information to the British Embassy for seven or eight months through a contact whose name I shall, however, withhold."

The gentlemanly gesture, devoid of meaning, looked like posturing. Tony winced, though ridicule, alas, was not their quandary.

A dry, triumphant whisper cut him short. "All that's known. No need to shield Gálvez; he's our informant. He's a boyhood pal of one of the Fräulein's past lovers. Just give us your other contacts."

Belmán, thought Tony. Carlota, what a sin you have committed.

"I have no other contacts."

"Well?" the grey man leaned toward Tony, resting a casual hand on the rope under her eyes, seeking further enlightenment from her. She refused to look down and did not answer.

"If you want to catch your plane you'd better hurry."

"Antonie, speak!" Stephan said shrilly.

"Why don't you, Count?" the grey man interposed mildly. "You might save her . . . if you still care to do so. She may not have acquainted you with your competition, but you certainly know the rest."

"I know nothing," said von der Heiden. "It seems absurd, but I don't. I actually think she's been framed. As you so brilliantly inferred, I have many hapless rivals, one is Fernando Belmán, another is Gálvez. Your sources of information."

"Then we'd better proceed," remarked his interlocutor as if he had withdrawn without listening further from a dialogue he judged futile. He glanced at the steel watch on his ashen wrist. "It's getting late, search him."

234

He got up and walked toward Tony who, having risen too, now shrank even closer against the wall. He put a lifeless hand into her low-cut gown, the other feeling around her skirt up to the tight waist.

"Nothing. Nothing there either? Let's get started then. If you please, Count, take the chair at the other end of this table."

He put paper and pen on the side table opposite the rope and pulled back the chair across from Tony, not without courtesy. "Please sit down," he repeated to Stephan, who had not moved, his face turbulent with senseless schemes, "and write as I dictate. The Fräulein can then add her postscript," he added with an almost social nod at her. He was positively relaxed now that everything was going according to schedule.

Stephan was no longer looking at Tony. He was staring straight at the man (who waited for him to sit while idly untwisting the rope, then desisting as if in ludicrous delicacy) when he heard her voice for the first time, shaken and abrupt, and noticed that she had taken a step forward. "Let us go, and I'll give you the microfilm I was taking abroad. If you let us both board the plane and see to it that it crosses the border!"

The grey man slackened momentarily as one would a rope. Stephan said, "Don't! Don't ask for too much. If they just let you go and let me live long enough to see that they keep their promise . . . "

The grey man smiled, but then he whispered. "We might, we might after all. We're no beasts, you know. Where's the stuff?"

Tony was trembling all over, her eyes were wild and her nostrils fluttered. "I'm not going to give it all. I need some security. I'll mail the rest to Heinrich once we've crossed the border."

She doesn't speak, she gasps, thought Stephan. Poor child, what does she think she's doing?

"You're quite naïve, Fräulein," said the man, his ghostly thin-lipped smile lingering meaningless. "Produce the first batch and we'll see. Where is it?"

Although she did not answer, he saw her shift toward the two small suitcases topped by a roomy travel purse.

"In the bag?"

"No, no . . ."

"Give me the key if you please. Or else we can keep the luggage. You'll bequeath it to us, won't you? Nothing could be simpler."

"I'm going to give you the key," she said. "Why shouldn't I? It was my suggestion."

She started toward her bag and, though the grey man took a swift long step, with a cat's leap reached it first.

How beautifully, thought Stephan, she would move in the open, playing tennis or riding over fences . . .

"All right," said the man, like someone who at this stage of the game could afford to be generous, and to the giant, "Come over here. And you, Count, if you please, stay where you are."

The thug curved around closer to where Tony was standing with the grey man, without for a second letting her or von der Heiden out of sight or range, his eyes going incessantly from one to the other, the muzzle of the gun poised midway between them, alert and quivering like a hound's.

Tony had set the bag down again but not let go of it. The grey man watched her kneel shakily before it. She fumbled with the lock and opened it, hesitating a moment before putting a reluctant hand inside. She turned around in obvious despair, looking from one of her persecutors to the other, at bay.

Stephan had seen that gaze in the eyes of the stag at the end of the hunt. My god, he thought, does she really expect something?

Alternately she looked at the gunman, the grey man, the gunman, in time with the latter's oscillating glance, returning with it as it fell on Stephan. The .22 hissed, the giant firing as the pistol went off again, so his shot struck wildly against the wall.

Three silenced shots and it was over. The gun dropped from Tony's hand, and she stood staring at Stephan who returned her stare speechlessly.

"I've done it," she said huskily at first, and then with hysterical exultation. "I've really done it. It worked!" She blinked and then asked, all sound gone from her voice. "But now, what?"

"That little gun saved you, not I," he said, half in contrition, half in wonder. "Who gave it to you?"

"Never mind, I had it." Strange that one could smile, however weakly, with two dead bodies in the room.

"You must leave right away," he said urgently, with a glance at his watch.

"And you will come with me. We'll bribe that rogue pilot with Mother's ruby. Father bought it from still another refugee, a Russian princess, after the revolution. It has already served us well."

"No, Antonie. It won't do. They certainly have other men near the plane. If they really meant to let you go—and that might be, because your full name is Antonie Herrnfeld y Guerida Paz—seeing you alone they might think their scheme has worked, though they'll probably expect a postmortem from their hangmen . . . Who knows? I still can't imagine that they would permit a witness of tonight to live, no matter who she is. Don't you want to call your cousin? He'd hide you until you have a chance to slip out."

"And the mess in my apartment?" asked Tony, gesturing toward the bodies without looking at them.

"That's right. You'll have to try."

"And so will you."

"No, Antonie. That would be suicide for both of us."

"What are you going to do?"

"They're not going to lay hands on me. You have my promise. But you must go now. Take my car." He pressed the key into her palm. "It's parked just around the corner. And when you stop over in Brazil, remember to send a telegram. But to your own name and address. I'll get it."

"Do you intend to stay here?"

"Yes," he said, adding with disgust, "I'll have to clean up."

"What are you going to do about it?"

"I'll take care of that. Hurry. Do you have anything in your suitcases except clothes? I mean, anything you could not do without?"

"No."

"Then change quickly and take an almost empty little travel case, so you can run if necessary. Don't wait for a cab. Take my car. Someone might be downstairs—in the house, or outside. I can't go down with you because I'm dead, or about to die. You understand?"

"Yes," she said and did not move.

"Hurry, dress!"

He propelled her gently toward the bedroom door, and she reached for his hand. "Come in there with me, don't stay here with . . . with . . . you know."

She stood in the soft light of the dressing table lamps, her fluttering hands straining at the hooks in the back of her dress. As she bent her head sideways, the weight of a long strand of hair coming loose tumbled the whole coiffure.

Stephan came to her aid with unsteady fingers. With the undoing of the waist hook, the heavy mass of lace sank to the ground around her. He knew that he should not have touched her. He was holding her to him, his blood crushing his temples, his breath hot on her nape, his hard pulse pressing in on her imperiously, fighting to regain composure.

"Stephan . . ." She turned around. "Stephan . . . if you really won't come away with me, I'll stay with you. Come, take me to you."

"No, my darling, you must go. Alas, we've lost our gamble. By the time we drew the right card it was too late. You can't stay with me." He drew back. "Dress quickly; quick, my darling."

"I need you more than you've ever needed me. Give me your love now, because if you make me go away there'll be no other time."

Trying to persuade him, she did not know whether she was afraid for him or to be without him. It did not matter, she could not leave him behind in this situation, must change his mind. "Come with me, one way or another. Love me and then we'll go to sleep . . . you'll never again have to go away at dawn. We may not have known how to live but we'll know how to die. I won't be afraid in your arms . . ."

"Don't tempt me, Antonie. Don't tempt me."

Obediently she stepped away from the lilac lace around her feet and slipped off her evening stockings. He averted his eyes.

"You don't know," she said, "that my mind was made up when I left Antonio's house," and she wondered if it were true. If she did not know, none of the doubt showed on her face; without the lace, she was once more the Grecian youth he had so often held in his arms and who now, only now, was surrendering to him.

"I don't want to go alone, I want you to take me. *Songe à la douceur d'aller là-bas vivre ensemble . . .*"

"*Le monde s'endort dans une chaude lumière,*" he took up almost inaudibly, as though in a dream. She opened her arms to him and his hand moved forward. He forced it back to his watch fob, looked at the time, and said harshly, "Your decision comes too late. Let's not be late again. Dress now."

She ducked as if under a whiplash while he turned and went to the door. When she came to him, dressed for travel, he said, "Remember the password. *Königskinder*. Good-bye, Antonie, and good luck. You have given me great happiness."

"Good-bye Stephan," she said meekly, trembling like a child after corporal punishment. She raised her head, pleading. "Stephan, come . . ."

"Go," he said with gentle determination.

He made no attempt to change anything about the room. He sat and waited, rising from time to time, oblivious of the rope, the dead bodies, passing a hand over the rows of books or the back of a chair where Antonie had often sat. He went into the bedroom where her perfume still hung in the air and her dress lay on the floor like a bird brought down by the hunter. The bed under its white cotton spread was like the bed of someone long since gone or dead. It made him feel cold, and he opened her wardrobe and buried his face in clothes that were alive with the scent of her body. Then he went back to wait again.

When dawn crept through the windows he was as empty as a shell. There was no emotion, no thought in him, except the anxious wait for a telegram in which he did not really believe. Only that; otherwise it was as if he had already ceased to exist.

When the grey sky turned pink and yellow, he grew restless. By now someone at the embassy waiting for a report must have begun to wonder where his trusted hangmen were. And if the wire did not come soon, Antonie had not crossed the border.

When the sun was hot on the window panes, the bell rang. Stephan went to the door and peered through the lookout. It was a Western Union boy. As he took the telegram from him, his fingers trembled with excitement.

When he had shut and bolted the door again, he ripped the envelope open so hastily that the sheet tore within. Not just the keyword *Königskinder*, she had set down the first line of the second verse: "Dear heart, can you not swim, not swim across the lake?"

He went to the telephone.

"Don Antonio? It's all right," heard a breath of relief on the end of the line, and continued in very rapid French: "Look at the socket in the hall closet . . . That's it. Thank you and good-bye, sir."

He hung up, went to the table where the grey man had left the rope, the paper, and the pen.

Buenos Aires, the 7th of March, 1942

I, Stephan Cornelius Adalbert von der Heiden, Second Secretary of the German Embassy in Buenos Aires, have killed the two German espionage agents and would-be assassins whose bodies will be found in this apartment. Antonie Herrnfeld, in whose defense I was forced to act, left the apartment and the country before the writing of this statement to escape further attempts on her life.

Stephan Count von der Heiden

He went out to the hall closet and, unscrewing the bulb, fitted the folded paper into the socket, then replaced the bulb and returned to where Tony's abandoned luggage stood. He stooped and picked up the .22.

EPILOGUE

RIO DE JANEIRO (AP) MARCH 9, 1942 — A Brazilian plane, bound for Lisbon, Portugal, exploded over Rio de Janeiro Bay shortly after take-off yesterday morning. According to officials, 20 passengers and a crew of four were aboard the plane.

Ten bodies charred beyond recognition have so far been recovered from the sea, awaiting identification. A gold ring with a large gem rumored to be the famous Fortnam Ruby was found on the remains of a female passenger. The British Embassy in Rio de Janeiro, claiming that the gem had last passed through British hands, has requested that the Brazilian government carry out a thorough investigation of the accident. According to Embassy sources speaking on condition of anonymity, there is a strong suspicion of sabotage.